Pretty Geraldi
the New York Sa

or, Wedded to Her C.___

Alex. McVeigh Miller

Alpha Editions

This edition published in 2024

ISBN 9789362093905

Design and Setting By

Alpha Editions

www.alphaedis.com

Email - info@alphaedis.com

Contents

CHAPTER I.

"If I could have my dearest wish fulfilled, And take my choice of all earth's treasures, too, Or choose from Heaven whatsoe'er I willed, I'd ask for you!

"No one I'd envy, either high or low, No king in castle old or palace new; I'd hold Calconda's mines less rich than IIf I had you!"

"There is more charm for my true, loving heart, In everything you think, or say, or do, Then all the joys that Heaven could e'er impart, Because it's you!"

She stood behind the counter in H. O'Neill's splendid dry-goods emporium on Sixth avenue—only one of his army of salesgirls, yet not a belle of the famous society Four Hundred could eclipse her in beauty—pretty Geraldine, with her great, starry, brown eyes lighting up a bewitching face, with a skin like a rose-leaf, and a low, white brow, crowned by an aureole of curly hair, in whose waves the sunshine was tangled so that it could not get free. Her round, white throat rose proudly from a simple, nun-like gown of fine black serge, unadorned save by the beauty of the form it fitted with easy grace.

She would have graced a queen's drawing-room, this lovely girl with her starry eyes and demure dimples, but untoward fate had placed her behind a glove counter in New York.

It was very cold up to ten o'clock that bright October morning, and the great throngs of fall shoppers were not yet out in force, so Geraldine had an idle moment in which to gossip with her chum, plump, gray-eyed Cissy Carroll.

They both belonged to an amateur dramatic society, and a generous manager had sent them tickets for the play that evening. It was of this anticipated pleasure that they were chatting joyously, when a low, deep, masculine voice spoke to Geraldine across the counter:

"Gloves, please."

She turned quickly toward her customer, and at the same moment a very exacting lady claimed Cissy's attention.

The shop was rapidly filling with elegantly dressed women of fashion, and they would have no more leisure that day.

Geraldine saw before her an elegant-looking gentleman—tall, broad-shouldered, graceful, with a clean-shaven face, clear-cut features, fair, clustering locks, and large, glittering, light-blue eyes, keen and clear as points of steel in their direct gaze, but with something unpleasant somehow in their admiring expression that made the pretty salesgirl drop her eyes bashfully, as he continued, easily:

"I have lost a bet of a box of gloves to a lady, and would like you to assist me in selecting some pretty ones to pay the debt."

"What size?" she asked, as she began pulling down the boxes.

"Sixes," he replied, and added: "She is a gay and pretty young girl—an actress."

"An actress!" Geraldine sighed, enviously, then smothered the sigh by saying, carelessly: "We both wear the same size of glove."

"Ah!" and the customer gazed admiringly at the slender, dimpled white hands sorting out the gloves, then continued: "And I am an actor, and it pleases me to tell you that I am Clifford Standish, the leading man in 'Hearts and Homes,' the society play you are going to see to-night."

He laid his elegantly engraved card before her, and she started with surprise and pleasure, faltering, eagerly:

"I—I am proud to know you—but how did you guess I was going to the theatre to-night?"

"I beg your pardon for listening, but I heard you and your chum talking about it while I stood at the counter waiting for you to notice me."

"Oh, did I keep you waiting? I am very sorry; and if the floor-walker had observed my inattention, I should have been scolded."

Clifford Standish drank in with keen delight the music of her voice, and thrilled with rapture at her rare beauty, so he answered, gallantly:

"He did not see you, and I was in no hurry, for it pleased me just to stand there and watch you. I was watching your spirited face and gestures and thinking that you would make a clever actress. You belong to an amateur dramatic society, do you not?"

"Oh, yes, and I enjoy it so much. It is the dream of my life to be an actress!" exclaimed Geraldine, impulsively, her eager, brown eyes shining like stars. Her beauty thrilled his blood like a draught of rare old wine, and he felt that here was the love of his life, for no woman had ever touched his heart as maddeningly as this one; so he answered, almost as passionately, in a swift, overmastering impulse to draw her within the circle of his life:

"A dream that may easily become a reality. Will you let me help you to become an actress? I am almost sure that I can secure you a position in my company."

"Oh, I would be so grateful," smiled Geraldine, her cheeks glowing crimson with joy.

"Then you will permit me to call on you and talk it over? Let me see—you will be at home this evening at seven o'clock, will you not? May I come for half an hour at that time?"

"If you please," she answered, eagerly, scribbling her address on the back of his card.

He took it with thanks, his keen, blue eyes gleaming with triumph at the success of his ruse, and then gave his attention to the gloves, which he paid for and directed to be sent to his hotel.

He lingered as long as he dared after the purchase, but another customer soon claimed Geraldine's attention, so he smiled and bowed himself away, leaving the young girl with a fluttering heart and blushing cheeks, the result of this chance, but fateful, meeting.

Geraldine and Cecilia were close friends, having come together from their country homes to seek employment among strangers in the great city. They roomed together in the third story of a cheap apartment-house, and Cissy, as her intimates called her, was like an older sister to the ambitious Geraldine.

Cissy was twenty-five, and her friend only eighteen, so she always assumed the role of adviser to her junior, and as they walked home from the store that evening, she said, reprovingly:

"My dear, I didn't like the young man who talked to you so glibly over the gloves this morning."

"Ah, Cissy, you don't know who that young man was, or you would be proud of his notice!" And Geraldine poured out a breathless account of her good fortune.

But, to her surprise, Cecilia answered, gravely:

"Oh, I heard a good deal that he was saying to you, and noticed, too, that he looked at you as if he would like to eat you up. But, dear Geraldine, please don't let him persuade you with his silly flatteries to go on the stage.

It's a hard life for a young girl, they say, and full of terrible temptations. Believe me, you are better off behind O'Neill's glove counter."

Geraldine's pride was cruelly wounded at Cissy's lack of sympathy in her pet ambition, and she answered, rashly:

"Cissy Carroll, you're just jealous, that's why you preach to me! I can't help being pretty and attractive, can I? And I know that if he had offered to make you an actress, instead of me, you'd have sung quite another tune."

Cecilia felt her friend's slur on her own attractiveness, and flushed with quick resentment.

She knew that she was not as beautiful as Geraldine, but she had the soft, plump prettiness of a gray dove, so attractive to many men, and she had not lacked for admirers, although, for reasons of her own, she was single still, so she tossed her pretty dark head, her gray eyes flashing scorn, and made no reply to the ungenerous attack.

Geraldine, still angry, continued, patronizingly:

"If you would like to be an actress, too, Cissy, I'll introduce the actor to you when he calls this evening, and ask him to get you a position."

"Pray, don't trouble yourself, for I sha'n't enter the room while he's there. I despise real stage people! They're most always shabby sheep, and their acquaintance no credit," returned Cissy, rudely, giving such mortal offense by the taunt that Geraldine did not speak another word to her on the way home.

They had two small rooms, and Cissy hastened to one to prepare their simple tea, so as to get ready for the theatre, but Geraldine hurried to beautify herself for her caller, putting on her best gown, a garnet cashmere, with velvet trimmings, and drawing her wealth of golden brown locks into the classic Psyche knot.

"Supper's ready!" called Cissy, curtly, from the next room.

"I don't want any, thank you," Geraldine answered, coldly, and, indeed, her excitement ran too high for her to eat.

So Cissy ate her solitary meal in snubbed silence, while the radiant Geraldine entertained her caller, for Clifford Standish soon came, and spent a delightful half-hour, having to tear himself away at the last minute to return to his stage duties. Then she and Cissy patched up a kind of truce, and went together to the play, returning at the close, Cissy silent and disapproving, and Geraldine more determined than ever to go on the stage.

The girls were very distant to each other after that, but Geraldine carried a high head, and clung to her purpose, encouraged by the handsome young actor, who called on her for a short while every evening, and gave her tickets to every performance, declaring that she inspired him to his best work by the rapt gaze of her appreciative eyes as she sat in the audience.

But Cissy would not accompany her friend again to the play, doing all she could in a quiet way to wean her from her infatuation, but in vain.

She thought that Geraldine was weak and vain and silly, and the latter believed that Cissy was jealous of her good fortune. She hoped that she would soon be able to go on the stage, and part from the girl who had grown so selfish and cruel. The breach widened between their once loving hearts, and neither tried to bridge it over by a kind, forgiving word.

Toward the end of the week, Geraldine said, coldly:

"I am not going to work to-morrow morning, Cissy. I asked for a day's holiday before I left the store yesterday."

"Why?" asked Cissy, curiously.

"Mr. Standish has invited me to go with him on an excursion to Newburgh to witness the firemen's parade there. The firemen are having a grand celebration, you know, with splendid music, a grand parade, and all sorts of firemen's games. I wish you were going, too, Cissy!" wistfully.

"Well, I don't, and I think you are imprudent to go alone with that strange actor—so there!"

"Well, come with us, Cissy, won't you? I don't think he would mind your going!"

"Oh, yes, he would! 'Two are company, three a crowd!'" Cissy quoted, flippantly, and she went alone to work the next morning, Geraldine having started at an earlier hour to take the day boat for Newburgh.

CHAPTER II.

A FRIEND IN NEED.

"I had a dream of Love.It seemed that on a sudden, in my heart,A live and passionate thing leaped into being,And conquered me. 'Twas fierce and terrible,And yet more lovely than the dawn, and soft,With a deep power. It roused a longingTo do I know not what—to give—ah, yes!More than myself! And—failing that—to *die*!"

"How lovely she is, this brown-eyed little beauty! My heart is really touched at last, and I would give the world to call her mine!" thought Clifford Standish, as he led Geraldine on the crowded boat and watched her sweet face glow with pleasure at the animated scene.

He said to her, in apparent jest, but secret earnest:

"There are some members of the crack company of the New York Fire Department on board this morning, going to Newburgh, to take part in the parade and games to-day. They are fine-looking fellows, in their bright, new uniforms, but I hope you won't lose your heart to any of them. I think fate has destined you for an actor's bride."

His ardent, meaning glance made the blood flow in a torrent to her cheeks, but she was saved the necessity of replying, for at that moment she saw a woman's handkerchief waved to him from the shore, and he exclaimed, in an embarrassed tone:

"I see a friend beckoning me. Will you excuse me for a moment?"

He ran hastily down the gang-plank, leaving Geraldine alone on the crowded deck among the good-natured throng of people in the nipping air of the early morning, for the sunshine had not yet pierced the fog that lightly overhung the beautiful Hudson.

But Geraldine did not mind the frosty air, for her dark-blue suit was both warm and becoming, and the merry crowd and the martial music played by the band inspired her to cheerful thoughts.

She passed the minutes so pleasantly in watching the animated faces about her that she did not realize how long Mr. Standish was absent, until suddenly the whistle blew, the gang-plank was drawn up, and the steamer moved away from shore, thrilling the girl with swift alarm over her escort's absence.

She looked about her with a keen, searching gaze, then back to the shore.

A crowd of people were leaving the wharf, but among none of them could she distinguish the stately form of Mr. Standish.

"What had become of her escort?" she asked herself, in terror, wondering if he had willfully deserted her like this.

A choking sob rose up in her pretty throat, and her eyes filled with frightened tears.

She thought, miserably:

"Oh, I wish I hadn't come! I wish I had listened to Cissy's warnings! Why did Mr. Standish treat me like this? He is a mean wretch, and I'll never, never speak to him again!"

Poor little Geraldine, so lovely and so impulsive, if she had kept to that resolution, this story would never have been written. Her life would have flowed on too quietly and happily to have tempted a novelist's pen.

But "fate is above us all."

She looked about her despairingly for a friendly face among all those strangers.

Her tearful eyes encountered the gaze of a fireman who had been covertly watching her ever since she came on board.

He was a magnificent specimen of athletic young manhood, his fine straight figure setting off to advantage his resplendent uniform of dark-blue, with fawn-colored facings and gilt buttons. His face was bold, handsome, and winning, with a straight nose, laughing dark-blue eyes, a dark, curling mustache, while beneath his blue cap clustered beautiful blue-black curls, fine and glossy as a woman's hair.

When Geraldine's appealing eyes met the admiring gaze of this young man it paused and lingered as if held by some irresistible attraction, and, advancing to her, he lifted his blue cap courteously from his handsome head, saying, kindly:

"You seem to be in trouble, miss. Can I help you?"

Thus encouraged by his kind look and tone, the girl faltered out her distressing plight:

"My escort went back on shore to speak to a friend, and was left behind. And I—I—don't know anybody—and have no ticket—and no money with me!"

Poor, troubled baby! How charming she was with those crimson cheeks and wet eyes, and that tremulous quiver in her low voice! The handsome fireman's heart went out to her so strongly that he longed to take her in his arms like a child, and kiss away her pearly tears.

But of course, he didn't obey that strong impulse. He only said, cordially:

"Don't let that little trifle worry you, miss. You must permit me to buy you a ticket, and to take care of you to-day, like a brother. Will you?"

How glad Geraldine was to find such a kind friend. Her heart began to rebound from its depression, and she exclaimed, gratefully:

"Oh, how can I thank you enough? I felt so frightened, so like a lost child, till you spoke to me! Yes, I shall be very grateful if you will buy me a ticket. I'll pay you when we get back to New York. And—and—till then, please keep this!"

She held out to him her sole ornament, a pretty little ring, and insisted, against all his entreaties, that he should hold it in pawn for her debt.

"You oughtn't to trust your engagement-ring to another fellow," he said, lightly, as he slipped it over his little finger.

Geraldine blushed brightly as she answered to this daring challenge:

"Oh, it's not my engagement-ring at all. I'm not engaged."

"I'm very glad to hear it," he replied, meaningly, then proffered her his card, on which she read, in a clear, bold chirography, the name: "HARRY HAWTHORNE."

Geraldine bowed, and said:

"I haven't a card, but my name is Miss Harding—Geraldine Harding. I would like your address, please, so that I may return your money to-morrow."

"I am usually at the engine-house on Ludlow street—Engine Company No. 17. Driver, you see; and our splendid horses—oh, but you ought to see how they love me," enthusiastically; then pulling himself up with a jerk; "but, pray don't trouble to return the money. It will be better for me to call, will it not, and return your ring?"

She assented, and gave him her address; then he found her a seat, and as their boat plowed swiftly through the frothing waves, they fell into a pleasant chat, during which he said, courteously:

"I saw you come on board with Standish, the actor. Are you a member of his company?"

"Not yet; but I hope to be one soon. I'm only a salesgirl at O'Neill's now, but Mr. Standish has promised to help me to become an actress."

She read distinct disapproval in his dark-blue eyes as he said:

"But you will have to study a long while before you can make your debut."

"No, for I've already studied a great deal, and acted several parts in the amateur dramatic company to which I belong. Mr. Standish says I can go right on as soon as I secure a position."

"Perhaps you will regret it if you go on the stage," he observed, abruptly.

"Oh, no; for it is the dream of my life!" smiled Geraldine.

"Will your friends permit it?"

"I'm only an orphan girl, earning her own living, so I don't need to ask any one's leave. And I'm glad of that, for I'm ambitious, and want to rise in life. I'm tired of being the slave of the public at a dry-goods counter," cried Geraldine, with sparkling eyes.

He gazed at her admiringly, but he did not hesitate to say:

"It is only an exchange of slavery from the counter to the stage. You will be the slave of the public still. If you would listen to me, I would persuade you to remain where you are—until some good man marries you, and makes you the queen of his heart and home."

Geraldine tossed her shining head, and gave him a saucy smile, and retorted:

"That sounds like my chum's preaching, but I shall not listen to either of you. My heart is set on a stage career."

Harry Hawthorne gave her a grave look, but made no reply in words, and for a few moments they kept silence, while the gay, lilting music of the band filled up the pauses, and the sun pierced through the fog and smiled on the majestic steamer plowing her way through the blue, sparkling waves.

Geraldine felt intuitively that he disapproved of her plans, and maintained a pouting silence until he remarked, genially:

"I have an idea!"

She looked at him, questioningly, and he continued:

"The wife of our captain is on board to-day, going to Newburgh. Now, wouldn't it be pleasant to introduce you, so that she could look after you while I'm taking part in the firemen's games?"

Geraldine felt as if he were tired of her already, and eager to put her in charge of some one else, and her heart sank with a strange pain, but she did not permit him to see her mortification, she only gave an eager, smiling assent.

"I should like it very much, if the lady will be so kind."

"Then I will go and bring Mrs. Stansbury, if you'll wait here for us," and smiling at her, a friendly smile that warmed her chilled heart like a burst of sudden sunshine, he bowed himself away, and left the little beauty sitting alone by the rail.

She leaned her elbows on the rail, her dimpled chin in her hands, and watched the foamy waves with tender eyes as she thought how bonny he was, her handsome new acquaintance. Almost nicer, indeed, than Clifford Standish, or at least he would be, but for his absurd prejudice against her going on the stage.

"Won't Cissy be surprised when I have another handsome caller? I suppose she'll be cross, and wonder where I got another string to my bow," thought the budding coquette, with artless vanity.

She decided not to tell Cissy of the actor's strange conduct, for she would only say that he did it on purpose, and that it served her right.

"And I shall not give her the chance to crow over me, and say, 'I told you so!'" murmured Geraldine.

In the preoccupation of her mind, she did not notice that the rail she leaned on was old and weak, and had been mended at that very place. In the sudden indignation at the thought of Cissy's contumacy, she leaned yet more heavily upon it, and, with a sudden snap, the frail support gave way, precipitating its lovely burden into the water.

"Heaven have mercy!" shrieked poor Geraldine, as she went downward over the side of the boat—down, down down, into the churning, frothy waves.

In a moment all was terror, bustle, and confusion, the passengers all crowding to the side to look over, almost precipitating another accident in the excitement.

"Give way!" cried a stern, ringing voice, as the tall form of the fireman pushed through the crowd, and he demanded, hoarsely:

"What has happened?"

And a dozen voices answered that there had been an accident to the young lady he had been with just now. The rail on which she leaned had broken, throwing her into the water.

"My God!" he cried, supplicatingly, and sprang over the side to the rescue of the drowning girl!

CHAPTER III.

A GALLANT RESCUE.

"Awake, awake, oh, gracious heart—There's some one knocking at the door!'Tis Cupid come with loving artTo honor, worship, and implore.Arise and welcome him beforeAdown his cheeks the big tears start.Awake, awake, oh, gracious heart—There's some one knocking at the door."

Several moments of keenest suspense ensued, while the noisy and excited crowd watched the water where Geraldine's fair head had gone down beneath the surface.

Harry Hawthorne made a bold and gallant dive through the eddying circles on the water, and for a few breathless moments, he, too, was lost to sight.

The people shouted, in dismay and pity:

"They are both lost! They have been sucked under the boat by the swift current!"

Every face grew sad at the thought, and some tender-hearted women burst into tears.

It seemed terrible that those two beautiful young lives should have gone down so suddenly and tragically into the darkness of death.

But, suddenly, a low murmur of joy rose above the lamentations.

"See! see!"

The dark head of Harry Hawthorne had reappeared above the waves.

In another moment it was seen that he held Geraldine clasped to him with one arm, her white, unconscious face and dripping hair upturned to the light.

Supporting himself as best he could with one free arm, he halooed, loudly:

"Boat! boat!"

Oh, what a ringing cheer answered him—shouts of joy at the rescue; shouts of praise at his bravery!

In the meanwhile the steamer had been stopped, and a little boat let down. The men rowed quickly to Hawthorne, and drew him and his burden into safety.

The whole affair had passed off very quickly, but only the strength and bravery of one man had saved pretty Geraldine from a grave beneath the deep, sparkling waves of the beautiful Hudson.

As it was, she had sustained no injury, and soon recovered consciousness, looking about her with dazed eyes, to find her rescuer kneeling by her side, gazing at her with eager, dark-blue eyes, full of yearning anxiety.

"Oh, you need not look so frightened, Mr. Hawthorne. She is all right now, and I'm going to take her down stairs and lend her some of my dry clothes!" cried a gay voice, and the pretty young married woman to whom he had been about to introduce Geraldine when she fell into the river, now took the girl in charge and led her down stairs, saying, cheerily:

"You'll be all right directly. I'm going to get you some wine, and have you lie down and rest a while when you get on some dry clothes. Oh, you don't know my name, do you?

"I am Mrs. Stansbury, and Harry Hawthorne was bringing me over to see you when you fell into the water. A mercy you wern't drowned, isn't it? You certainly would have been, only for his bravery."

Closeted in the little state-room, she continued:

"How fortunate that I brought along a little steamer trunk, expecting to spend several days with my mother in Newburgh. I can lend you an outfit, for we are almost the same size, aren't we? But I'll wager that Harry Hawthorne will not be able to borrow a suit big enough for him, and will have to remain 'in durance vile' until his own clothes are dry."

Her words proved true, and she and Geraldine did not see the handsome fireman again until just before they landed, when he joined them, looking fresh and bright, and none the worse for his ducking, excusing his absence by saying, gayly, that he had been hung over a line to dry.

His eager eyes sought Geraldine's, and he said, tenderly:

"You feel no worse for your wetting, I hope?"

"No, indeed, thanks to the coddling of Mrs. Stansbury and the other ladies, but"—and her low voice broke with grateful emotion—"how can I ever thank you enough?"

"Let my own keen joy in saving your life be my reward," he answered, lightly, but with an undercurrent of joy in his deep, musical voice, for it seemed to him that had she perished beneath the cruel, darkling waves, life would never have seemed the same to him again.

Yet he knew that it might never be possible to win her for his own. His rival, the handsome actor, might already be lord of her girlish heart.

The bustle of landing cut short any further interchange of words between them, and when they stepped on shore, Mrs. Stansbury said, in her cordial way:

"I have claimed Miss Harding for my mother's guest, and she will go with me to the ball to-night, and return to New York with you to-morrow. Now, I see mamma's carriage waiting. Will you come with us to luncheon before we go out to the parade?"

"I thank you, no, for some of the fellows are waiting for me now. But I will see you later. *Au revoir!*"

He smiled frankly at Geraldine, touched his cap, and hurried away, seeming to take away some of the sunshine with him, for her heart had gone out to him in a great wave of tenderness that blotted out the memory of Clifford Standish as though he had never existed.

She looked at her companion, and asked, naively:

"Why did you say I would go to the ball? I have no dress to wear."

"What does that matter? I have several sisters. One of them can lend you a white silk, I'm sure. Why, you pretty darling, I wouldn't have you miss that ball for the world! Perhaps you will meet your fate there!"

CHAPTER IV.

"TWO SOULS WITH BUT A SINGLE THOUGHT."

"In peace, Love tunes the shepherd's reed;In war, he mounts the warrior's steed;In halls, in gay attire is seen;In hamlets, dances on the green.Love rules the court, the camp, the grave,And men below, and saints above;For love is heaven and heaven is love."

It seemed like a pretty act in a new play to Geraldine, the crowding events of that delightful day.

To be welcomed so cordially by Mrs. Stansbury's gentle mother, to ride through the crowded and gayly decorated streets, in the private carriage, to the hospitable red brick house full of pretty fun-loving girls, and to be installed as an honored guest in a dainty chamber, was a treat to the little working-girl whose life flowed in such a narrow groove of toil and poverty, and she thought, generously:

"Oh, I am very fortunate to find such kind friends, and I will always love them for their goodness to me. How I wish Cissy had come with me, for she would enjoy this so much."

Mrs. Stansbury entered with a great fluff of silk and lace over her arm, saying, cheerily:

"Here's the ball-gown I promised for to-night—Carrie's gown that she wore when she graduated last year. No, she doesn't need it. She has a blue silk-and-chiffon affair for the ball; so you'll be all right, won't you? And now let's go and have our luncheon, for we must hurry down town, where we have windows engaged to sit in and watch the parade. Oh, dear, I'm so sorry that my hubby, the captain, couldn't get away and come with us!"

They had a delightful luncheon, very enjoyable after their morning on the water, then the party of six—Mrs. Stansbury, her mother, Mrs. Odell, and her three daughters, Carrie, Consuelo, and Daisy, with pretty Geraldine— set out for the centre of attraction, Newburgh's "triangular square" at the junction of Water and Colden streets. Here the party had two large plate-glass windows over a splendid dry-goods store. From this vantage ground the scene presented, as the magnificent parade filed past, was one to be treasured long in memory.

It was a glittering spectacle, with thirty companies in line, and almost as many bands. Newburgh had not seen such a great day as this for years, with its glorious sunshine, brilliant uniforms, dazzling apparatus, splendid music, and throngs of appreciative people.

The crowd was enormous, the broad pavements packed with a living mass of humanity; the door-ways, balconies, windows, house-tops, a sea of faces. When the dazzling pageant swept by, the effect was kaleidoscopic. The bright gay uniforms of the fine-looking men, the beautiful caparisons of the prancing horses, the heavily plated, imposing engines, the light and graceful carriages, with their paintings and stripings, their images and lamps, their glass-and-gold reel-heads, their silver and gold jackets—all gleamed and glittered in the flashing sunlight like an Arabian Night's dream, and the hearty applause of the gazing crowds made the welkin ring.

Geraldine was charmed with everything, and her lovely, smiling face caught the upraised admiring glance of many a gallant fireman as the long column of thirty companies swept past to the ringing martial music of the accompanying bands. She forgot all her resentment against Cissy in her poignant regret that her chum was missing all this splendor and enjoyment.

But, strange to say, not one regretful thought wandered toward her lost cavalier, Clifford Standish.

She had forgotten him for the time, and her whole soul was thrilled with the present—permeated, enraptured with the thought of Harry Hawthorne, the handsome, dashing fireman who had so nobly saved her life. She loved him already, but she did not know her heart's language yet—her heart that had already elected him its king.

What though his position was an humble one, it was equal to hers, and Geraldine had never reflected that beauty like her own ought to win her a fine rich lover. She was in a whirl of bliss at the all-pervading thought that she had met her fate at last.

"He is mine, and I am his," ran the secret voice of her tender heart.

She watched the firemen eagerly as they paraded past, hoping for a sight of his face among them, so she did not hear the door open behind her until a hand touched her shoulder and she looked up with a start, her voice unconsciously betraying the rapture of her heart as she cried:

"Oh-h-h!—I thought you were in the parade!"

He smiled, radiantly, his heart thrilling with joy.

"No, I am not in the parade. That is, I chose not to be. You see, my company did not come, to take part, only a few of us fellows, so we can do as we like. We were offered seats in the carriages with the visiting firemen, and the others accepted. But I—I thought I would return and remain with you ladies."

His voice said "ladies," but his eyes said "you," and Geraldine thrilled deliciously.

Oh, how gay and happy she felt—happier than she had ever been in her whole life before. The dawn of love made the whole world roseate with sunshine.

And never had she looked more beautiful. The joy in her heart sent the warm blood leaping through her veins and made her eyes brighter, her cheeks redder, until she was dazzlingly lovely.

Harry Hawthorne remained with the party all the rest of the afternoon. Other young men joined them presently, admirers of the pretty Odell girls, and later on they repaired to the County Fair Grounds to witness some of the firemen's games taking place there.

Seated on the grand stand, by the side of Geraldine, Harry Hawthorne felt as proud and happy as a king, for the same sweet wine of Love that thrilled the girl flowed intoxicatingly through his veins.

"For what was it else within me wroughtBut, I fear, the new strong wine of Love,That made my tongue to stammer and tripWhen I saw the treasured splendor, her hand,Come sliding out of her sacred glove,As the sunlight broke from her lip?"

The tournament and games of this afternoon were only a repetition by Newburgh firemen of the ones that had been participated in the previous day by the visiting companies—"consolation races," the chief merrily called them.

But the grand stand was packed and the entertainment was novel and interesting, as evidenced by the frequent applause of the crowd.

The exercises after the pretty tournament consisted mainly of hose-racing contests, in which firemanic skill was displayed at its best.

"You must explain the game to me. You see, I never thought much about firemen before, although I am deeply interested in them now," pretty Geraldine said, naively, to her delighted companion.

He thanked her with a kindling glance of pleasure, and answered:

"It will give me pleasure to explain it all to you, Miss Harding. It is very simple indeed, depending on the skill and dexterity of the men. In the first place, the rules of the game require fifteen men. They must run two hundred yards to the hydrant, with a hose cart, and from that point lay one hundred yards of hose, make a coupling, and screw on the pipe. But these technical terms are Greek to you, of course, so I will try to make it clear to you as they proceed."

He did so, and Geraldine, who was beginning to love all firemen, for the sake of the splendid one by her side, watched the contest with breathless interest.

But now arose a difficulty.

The Newburgh company had only fourteen good runners, and they must have a fifteenth one.

But the rules of the race required that no company should make use of the services of a member of another company.

It was finally decided that as the race was not for a prize, but simply for practice and amusement, the rule might be waived for one in favor of a visiting fireman.

Then a murmur arose among the firemen that suddenly swelled to a clamorous shout:

"Hawthorne! Hawthorne!"

Mrs. Stansbury, who sat on the other side of Geraldine, looked round, and exclaimed, gayly:

"They are calling you, Mr. Hawthorne. Why don't you go?"

"I prefer remaining here," he smiled back, though a slight flush rose to his brow as the calls continued more clamorously:

"Hawthorne! Hawthorne! Hawthorne!"

All eyes turned on him as he sat unmoved, and a delegation of firemen came to insist on his joining the race.

"Oh, do go, Mr. Hawthorne. I think it will be grand to join the race!" exclaimed Geraldine, enthusiastically, and he rose at once like a gallant knight who has no other wish than to do the behest of his lady-love.

Mrs. Stansbury whispered as he went away:

"He will win the race for them. He is a magnificent athlete, my husband says. And as for horses—well, you should see him control them! They love and obey him like a master, and he has a passion for them. He is a splendid fellow, though there is something rather mysterious about him. He has been driver for No. 17 two years, yet no one knows where he came from or aught about his family. But he is educated above his position, and has betrayed that he has lived abroad. We think he is English or Irish—perhaps a mixture of both. But, anyway, he is just magnificent, and the men and the horses both worship him alike. He has been a hero at dozens of fires, and has several medals of honor, but he will not accept promotion. He says he loves the horses, and will not give up driving. But look! the team is about to start!"

Every word she uttered only made Geraldine love Hawthorne more dearly, for what woman does not love a hero?

Geraldine watched the contest with flashing eyes; but, needless to say, she saw but one man, and she soon realized that the most thunderous applause was given to him.

"He is the swiftest runner of them all!" cried Carrie Odell. "Look how the men are dropping off! They cannot stand it. Seven, eight, nine, ten, have given up. Oh-h-h!"

"Another! And another!" cried her sister, Consuelo, and so it kept on till when they reached the finish they had only two men to open the hydrant, and screw on the pipe—a simple operation it would seem to a novice, but it is just here that the race is won or lost. Under the moment's excitement the couplers will likely find their nerves unsteady after the long run. But these two men made no false moves. They put on the pipe with indescribable speed, then ran on the remaining hundred yards to the judge's stand, Harry Hawthorne coming out ahead amid the deafening cheers of his admirers.

The judges took the time at the very instant that the pipe touched the ground, and after examining the coupling they found it all right, and announced the time as forty-six and one-fourth seconds.

The victors retired amid tumultuous applause, and another team prepared to run, Hawthorne returning very soon to Geraldine's side to sun himself in her admiring eyes.

"You were splendid, and I was proud of you!" she cried, innocently, unconscious of the tenderness her words implied.

"Thank you. I am proud that I pleased you; but I was sorry they made me run. I was trying to keep rested and fresh to dance with you at the ball to-night," he answered, lightly.

"And now you will be too tired—I am sorry for that."

How frankly she could talk to him, and yet they had been strangers only this morning; yet it seemed as if they had known each other years and years.

"No, I shall not be too weary to dance with you," he answered, tenderly.

Then others of the party claimed his attention, and Geraldine sat in a happy dream, thinking how heavenly it would be dancing with him to-night.

Presently the games were over, and the weary, happy throng departed—the Odells and their guests to make ready for the grand fireman's ball they were going to attend that night.

"Oh, I wonder what Cissy will say when I don't come back to-night? She will be uneasy about me; perhaps angry. But she will forgive me when I tell her how it happened, and what a lovely time I had," thought Geraldine.

But again she did not even think of Clifford Standish, or even wonder what had become of him. She was full of the dear, delightful present.

How delightful it was to be dressing for a grand ball, in white slippers and a fairy-like gown of white silk, and with white roses for her breast and hair. Geraldine felt like a Cinderella going to the ball with a prince, for Harry Hawthorne was coming to be her escort, and to her he was the handsomest man on earth, a veritable Prince Charming.

She looked at her reflection in the long mirror, with artless delight at her own beauty.

"How pretty I look! I hope he will think so, too, but perhaps he knows some one more beautiful," she murmured, uneasily.

CHAPTER V.

RIVALS AND FOES.

"We meet where harp and violinWere singing songs of mirth,Where creatures floated in the spaceAlmost too fair for earth.He moved amid the surging crowd,And by one single glanceMy heart was lost, forever lost,While swinging in the dance."

Oh, how Geraldine enjoyed the first two hours of the ball!

It was one of the most brilliant affairs ever given in Newburgh.

The dazzling lights shone on an animated scene, adorned with rich floral garnitures, and brightened by the rich uniforms of the firemen, mixed with the sober black of the ordinary citizen, and the gay gowns of the beautiful women.

Geraldine, with her golden fluff of hair, bright brown eyes, and shining white attire, was the cynosure of all eyes, and many a gallant fireman envied Harry Hawthorne, who was her partner so often in the joyous dance.

True, she would dance with any of them to whom he introduced her, but each one saw by the wandering glances of her brown eyes that Hawthorne was first in her heart and thoughts.

So the first two hours passed by like a dream of bliss.

Geraldine loved music and dancing and gayety, with all her heart. She loved, too, the congenial new friends she had made, and lost in the delightful present, she forgot for a time her feverish ambition to become an actress and shine upon the stage.

What exquisite rapture may be crowded into two hours—rapture that will linger in the memory till death blots out all. So it was with Geraldine.

When Hawthorne pressed her hand in the dance, and looked into her eyes, drinking in deep draughts the intoxication of her beauty and sweetness, the girl thrilled with a rapture akin to pain, and those moments of dizzy, subtle bliss so dazzling in their brightness, returned to Geraldine through all her life as her happiest hours—that hour in a woman's life when First Love "is a shy, sweet new-comer, and Hope leads it by the hand."

"New hopes may bloom, and days may come,Of milder, calmer beam;But there's nothing half so sweet in lifeAs love's young dream."

How sad that a shadow should fall so suddenly over Geraldine's happiness!

But as she stood at a window, panting from the dance, rosy and smiling, as she talked to Harry Hawthorne, a shadow suddenly came between her and the light, pausing by her side till she looked up and saw—Clifford Standish!

Alas! that his shadow should ever come between her and the dawning happiness of her life!

Alas! that she had ever met him, the handsome, unscrupulous actor, who stood there scowling at his splendid rival!

"Mr. Standish!" she exclaimed, with a violent start, and a strange feeling of annoyance, and he answered, impressively:

"How glad I am that I have found you at last!"

"Have you been looking for me?" she asked, coldly.

"Everywhere! And I beg ten thousand pardons for my seeming desertion of you. It was wholly an accident, and the fault of my friend, who detained me talking one minute too long. I followed you on the next steamer, but it was several hours late, and all the time my mind was distracted over what would become of you. Of course I knew you would find friends—a beautiful girl alone in a crowd will always find a protector; but," sneeringly, "not always a safe one!"

"I beg your pardon. It was I who protected Miss Harding," began Harry Hawthorne, wrathfully, and the girl started, and exclaimed:

"Mr. Standish, this is Mr. Hawthorne, a very kind gentleman who paid my fare on the boat after you left me without a ticket, and afterward jumped into the river and saved my life when I fell overboard. I owe him a debt of gratitude that I can never repay."

They bowed coldly, trying not to glare, each seeing in the other a dangerous rival.

Clifford Standish was not pleasant to look at with that steely glare in his large, light-blue eyes, and that angry compression of his shaven lips as he said, coldly:

"I thank you, sir, for your care of my friend during my enforced absence from her side. I will repay you the boat fare, and remain deeply indebted to you for saving her life. Of course it goes without saying that I shall now be honored with her company again, thus relieving you of her care."

Harry Hawthorne, with a dangerous flash in his dark-blue eyes, retorted, calmly:

"I beg your pardon. Her engagement with me for this evening gives me a right that I shall not relinquish unless at her desire."

Both looked at the beautiful, flushed face of the girl. She comprehended the sudden hate between them, and said, tremblingly, but with the sweet tones of the peacemaker:

"I think Mr. Hawthorne is right. My engagement with you was for to-day, and we were to have returned to-night, you know. But after you left me alone on the boat, I made new friends, and a very sweet, kind lady, well-known to Mr. Hawthorne, took charge of me and invited me to be her guest while I staid in Newburgh. It was under her chaperonage I came to the ball, and, with her consent, I accepted the escort of Mr. Hawthorne. I cannot break my engagement with him, and I have promised, also, to go back to New York in his care to-morrow."

Every word she uttered maddened him with secret fury. His face was livid as he almost hissed:

"I should like to see this lady who chaperoned you here. How do I know that she is a proper person!" he began, insolently, but at that moment a lady tapped him smartly on the arm with her fan, exclaiming:

"Ha, ha, ha! I like that, Mr. Standish! A proper person indeed. Well, I'm the person, and if you have any fault to find with me, my husband, Captain Stansbury, will settle it with you."

"Miss Odell!" he exclaimed, recoiling in surprise from the sight of the face of an old acquaintance.

"Mrs. Stansbury, please," she corrected him, then went on, gayly: "Do you remember our flirtation at Asbury Park three years ago? I haven't seen you since, have I? Well, I've been married two years now to the finest man in New York. But my sisters are single yet. Come with me and pay your respects to them before the german begins."

She dragged him reluctantly away, and then Hawthorne said, angrily:

"That fellow was inclined to be insolent, and I could scarcely refrain from pitching him neck and heels through this window!"

"Oh, please, please, do not get into any trouble with him on my account!" pleaded Geraldine. "He has been very kind to me, really, and I should not wish to offend him!"

"Do not tell me he is your lover—that you care for him!" exclaimed the young man, jealously.

"N-n-o, he is only a friend!" she faltered, and was glad when her partner for the next dance came to claim her hand.

She knew in her heart that Clifford Standish regarded her with more than a friendly liking, but she was not prepared to own it to impetuous Harry Hawthorne, so she was glad to get away from his inquisitive looks and words.

But the joy of the evening was ended now for pretty Geraldine.

Clifford Standish soon escaped from the Odell girls, and haunted Geraldine the rest of the time, not offensively, but with the assurance of a favored lover, torturing the poor girl who could not bear to wound his feelings, but whose reserved and distrait manner did not discourage his persistent gallantry, for he stood his ground, debarring the lovers from any pleasure in each other's society.

Once Hawthorne whispered to her, fiercely:

"There comes that cad back. He is annoying you. I see it by your altered looks. Will you not allow me to pitch him out of the window?"

"No—oh, no, you must not make a scene!" she shuddered, apprehensively.

"Then tell him yourself that you are weary of his persistent following," he urged.

"Oh, no, I cannot wound him so. He has been kind to me, and means no harm," she said, trying to make excuses that she felt he did not deserve.

But she escaped from the ball as soon as she could, glad to be rid of him, and spent a restless night, repenting the encouragement she had given Standish before she met Hawthorne.

"They both love me, and I can see that they will be bitter foes," she thought, in terror of some unknown evil.

The next morning Standish came at an early hour to call. He was acquainted with the girls, and they tried by merry banter to drive the threatening gloom from his brow; but all their efforts were dismal failures. He had eyes only for Geraldine, who was pale and perturbed under his reproachful glances, that seemed to say, bitterly:

"You are a cruel little coquette. You encouraged me to love you until you met that other fellow, and now you wish to throw me over."

CHAPTER VI.

FORTUNE, THAT FICKLE GODDESS, FAVORS STANDISH.

"Her winsome, witching eyesFlash like bits of summer skiesO'er her fan,As if to say, 'We've met;You may go now and forget—If you can.'"

SAMUEL M. PECK.

It was a great relief to Geraldine when Harry Hawthorne arrived with a cab to take her to the boat. Now at last she could escape her angry lover.

He rose, indeed, to take leave of the family, but he said to her:

"I shall see you again, Miss Harding. I go back to New York on the same boat."

He did so, but he did not judge it prudent to incur the wrath of Hawthorne by too persistent attentions. He preserved a coolly courteous demeanor toward both, devoting himself to some other friends whom he met on the boat.

But, toward the last, he approached Geraldine again, murmuring, pleadingly:

"I should like to call on you this evening, if you will permit me."

She blushed, and stammered:

"Please excuse me, as I have another engagement."

He saw her timid glance turn toward Hawthorne, and readily guessed that she had made an engagement with him.

Stifling an execration between closely drawn lips, he muttered:

"To-morrow evening, then?"

"Oh, yes, certainly," she answered, but with an air of restraint that made him furious.

"She would like to refuse if she dared, the little flirt," he thought, and when Geraldine and Hawthorne left the boat together, he looked after them pale with rage.

At that moment Cameron Clemens, one of the actor-friends he had met on the boat, slapped him on the shoulder, and said, teasingly:

"Hallo, Standish! that was a stunning little beauty! But what are you glowering at, man? Jealous, eh?"

"Jealous of a beggarly fireman? Bah, no! The little coquette will throw him over to-morrow."

"And pick you up again, eh? Consolatory, by Jove! But who is she, anyhow?"

"Oh, nobody but a salesgirl from O'Neill's. She scraped acquaintance with me in the store some ten days ago, and has been begging me to get her in my company ever since. You know how the pretty girls always run after actors, Clemens."

"And how ardently the actors encourage their attentions; oh, yes," smiled the other, who was a very handsome young fellow himself. He added, after a moment: "Is the girl stage-struck?"

"Yes, decidedly—member of an amateur dramatic society, and all that, you know. Wild to go on the stage, and I intend to get her in our company, just before we go on the road next week."

"But there's no vacancy."

"I'll get that little soubrette turned off. I owe her a grudge anyhow. She slapped my face when I tried to kiss her in a dark corridor one night."

"Oh, don't take revenge for that. She's a good little girl, that Bettie," said Cameron Clemens, who, although he was the villain in the play where Standish had the part of hero, was kind and generous at heart.

But Clifford Standish could not be brought to relent.

"She can get another place," he said, carelessly. "The manager can't afford to displease me. I'm drawing full houses every night. So out goes prudish Bettie, and in comes pretty Geraldine!"

"You don't think you can kiss her in a dark corridor, do you?"

"I shall kiss her when I please. In fact, I intend to marry the little beauty; so no attentions in that quarter, my friend."

"All right. I'll keep off the grass," returned the young actor, slangily, and turning to his friend, Charlie Butler, they went away together, leaving Standish to some bitter reflections, for his bravado was all put on. He feared that Geraldine was lost to him forever.

"He will be with her this evening, that villainous fireman, while I am plodding away on the stage," he thought, angrily.

But a most untoward fate helped him on when he feared that the game was lost to him forever—helped him on, and blighted all the springing hopes of poor Harry Hawthorne.

A morbid curiosity over his rival led him to stroll down on Ludlow street that afternoon, in the neighborhood of the engine-house, and he saw the horses dashing out attached to the engine, and the hated Hawthorne on the driver's seat, handling the reins with consummate skill, his handsome face aglow with excitement. An alarm of fire had come in, and he was hastening to the scene.

Clifford Standish hated his manly rival more than ever at this moment, but he impulsively joined the crowd that was running after the engine, intent on seeing the fire.

On went the engine in splendid style, the horses obeying Hawthorne's hand lovingly, their sleek sides shining, their manes streaming, their fine heads erect, their large eyes flashing, a sight to win the admiration of every gazer. Flying like the wind, their hoofs striking fire from the pavement, they turned the corner, and—— Alas! what was that shriek that went up from hundreds of throats?

Their splendid onset was defeated. In turning the corner the wheels struck a car track at an angle, and the engine was overturned, the gallant steeds struggling in the dust with their noble driver.

Clifford Standish rushed forward with demoniac glee, muttering:

"My rival is dead beneath the engine! I am free of him forever!"

CHAPTER VII.

THE POWER OF LOVE.

"To look for thee—sigh for thee—cry for thee,Under my breath;To clasp but a shade where thy head hath been laid,It is death.

"To long for thee—yearn for thee—burn for thee—Sorrow and strife!But to have thee—and hold thee—and fold thee,It is life, it is life!"

It almost seemed as if Clifford Standish was destined to realize his diabolical hopes of his rival's death.

When Harry Hawthorne was drawn from his perilous position at the heels of the horses, he was found to be unconscious, and the blood pouring from a wound on his head.

An ambulance was called to convey him to the hospital, and the physician in charge looked very serious over the case.

"It is impossible to say yet whether he is mortally injured or not. He may simply be stunned from the bad cut on his head, or he may have sustained internal injuries," he said to the anxious crowd about him, and then the wounded man was lifted carefully into the ambulance, and driven to the Bellevue Hospital.

Clifford Standish turned away from the scene with a diabolical smile of triumph on his thin lips, hissing cruelly:

"The Fates have played me a good turn, and I will make the most of my opportunity. Whether Harry Hawthorne lives or dies, I will come between him and Geraldine so effectually that when he returns to her it will be impossible to win her from me. Of course, I shall not go near her this evening. She must be kept in ignorance of his accident, if possible, so that she may think he has forsaken her. Ha, ha, ha! what a weary waiting she will have for him this evening, and how angry she will be because he has broken his engagement."

Geraldine did, indeed, have a weary waiting for her lover, and her disappointment was keen and bitter at his failure to come.

But so absolute was her faith in him that she did not become angry, but thought, excusingly:

"I do not know."

"You have not heard from him?" he exclaimed, in surprise.

"Not a word," she sighed, then added, quickly: "But I don't think he meant to break his engagement. Perhaps there was a fire, and he had to go."

"Very likely—but, then, he should have sent you an apology early this morning."

"Do you think so? Oh, I suppose he will come and explain in person," said Geraldine, with assumed indifference.

Another customer bustled up to claim her attention, and he bowed himself away, secretly exultant over the fact that she was utterly ignorant of Harry Hawthorne's fate.

"There is no one to come and tell her, and even if it gets into the papers, she is not likely to read it. A poor working-girl has little time for reading," he reflected.

Again his evil genius favored him.

When he went for his call on Geraldine that evening, he found a messenger-boy in the street with a letter for her from the Bellevue Hospital.

He took the letter from the boy, and gave him a quarter.

"I am going in to see Miss Harding now. I will deliver the letter," he said, affably, and the boy, who was in a hurry to get home to his supper, thanked him for the service, and turned away, rejoicingly.

The triumphant actor hid the letter in his breast, congratulating himself on having so easily obtained possession of it.

"I am very fortunate, for had the fickle little beauty received it, all would have been explained between them."

Geraldine came to the door to receive him, and he saw at once how much she had changed toward him by the simple fact that she had not adorned herself in her best gown, as usual, but wore her simple shop-gown of black serge.

She did not care whether she looked fair to him or not, and he quickly realized it, for he was an adept in reading the complex nature of woman. But he hid his chagrin, saying, admiringly:

"Perhaps you do not realize how pretty and demure you look in that black gown."

"Thank you," Geraldine said, listlessly, as she sank into a chair opposite, and tried to seem friendly and interested.

CHAPTER VIII.

"A GIRL HAS A RIGHT TO CHANGE HER MIND."

"Reprove me not that still I changeWith every passing hour,For glorious nature gives me leave,In wave and cloud and flower.And you and all the world would do—It all but dared—the same;True to myself—if false to youWhy should I reck your blame?"

It made Clifford Standish secretly furious to see how near he had come to losing the charming little beauty on whom he had set his burning heart, and of whom he had felt so sure but a few days ago.

Her pale and pensive looks, her drooping eyes, her pathetic red mouth, all told that her heart was far away, and in his heart he cursed himself for inviting her to go on that fateful excursion to Newburgh, by which he had almost lost her forever.

But he had one chance now to retrieve his misstep, and he set about improving it.

"Well, I will tell you the promised good news!" he exclaimed. "I have at last secured you the wished-for position in my company."

"Oh!" cried Geraldine, starting, and clasping her little hands convulsively together.

But the exclamation was one of dismay rather than of joy.

His quick ear detected it, but he pretended to misapprehend her, and continued:

"I knew you would be delighted to hear it."

"Ye-es," she faltered, weakly; then bracing herself to escape the engagement. "But—but—perhaps I ought not to go on the stage. Cissy is opposed to it."

"Yes, I know—you told me that at first, but you said, also, that you did not care for her opinions—that you should do as you pleased."

Geraldine could not contradict him. It was perfectly true.

She sat speechless and embarrassed, feeling like a little bird caught in the fowler's net, while he continued, smoothly:

"Don't be afraid of Miss Carroll's displeasure. It's only envy and jealousy."

Geraldine, in her resentment against Cissy, had said this to him, too, and she comprehended that he was cleverly turning her own weapons against her now. She could only sit mute and miserable, with a forced smile that was more pathetic than tears.

"'If I could leave this smile,' she said,'And take a moan upon my mouth,And let my tears run smooth,It were the happier way,' she said."

Clifford Standish continued:

"The position offered you is not as good as I could wish, but I shall manage to get you a promotion soon. Our soubrette is going to leave, and you can take her place as soon as you wish."

It was strange how tenaciously Geraldine's mind clung to the dread of Harry Hawthorne's disapproval. She did not wish to go on the stage now, and was eager for a loophole to escape.

"Oh, I don't think I'd like to take a soubrette's place," she cried.

"But last week you said you wouldn't mind it."

"Oh, why do you keep throwing up things I said last week?" she burst out, pettishly.

"Do you wish to forget them so soon, Miss Harding? Then you must be very fickle-minded, and I am sorry that I had that poor soubrette discharged for your sake!"

"For my sake! Oh-h-oh!"

"Why, certainly; because you were so anxious for a place, and I wished to please you above all things," tenderly; "and, of course, you know the manager dare not refuse anything reasonable that I ask, so I persuaded him to discharge poor Bettina."

"Oh, let her keep the place, do! It was cruel to turn her off."

"It is too late to replace her now. She has accepted an offer from a company that is going to remain in New York, and I shall have no end of trouble getting another girl to fill the place. I thought you wanted the chance so badly," reproachfully.

Geraldine flushed crimson, and the tears she had been fighting back brimmed over in her eyes.

"Oh, I have acted abominably," she sobbed; "but—but—a girl has a right to change her mind, hasn't she?"

"Certainly, if she doesn't mind putting every one out," stiffly.

He rose as if to go, walked to the door as if in anger, then relented, and stood looking back with intense eyes that compelled her to look at him deprecatingly.

Having gained this point, he said, gently:

"We are going on the road with our company in one week, and as our soubrette can stay with us a few days longer, I'll give you three days to make up your mind whether you will take the place or not. For who knows but that you will change your mind again?" and still smiling kindly at her, he quoted:

"'Tis helpless woman's right divine,Her dearest right—Caprice!"

"Please go now," she answered, burying her face in her hands.

"I am going now, but I shall come back to-morrow evening, and hope to find you in a brighter mood," he answered, going out softly and closing the door.

He had purposely refrained from speaking of Harry Hawthorne, but he guessed well that it was he who had influenced her against the stage.

"Curse his meddling! But it shall avail him nothing. I shall conquer in the end. I have sworn to make her mine, and mine she shall be, the coquettish little darling," he muttered, resolutely.

The days came and went, while Geraldine waited patiently for the coming of Harry Hawthorne—waited all in vain, for he continued very ill at the hospital, and the note he had dictated to a nurse acquainting her with his accident she never received. It had fallen into the hands of his triumphant rival, Standish, who kept it hidden safely from that yearning young heart.

CHAPTER IX.

THE ACTOR MAKES HAY WHILE THE SUN SHINES.

"Go! let me pray, pray to forget thee!Woe worth the day, false one, I met thee!Ever till then, careless and free, love,Never again thus shall I be, love.Through my soul's sleep thine the voice breaking,Long shall I weep, weep its awaking,Weep for the day when first I met thee,Then let me pray, pray to forget thee!"

Two more days passed by, and still Geraldine heard nothing of Harry Hawthorne.

"Is it not strange—the way he has acted?" she said, at last, to Cissy, who answered:

"Yes; he has behaved so shabbily that you ought to put him out of your thoughts, dear."

"Oh, Cissy, do you believe that he never meant to come? That he was unworthy?" almost piteously.

"I'm afraid so, Geraldine, for even if something had happened to keep him away that evening, he has had ample time to explain and apologize since then; but he has not done so, and it looks as if he was a sad flirt, and only amused himself with you for the time, without giving you another thought since he left you."

Cissy believed what she said, and meant only kindness, but her frank words quivered like a thorn in Geraldine's heart.

Oh, how could she think of him as an unprincipled flirt, awakening an interest in a young girl's heart only for his own amusement?

But still she knew that such men existed, and that many broken hearts lay at their door.

The dread that Harry Hawthorne might be one of these heartless men awoke to life within her a fierce and burning pride.

"No man shall break my heart. I will forget Harry Hawthorne," she vowed, bitterly, to herself; and when the actor came that night, he found her bright and gay as of yore. She had put on over her tortured heart that mask of smiles which many a woman wears through life to deceive a carping world.

"'I have a smiling face,' she said,'I have jest for all I meet,I have a garland for my head,And all its flowers are sweet,And so you call me gay,' she said.

"'Behind no prison grate,' she said,'Which slurs the sunshine half a mile,Live captives so uncomfortedAs souls behind a smile.God's pity let us pray,' she said."

Clifford Standish was charmed with her new mood. He saw that a reaction had begun.

"I am glad to see you so happy, for I am sure that you have decided to go on the road with us," he exclaimed, coaxingly.

She shook her head, and laughed, gayly:

"Do not be too sure. You know you have given me until Sunday night to decide."

"But that is not far off—only twenty-four hours," he said, with a smile, for he felt sure of victory. As she made no reply, he continued:

"I have made a charming invitation for you for Sunday afternoon. Some of the leading members of our company are going to skate in the park to-morrow—you know this cold snap has frozen the lake beautifully—and they want me to bring you. Will you come?"

"Yes," replied Geraldine, quickly, glad of a diversion for Sunday afternoon, so that she need not mope alone with her miserable thoughts of how Harry Hawthorne had flirted with her for his own amusement.

For she had begun to lose faith in her handsome lover now. The leaven of Cissy's words had worked steadily in her mind.

And a cruel self-shame that she had given her love in vain was at war with the tenderness of her heart.

"Thank you. I am so glad you will go. I know you will like the trip and the company," he said; then, in a changed tone: "By the way, did that fireman ever keep his promise to call on you?"

"No," she answered, carelessly.

"Have you heard anything about him?"

"No, indeed, and I had almost forgotten the man until you recalled him to my mind," she returned, fibbing unblushingly.

"Ah! Then you will not mind what I have to tell you?" deprecatingly.

"Of course not. What is it?" carelessly.

"Well, of course, I thought it rude and strange his not keeping his appointment with you, and thinking something might have happened to the fellow, as you feared, I made some indirect inquiries at the engine-house, and found that he had returned to Newburgh the same day he brought you back to New York."

"Indeed?" she returned, with a paling cheek, whose pallor she could not control.

"Yes, he had gone back, but I did not like to tell you the truth. I waited for developments. But, to-day, I met Mrs. Stansbury on the street, and she told me something—well, see if you can guess?"

"Something very amusing, no doubt," she replied, carelessly.

"She told me she had just returned from Newburgh, and that she had left Hawthorne there, courting her sister, Daisy Odell. It seemed that he had been in love with the pretty little black-eyed thing some time, and fearing that she might get jealous of the attentions he had to pay you the day you were thrown on his care by my accidental desertion, he returned to make his peace with her, and has been lingering by her side ever since. Mrs. Stansbury was vastly amused over it all, and said to me, 'He flirted shockingly with that pretty little salesgirl, didn't he? but I hope she knew it was only fun! Give my love to her when you see her again!'"

Geraldine treated the matter with a seeming careless indifference, but, oh! the tumult of wounded love and pride that raged within her girlish breast!

"I was so fond of that woman, and she was only kind to me for the sake of a little amusement," she thought, with hot and burning cheeks at his tone when he repeated Mrs. Stansbury's contemptuous epithet, "that little salesgirl!"

To herself she said, angrily:

"I will not be a poor salesgirl any longer, to be twitted with my humble position in life. I will become an actress, and my talents will make me famous, so that these people will go to see me act, and be proud to say, 'I knew her once, but she is so rich and grand now that she would not stoop to renew the acquaintance.' As for Harry Hawthorne, who knows but that I may be able to pay him back some day for the slight he put on me! I am no longer grateful to him for saving my life; for why should he have saved it, only to plant a thorn in my heart?"

But she did not tell Cissy what the actor had told her about Harry Hawthorne. She could not bear to confess her humiliation.

But she went with Standish to the park the next day, and while skating on the lake a vision of beauty and grace that attracted the eyes of admiring hundreds, she told him that she had decided to go with the company on the road.

"Although Cissy is very angry with me, and vows that I will repent it in dust and ashes," she added, uneasily.

"Don't listen to her croaking. She only envies your good fortune," he returned, reassuringly. "Why, you will soon be rich and famous, Miss Harding, for your beauty and talent will win you rapid promotion on the boards. Do you see how all those strangers have watched you on the ice to-day? It is because your face has already won you the sobriquet of 'the prettiest salesgirl in New York.' Soon it will be changed to 'the prettiest actress on the stage.' Will not that sound better?"

CHAPTER X.

A CRUEL DISAPPOINTMENT.

"Love, dear friend, is a sacred thing!Love is not tinsel, silver or gold!Love is a fragment of Heaven's own gate,Broken in halves by God's hand, Fate,And given two kindred spirits to holdWho would colonize in our earth unknown,'Tis whispered them: 'You may be thrownFar apart—'"

Harry Hawthorne remained in the Bellevue Hospital ten days only, it having been discovered that his injuries were not internal, as at first feared.

His temporary unconsciousness had resulted from the severe cut on his head, and as this healed nicely, he grew better, and asked for his discharge from the hospital. Indeed, he would have recovered sooner but for a painful suspense and anxiety that augmented fever and restlessness.

The young fireman had been so deeply smitten by the charms of pretty Geraldine, that during his enforced confinement, the thought of her had never been absent from his mind. Love had sprung to life full grown within his breast.

When he was discharged from the hospital, he could not wait until evening to call on her. The ready excuse of the need of a pair of gloves took him to O'Neill's.

He did not wear his fireman's dress, but attired himself in an elegant suit of clothes, such as gentlemen wear to business. Thus arrayed, and looking as much the aristocrat as any Fifth avenue millionaire, he entered the store and went at once to the glove counter, his heart throbbing wildly at thought of seeing Geraldine again, and making an appointment to call on her that evening.

A whole row of smiling, pretty girls confronted him, but among them all he could not see his heart's darling, the lode-star of his dreams—sweet Geraldine.

He accosted the nearest girl—a plump, gray-eyed beauty—who fortunately proved to be Miss Carroll.

"I wish to have Miss Harding show me some gloves. Is she here?"

Cissy Carroll shook her dark head, and answered:

"Geraldine does not attend here any more. Can I show you the gloves?"

"If you please," he replied, and as she placed them before him, he took a pair, mechanically, in his shapely hand, but continued:

"I beg your pardon, but has Miss Harding gone to another store? She is a friend of mine. I wish to see her very much."

"Your name?" asked Cissy, with a quick suspicion of the truth, for he realized in his person Geraldine's description.

"I am Harry Hawthorne."

"I thought so. And I am Miss Carroll. Perhaps you have heard Geraldine speak of me?"

He smiled, and answered:

"Yes, as her 'chum Cissy.' She told me, also, that you roomed together."

"We did—but Geraldine has left me now."

She read the palpable disappointment on his face, and added, quickly:

"She had a talent for acting, and has gone upon the stage."

She saw him start as if she had struck him a blow in the face, and he grew lividly pale, as he asked:

"At what theatre?"

"Oh, she has left New York, and gone on the road with a stock company— the one that played 'Hearts and Homes' two weeks here. You may remember Clifford Standish, the leading man. He procured the situation for Geraldine."

Then, as she saw from his face that he was taking it quite hard, she added, with womanly curiosity:

"But how happens it that you are not acquainted with these facts? The papers had some very flattering paragraphs about the beautiful salesgirl who had left a New York store to adopt a stage career."

"I—I—haven't read the papers," he murmured, faintly, like one recovering from a blow.

"Oh, then you must have been away from New York—and poor Geraldine expecting you to call every evening. Why didn't you let her know?"

"I haven't been away from the city, Miss Carroll."

"Then why did you act toward her so shabbily?"

"Shabbily! Why I had a note written to her from the hospital, explaining that an accident had overturned my engine and seriously wounded me. I've been in Bellevue Hospital ten days, Miss Carroll. Look," and he showed her the scar on his head.

"Oh, it's a wonder you were not killed," said the girl, sympathetically.

"They thought I was at first, for I didn't recover consciousness until the next day. Then, as soon as I could think clearly at all, I thought of my broken engagement of the evening before, and wondered what she would think of me. I persuaded the nurse to write a little note for me, as I was too shaky myself, and sent it by the messenger-boy at the hospital. I hoped she would write me a line of sympathy, and that—perhaps—she might even be sorry enough to come and see me there. But I never received a word!"

"She did not receive your note. Your failure to come was a mystery to her always, Mr. Hawthorne."

"Why, that is very strange. I'll go back to the hospital and see that messenger. But—will you give me her address now?" eagerly. "I will write to her and explain."

Cissy blushed vividly, and said:

"I am sorry that I cannot, but the fact is I don't know where she is, for—we parted in anger, vowing to have no more to do with each other. I disliked Clifford Standish, and tried to persuade her not to go on the stage. She went in defiance of my advice—so she has not written to me."

———

CHAPTER XI.

A CRUSHING SORROW.

"Till now thy soul hath beenAll glad and gay;Bid it arise and lookAt grief to-day!For now life's stream has reachedA deep, dark sea,And sorrow, dim and crowned,Is waiting thee."

Miss Carroll was sorry for the young fireman, as she saw how pale and troubled his handsome face became at her tidings.

She exclaimed, sympathetically:

"Maybe Geraldine will get over her anger and write to me yet. She never stays angry long at a time. So, if she writes, I'll let you know."

"Thank you, a hundred times over," gratefully, "and may I call on you sometimes, to inquire?"

"Certainly," replied Cissy, who liked him as much as she had despised the actor. Almost every one has antipathies. The actor was one of Cissy's, no doubt.

Harry Hawthorne thanked her for her courtesy, paid for his gloves, and walked away with such a princely air that all the pretty salesgirls followed his exit with admiring eyes, and there was a swelling murmur of ejaculations:

"Oh, what a handsome fellow!"

"Isn't he perfectly magnif'?"

"Who is he, Cissy? A Fifth avenue millionaire?"

"Oh, no, indeed, girls; don't lose your wits! He's a fireman at the Ludlow street engine-house, that's all."

"Oh, then he must be a prince in disguise; and, come to think of it, millionaires are not usually good-looking, any way. I might have known he was poor, from his beauty. He was talking to you about Jerry Harding, wasn't he? Is she his sweetheart?"

"Perhaps so. Don't bother me! I don't know," laughed Cissy, cutting short their merry chatter.

Meanwhile the object of their admiration hurried away and returned to the hospital.

He had no trouble in finding the messenger-boy who had taken his note to Geraldine, and the youth, unconscious of having done wrong, very readily admitted that he had given the note to a gentleman, who said he was going in, and had offered to hand the letter to the lady.

"No harm done, I hope, sir?" he said, regretfully.

"Yes, more harm than you know. The man kept the letter, so the young lady never received it. It was something very important, too; and now she has gone away, and the mischief you did can never be undone."

"Oh, my! what a pity!" exclaimed the boy, readily guessing that here was a broken-off love affair. He looked pityingly at Hawthorne a minute, then continued: "I'm very sorry I made such a mistake. I thought the fellow was a gentleman. But I know him, and I'll get even with him for that trick—you see if I don't!"

"Who was he, Rob?"

"Why, that Standish that plays in 'Hearts and Homes.' An elegant swell, don't you know? Gave me a quarter, like a lord. But I'll hunt him up, and get back that letter."

"You are too late, Rob. He has gone on the road with his company."

"Whew! And the lady gone, too, with him?"

"Yes."

"Oh, what a kettle of fish! Of my mixing, too! Indeed, Mr. Hawthorne, I'm sorry; and, if I ever get a chance, I'll do that fellow up for his treachery, the villain!" cried the boy, so earnestly that the listener could but smile, for he had no faith in the possibility of such an event taking place.

He walked away, bitter at heart over the actor's treachery.

"He kept that letter, and managed to make trouble between us somehow, the cunning wretch!" he mused, sadly enough, for the case looked hopeless now.

Standish, having gained such a signal advantage over him in taking pretty Geraldine away, would follow it up by wedding her before his return.

"If I could find out where she is on the road, I might still write and explain all," he thought, with a gleam of hope that quickly faded as he recalled the treacherous nature of his rival.

"If I wrote to her, he would intercept my letter. He will be on the watch for that. There is no use trying and hoping. I have lost her forever—bonny, brown-eyed Geraldine!" he sighed, hopelessly.

As he returned to his work at the engine-house, he felt as if he had just closed the coffin-lid over a well-beloved face.

Such hopes and dreams as had come to him since he met fair Geraldine were hard to relinquish; they had brought such new brightness into his prosaic life; but he felt that all was over now.

True, he felt that he had made a strong impression on the girl's heart, but his rival would soon teach her to forget that he had ever existed.

But in a few days hope began unconsciously to reassert itself. He decided to call on Cecilia Carroll to inquire if she had any news.

He went that evening, and she told him that Geraldine had not written yet.

"But I found out from a manager the proposed route of the company, and I have written to her, and told her about you," she added, out of the kindness of her heart.

"Clifford Standish will take good care that she never receives your letter," he said, bitterly, as he told her how the actor had intercepted the note he had sent to Geraldine.

"I suspected as much, the grand villain!" cried Cissy, indignantly. "So now I shall write to her again and expose him!"

She did so, but no answer came to either of her letters.

Clifford Standish was too wily to permit Geraldine to receive them. He easily got possession of her mail, and destroyed it without a pang of remorse at his selfish heart.

- 45 -

CHAPTER XII.

THE LETTER THAT NEVER CAME.

"Write me a letter, my dear old friend,I love you more and more,As farther apart we drift, dear heart,And nearer the other shore.The dear old loves and the dear old daysAre a balm to life's regret;It's easy to bear the worry and careIf the old friends love us yet."

Yes, pretty Geraldine, piqued and unhappy over her cruel disappointment in love, had joined the Clemens Company, the manager of which was also one of the actors—Cameron Clemens. He played the clever villain in "Hearts and Homes," his special play, while Clifford Standish took the hero's part.

Geraldine threw her whole heart into her work, and succeeded so well that she was promoted in a week, owing to the illness and withdrawal of the second lady from the company. It was the part of an *ingenue*, which just suited Geraldine's youth and *naivette*. She could act it to perfection without laying aside her pretty naturalness of manner.

They traveled from town to town, staying just a night or two in each place, usually drawing full houses, and Geraldine proved a great attraction, winning always so much admiration that it was a wonder her pretty little head was not turned by flattery.

It might have been had not her heart been so sore over its brief, broken love-dream.

To have known a man but two brief, bright, happy days, and not be able to forget him, it was absurd, she thought, in desperate rebellion against her own heart.

And yet, through the busy weeks of travel, study, and acting, Harry Hawthorne's image staid in her mind, and his voice rang through her dreams, sweet and low and tender as it had always been to her whenever he spoke.

In her waking hours she knew him light and false; in her dreams he was always tender and true, and inexpressibly dear.

"Last night in my deep sleep I dreamed of you—Again the old love woke in me and thrivedOn looks of fire, on kisses, and sweet wordsLike silver waters purling in a stream—A dream—a dream!"

Through all the changing days in which the silent struggle against a hopeless love went on in her young heart, Clifford Standish was ever near, patient, tender, devoted, telling her with his yearning eyes the love she was not ready to listen to yet.

And in spite of herself, Geraldine found a subtle comfort in his devotion.

It was a balm of healing to her proud heart, so deeply wounded by Harry Hawthorne's trifling.

Many hearts have been caught in the rebound in this fashion, many true loves won.

True, there are many proud ones who do not prize a love they can only have because it has been scornfully refused by another.

They will say, resentfully:

"I will not accept a love that is given me only because it was left by one who did not prize it."

Others, more humble, will gladly accept the grateful love of a wounded heart that finds consolation in their tenderness.

Clifford Standish, madly in love with Geraldine, was glad to accept such crumbs of love as might fall to him from the royal feast that had been spread for Harry Hawthorne.

So he hovered by her side, he paid her the most delicate attentions, anticipating every wish, and found ample reward as he saw himself gaining in her grateful regard.

At the same time the arch-traitor was intercepting the few letters that came to her, and the ones she wrote to Miss Carroll.

For Geraldine had long ago gotten over her pet with her friend, since she know in her heart how dear she was to Cissy, and that the girl had advised her for her own good.

Geraldine had found out that the career of an actress—even a young, pretty, and popular one—is not always strewn with roses.

She had to study hard, and she did not enjoy traveling all day, or even half a day, and then appearing on the boards at night. Sometimes the hotel accommodations of country towns where they stopped over were wretchedly indifferent. Sometimes her head ached miserably, but she must appear on the boards, all the same. And the free-and-easy ways of some of the company did not please the fastidious taste of the girl.

Now and then she found her thoughts returning to the old days behind the counter at O'Neill's with Cissy and the other girls, with an almost pathetic yearning. Secretly she longed to be back again.

How she wished that Cissy would write to her now, and beg her to return, so that she might have an excuse for following the dictates of her heart.

At last, believing that Cissy was too proud and stubborn to write first, she penned her a long, affectionate letter, through which breathed an underline of repentance and regret that her chum would be sure to answer it by writing:

"Come home, dear. I told you that you would get sick of being an actress."

But Geraldine was too weary and heart-sick to care for a hundred "I-told-you-so's" from the triumphant Cissy. What did it matter so that she got back to her dear old chum again and their cozy little rooms, and even to what she had once called her slavery behind the counter.

She recalled what Harry Hawthorne had told her about it being a slavery of the stage, too; then put the thought from her with an impatient sigh.

"What do I care what he said about it?" indignantly, then sighing, "even though I have found it to be, alas, too true!"

She wrote her letter to Cissy, and after that her heart felt lighter. She knew her chum would be glad to get the letter—glad to have her back.

"Dear, I tried to write you such a letterAs would tell you all my heart to-day.Written Love is poor; one word were better!Easier, too, a thousand times to say.

"I can tell you all; fears, doubts unheeding,While I can be near you, hold your hand,Looking right into your eyes and readingReassurance that you understand.

"Yet I wrote it through, then lingered, thinkingOf its reaching you what hour, what day,Till I felt my heart and courage sinkingWith a strange, new, wondering dismay.

"'Will my letter fall,' I wondered, sadly,'On her mood like some discordant tone,Or be welcomed tenderly and gladly?Will she be with others, or alone?

"It may find her too absorbed to read it,Save with hurried glance and careless air;Sad and weary, she may scarcely heed it;Gay and happy, she may hardly care.

"If perhaps now, while my tears are falling,She is dreaming quietly alone,She will hear my love's far echo calling,Feel my spirit drawing near her own.

"Wondering at the strange, mysterious powerThat has touched her heart, then she will say:'Some one whom I love this very hourThinks of me, and loves me far away.'"

Poor Geraldine! what a hopeless waiting she had for the letter that never came!

How could he bear the wistful light in her sad brown eyes, the wretch who had robbed her young life of happiness?

In his keeping rested the letters of the two fond girls to each other—the letters that would have brought happiness to three sad hearts.

And the weeks slipped into months while they echoed in their souls the poet's plaint:

"The solemn Sea of Silence lies between us;I know thou livest and thou lovest me;And yet I wish some white ship would come sailingAcross the ocean bearing news of thee.

"The dead calm awes me with its awful stillness,And anxious doubts and fears disturb my breast.I only ask some little wave of languageTo stir this vast infinitude of rest.

"Too deep the language which the spirit utters;Too vast the knowledge which my soul hath stirred.Send some white ship across the Sea of Silence,And interrupt its utterance with a word."

It was two months now since they had gone upon the road, but not a word had Geraldine received. It seemed to her as if the past days were a dream, so different was her life now—all whirl, confusion, and excitement.

Once she had thought this would be charming. Now she found it the reverse.

How glad she was to hear that the company would go back to New York in time for Christmas. She was so tired of the West, where they had been all these weeks.

When they were on their homeward way, they stopped over for a night at a pretty West Virginia town a few hundred miles from New York.

They had come straight through from Chicago, and the stop-over was very agreeable to the weary members of the company.

They arrived in the afternoon, and the tired travelers, after resting a while at their romantic hotel on the banks of the beautiful Greenbrier River, set out to explore the little town of Alderson, first hurrying to the post-office for their letters, which they expected to be awaiting them there.

Geraldine did not expect any mail, poor girl! She waited at the door while Clifford Standish went in and came out with a little budget for himself.

"Nothing for you, Geraldine. It seems that Miss Carroll is still unforgiving," he laughed, without noting the sensitive quiver of her scarlet lips.

They walked on, and she pretended to be absorbed in contemplation of the beautiful mountain scenery, while he ran over his letters.

"Let us cross the railroad and walk on the bridge over there," she said, at last.

It was a beautiful sunny day, very calm and mild for December. They loitered on the broad bridge that spanned the romantic river between the two towns, Alderson and North Alderson, and while she watched the lapsing river and the mountain peaks against the clear blue sky, he read to her bits of his letters from New York.

"Here's one that will interest you," he laughed, meaningly, and read:

> "'Well, old fellow, there's nothing that I know in the way of interesting news just now, unless that a girl you used to be sweet on is going to be married to-morrow. It's little Daisy Odell, you know, of Newburgh. She's been visiting a married sister here, and caught a beau. He's a fireman named Harry Hawthorne, a big, handsome fellow, the hero of several fires. The marriage will take place at Mrs. Stansbury's, and I've an invitation to it.'"

He looked from the letter to her face, and saw that she was deadly pale and grief-stricken.

"Oh, will you let me read that for myself?" she gasped, as if she could scarcely believe him.

"Why, certainly," he answered, but as he was handing her the crumpled sheet, the wind caught it somehow, and fluttered it beyond reach over the rail and down into the river.

"Oh! oh! oh!" he cried, with pretended dismay, but his outstretched hand could not grasp it.

"It's gone; but no matter—the news must be true, for Charlie Butler wrote it, and he always tells the truth," he said, carelessly.

And how was the unsuspecting girl to know that no such words were written in the letter, and that it was from a woman, instead of Charlie Butler?

CHAPTER XIII.

TORTURED TO MADNESS.

"So the truth's out. I'll grasp it like a snake;It will not slay me. My heart shall not break.

"I was so happy I could not make him blest!So falsely dreamed I was his first and best!

"He'll keep that other woman from my sight;I know not if her face be foul or bright;I only know that it is his delight."

Geraldine was proud, very proud—and she thought she had quite overcome her hopeless love for Harry Hawthorne.

But the sudden, unexpected news of his marriage, that she never thought of doubting, struck her with the suddenness of an awful blow, beating down pride and reserve at one terrible stroke.

She realized all at once that her heart had still kept alive a little fire of hope burning before the shrine of its unacknowledged love. The quenching of this spark of hope was almost like the going out of life itself.

The other members of the party had gone on to the other side of the bridge and she was alone with Clifford Standish—alone with the agony of soul that blanched her sweet face to death-like pallor, and made her clutch at the rails, gasping out that she was ill, dying.

The arch-villain caught her swaying form and held it tenderly in his arms, while her white, unconscious face rested against his shoulder.

Some country people walking over the bridge at that moment stared in amazement, and going on to town, reported that, "those actor-folks were carrying on dreadful on the bridge—hugging right before folks."

But neither of the two participants was troubled over this sensation, Geraldine being unconscious, and Standish too much absorbed in her to heed aught else.

In a minute or two she sighed and opened her eyes.

"Oh!" she cried, as she met his eyes gazing deep into hers, and tried to struggle from his clasp.

"Wait. You cannot stand alone yet," he said, tenderly, then murmured: "Oh, Geraldine, it breaks my heart to find that you loved him, that low fireman, so unworthy of you; while I—I—have worshiped you ever since the hour I first saw you behind the counter, so bright and beautiful. I have been trying to win you ever since, and hoped—vainly hoped, as I see now—that I was succeeding. Oh, how did he succeed—this man you saw but a few hours—in winning your love?"

She struggled from his clasp, her strength returning, her face hot with blushes of fierce shame.

"It—it—is not true that I love him—no, no, no!" she faltered, wildly.

"But, my dearest girl, you fainted when you heard of his marriage."

"Oh, no, it was not that. I was tired, ill—from traveling, you know," cried poor Geraldine, who would have died rather than admit the truth which her pale, pale cheeks and trembling lips told all too plainly by their mute despair.

But her denial suited the actor's purpose, and he cried, gladly:

"Oh, I am so happy to hear you say you did not care for him. I feared—feared—that your kindness to me, your sweet smiles and ready acceptance of my attentions were only cruel coquetry."

"Oh, no, no," she murmured, helplessly, feeling herself drawn to him by every word he said.

Had she given him cause, then, to believe she meant to accept him?

He caught her hand, and continued, fondly, eagerly:

"Oh, Geraldine, dare I hope you care for me after all? That you will let me love you, and you love me a little in return? Will you—be my wife?"

He saw her shudder as with a mortal chill; then pride came to her aid. She let him keep the hand he had taken, and she answered, faintly:

"Yes."

And then a great horror of what she had promised rushed over her. How could she be his wife when she did not love him? Such a marriage would be sacrilege!

Her head drooped heavily, and her eyes were half-closed as she listened despairingly to the words of grateful joy he poured out. Not one of them found an echo in her heart.

Until now she had been grateful to him for his kindness, but a sudden aversion took root in her heart now, and she felt that she would rather die than be his wife.

But, to save her life, she could not have opened her lips to take back her promise.

She knew how angry he would be, how he would accuse her of trifling and coquetry. She could not bring down on herself the weight of his wrath.

But to the day of her death Geraldine would never forget that hour on the bridge at Alderson—that hour into whose short compass were crowded so much pain and regret that she longed for death to end her misery.

Mechanically she heard the whistle of an approaching train coming over the track at the end of the bridge. The rumble and roar blent with the rush of the river in her ears as she said, wearily:

"Let us return to the hotel. I—am—so—tired!"

Alas, poor girl! it was a tired heart!

They walked back toward the railroad, and the train came rushing on with a thunderous roar.

There was not one thought of suicide in her mind—she had always thought it a weak and cowardly act—but somehow a mad longing for death—because life was so bitter—seized on unhappy Geraldine.

The train was so close that they must wait for it to pass before they could cross.

She darted suddenly from the side of Standish and threw herself face downward across the trembling rails.

CHAPTER XIV.

A THEATRE PARTY.

"Time flies. The swift hours hurry byAnd speed us on to untried ways;New seasons ripen, perish, die,And yet *love stays*!

The old, old love—like sweet at first,At last like bitter wine—I know not if it blest or curstThy life and mine."

Harry Hawthorne called on Miss Carroll several times, but she always had the same discouraging story to tell—no answer from Geraldine to the letters she had written.

He gave up going at last, and tried to resign himself to his cruel disappointment.

"If she ever cared for me in the least, that villain Standish with his infernal arts, has turned her against me forever. But let him look out for himself if he ever returns to New York. We shall have a reckoning then, over my letter to Geraldine that he intercepted," he said to himself, bitterly and often.

Those were dreary days to the young fireman after he came out of the hospital and found Geraldine gone. People had always called him cold and unsocial somehow, and he became more reticent than ever now, going nowhere at all except when Captain Stansbury fairly dragged him to the house.

Mrs. Stansbury, as soon as she returned from Newburgh, had been anxious to renew her acquaintance with Geraldine, but meeting Standish on the street one day and asking after her, she was told that the young girl had lost her position at O'Neill's because of her trip to Newburgh and had gone back to her country home in consequence.

"Oh, I am so sorry, for I wished to cultivate her acquaintance, she was such a lovely girl!" the good-natured young woman said, regretfully:

"Yes, very pretty, but a shocking flirt! I got acquainted with her on the street by a handkerchief flirtation," laughed the actor, and he saw that the leaven worked. Mrs. Stansbury did not approve of forward girls, and her eagerness to see more of pretty Geraldine was at once abated.

She knew no better until weeks later, when her husband brought Hawthorne home for dinner, and discussing the pleasant times they had

had at Newburgh, he told her of Geraldine's going on the stage with Standish.

Little by little all came out, and she exclaimed:

"Mr. Standish must have lied to me in saying that she had lost her place and gone home to the country, and that he made her acquaintance by a street flirtation."

"It was cruelly false," answered Hawthorne, who had heard from Cissy the whole story of the beginning of the acquaintance of the wily actor and the pretty shop-girl. He continued:

"He wished to prevent your further association with Geraldine, so as to keep her away from me."

"And he really intercepted your letter to her? I did not dream he was such a villain."

"He shall answer to me for that injury when we meet again," he said, so sternly that she saw that he was in bitter earnest.

She admired him for his manly resentment, and said, cordially:

"I do not blame you for wishing to punish him. Any manly man would do likewise. As for Geraldine, when she learns of his perfidy, she will turn from him in disgust."

"Unless she has learned to love the villain. Women are so faithful in their love even when the object is unworthy," he sighed.

Changing the subject, she continued:

"Do you know that Sister Daisy is to be married the week before Christmas?"

"Your husband told me."

"Yes? Well, the bridal party are to spend Christmas with me. The other girls—Carrie and Consuelo—are coming, too. I intend to have a theatre party on Christmas Eve—a box to ourselves—and I want you to join us, won't you? And bring some pretty girl with you, for my sisters will have their beaus."

"I don't know any girl," he began, then suddenly remembered pretty Cissy Carroll.

"Oh, yes, I'll join the party if I can get leave. And there's a girl I know— Miss Carroll—the very intimate friend of pretty Geraldine. I'll bring her, if she will accept an invitation."

"Very well, and you may take me to call on her in the meanwhile, and then I can ask her to the dance I'm going to give the girls," replied amiable Mrs. Stansbury.

And so it was arranged that Cissy made the acquaintance of the Stansbury clique, and fell in love with them as deeply as Geraldine had done.

And on Christmas Eve they all filled a box at the theatre—and a merry party they were, for even Harry Hawthorne unbent from the grave reserve that was habitual to him of late, and tried to make himself entertaining to gentle Cissy while the orchestra played and they waited for the first act.

"What is the play?" asked Hawthorne, for Captain Stansbury had secured the tickets, and reserved the name of the piece as a surprise to the party.

"It's 'Laurel Vane'—a society play, by a well-known author—and it is to be presented for the first time to-night," replied Captain Stansbury.

"I hope it is a good company," said his wife.

"Oh, yes—excellent. The Clemens Company. I know the manager well."

There was a start from all, and Mrs. Stansbury said, nervously:

"But I thought that company was on the road."

"They returned to New York yesterday, with this new play," replied the captain, who was not in the secret of Clifford Standish's villainy.

The orchestra stopped playing, and the curtain rose.

CHAPTER XV.

GERALDINE WOULD NEVER FORGET ALDERSON.

It thrills one like a draught of rarest wine,The fine, pure air, the sunshine, and the scene,The mountains, and the river where it glides,A silver chain between its banks of green;And yonder, where the town lies white and low,On flowery banks so fair beneath the sun,Oh, Alderson sweet village I may goFull many a mile, nor find a fairer one!

MRS. ALEX. McVEIGH MILLER.

Poor, pretty Geraldine, if she had ever thought of death at all, she had never dreamed of ending her life like this beneath the wheels of this great panting, shrieking iron monster, rushing down upon her as her beautiful form lay across the bright steel rails where she had thrown herself in the extremity of despair!

But, frantic with hopeless love and terror at the promise she had just given—the reckless promise of her hand without the heart—reason had momentarily deserted its throne, and, conscious only of a mad desire to escape from life's tragedies of woe, she rushed forward in front of the train, and laid her golden head down upon the pillow of death, like one lying down to pleasant dreams.

And although her suicidal act was seen by fifty pairs of eyes, it was too late for even the most heroic hand to snatch her from her impending doom.

The locomotive was so close upon her the moment she fell before it that the immense cow-catcher touched her, and—even as the horrified shriek of Standish rang upon the wintry air—it seemed to draw her beneath the horrible grinding machine!

Did Heaven, in pity and mercy, intervene to save the rash girl from the consequences of her mad attempt at self-destruction?

Not once in a hundred cases is a human life saved by being caught and thrown upward by the projecting cow-catcher in front of the monster locomotive.

Yet once in a while such a fortunate intervention occurs, and a fatal disaster is prevented.

To poor, reckless Geraldine, who had placed herself beyond the reach of human aid, this accident happened, or our story must have ended here with the tragic close of her short life.

It almost seemed as if invisible angels must have caught up her doomed form from the track and placed it on the great shovel-like projection in safety, so miraculous seemed the saving of her life.

And a moment later the train, which had been slowing up as it entered the town, came to a full stop at the station, and the horrified engineer, who had been utterly unable to prevent what had seemed to happen, saw Geraldine's form lying on the platform of the cow-catcher, where it had rebounded at the first touch, and a cry of thanksgiving rose from his throat, echoed by a hundred other voices of those who had seen it all, and who now rushed to the spot in wild haste.

Quiet little Alderson had a sensation that day never to be forgotten in after years, when the express train rushed into the station bearing on its very front that form of a beautiful girl driven wild by sorrow, until she had tried to end her life in this terrible fashion.

What kind and eager hands drew her from her perilous position; what sympathetic eyes gazed on her beautiful white face as they laid her down on the platform, quite unconscious, for she had swooned when she threw herself on the track.

Every doctor in town was speedily on the scene. They vied with each other in their efforts to restore her to consciousness.

And in a few minutes Geraldine opened her heavy-lidded eyes with a blank gaze, and saw herself surrounded by a sympathetic, though curious crowd, and, as in a dream, heard Clifford Standish eagerly explaining to the people:

"Oh, no, indeed; you are mistaken. It was not an attempt at suicide; it was only a fool-hardy attempt to cross the track before the engine. She declared that she could do it safely, and dared me to follow her, darting from my side before I could restrain her, for I would not have permitted the rash venture otherwise. Still, I believe she would have accomplished the feat and cleared the track by a hair's breadth, only that her foot slipped and threw her down at that fatal moment."

Bending down to Geraldine's ear, he whispered, warningly:

"Do not contradict what I have told them, or they may put you in prison for attempted suicide, as they do in New York."

The people thought he was her lover, whispering to her of his joy at her safety, and in a moment he confirmed the belief by saying aloud:

"She would be distressed if any one accused her of trying to kill herself, for she is one of the happiest girls in the world. In fact, while we were standing on the bridge she had promised to marry me."

"Yes, I say him hugging her on the bridge, myself," said the old countryman who had passed them, and a smile went around, and then a cheer for the fair young life saved for a happy wedded future.

They carried her to the hotel that was but a few yards away, and it was found that she had sustained some bruises on her side, that was all. She would be able to go on with the company.

And a great revulsion of feeling took place in her mind—joy that her life was spared, horror at the momentary insanity that had driven her to that awful deed. Life grew sweet again, in spite of her great sorrow.

When the sympathetic women left her alone that evening in her room, she knelt down in a passion of repentance, and prayed God to forgive her for her great sin in trying to throw away the life He had given.

And she prayed Heaven to help her to forget Harry Hawthorne, and to love Clifford Standish, the man she had promised to marry.

"Surely he is good and true, and deserves my love," she thought, in an impulse of gratitude to him for the way he had shielded her when the people talked of suicide. She was ashamed of the truth now—glad for them to think it had been an accident.

"I will never be so foolish and so wicked again," she thought, in her keen remorse for her sin.

She spent a wakeful, restless night in spite of the sedatives the kind Doctor Spicer had administered before he went away. The hotel was so close to the railroad that she could hear the trains thundering by all night long, and the sound made her shudder with terror at thought of the heavy iron wheels that had come so near to crushing out her fair young life.

She was glad when morning came, and they boarded the train for New York.

She was eager to get away from this place, yet she would never forget Alderson, with its beautiful mountains, its romantic, winding river, and the bridge where she had stood with Standish, listening to the cruel words that had extinguished the last spark of hope in her breast and driven her mad with despair.

No, she would never forget beautiful Alderson, on the rippling, winding, singing Greenbrier River, set like an emerald chain between its romantic banks, overshadowed by wooded mountains, but she would remember it always with a horror it did not deserve, poor Geraldine, because of its tragic associations.

CHAPTER XVI.

"CALL PRIDE TO YOUR AID, GERALDINE."

"It is a common fate—a woman's lot—To waste on one the riches of her soul,Who takes the wealth she gives him, but cannotRepay the interest, and much less the whole.

"'Tis a sad gift, that much applauded thing,A constant heart; for fact doth daily proveThat constancy finds oft a cruel sting,While fickle natures win the deeper love."

We must return to our description of the scene in the theatre when the curtain rose on the first act, and the eager eyes of the large audience turned upon the stage.

The heroine of the play, Laurel Vane, a beautiful girl, left penniless and alone by the death of her only surviving parent, was discovered weeping in the shabby room from which she would soon be turned out, because she had no money to pay her rent.

Enter the handsome villain, Ross Powell, who declares his love for Laurel, and makes wicked proposals.

Repulsed with scorn, he departs, vowing vengeance on the scornful little beauty.

Desperate with misery, Laurel seeks a beautiful young lady, the noble daughter of a publisher, for whose magazine her father had written until his death.

"She is a sister-woman, and will help me in my trouble," thought the poor girl.

Between this splendid Miss Gordon and her clever maid, a plan was formed by which the orphan girl (by sailing under false colors) became the honored guest of wealthy people, and afterward the bride of a proud aristocrat, who thought he had married the peerless Miss Gordon, and had never heard of poor little Laurel Vane, who was his worshiped wife.

Upon this conspiracy hung all the plot of the play, and the leading parts were taken, first by Clifford Standish, leading man, the part of the hero, St. Leon Le Roy; the part of the heroine, Laurel Vane, by Geraldine Harding; the villain, Ross Powell, by Cameron Clemens; and Miss Gordon by Madeline Mills, the usual star of the company, although she had yielded precedence in this case to Geraldine, who looked so exactly the part of the *ingenue* heroine, with her starry brown eyes and curly golden hair.

But it is not necessary to our story to go into the details of the play. Although it enthralled the attention of the sympathetic audience, it held even greater interest for the party in the Stansbury box, because they knew two of the actors so well.

How it thrilled Harry Hawthorne to see pretty Geraldine again, even though he deprecated her stage career so bitterly.

As for Cissy, the tears sprang to her eyes when she first saw her lost friend, looking so familiar in the same simple black serge gown she had worn behind the counter when she was only a salesgirl at O'Neill's great store, and which answered excellently well for the mourning gown of the orphan heroine. Indeed, that floating mass of golden locks was glory enough to lend beauty to the shabbiest attire.

They watched her with absorbing interest through the changes of the play, but for a long time Geraldine did not perceive them. She was absorbed in her work, and did not cast coquettish glances at the boxes, like the other actresses. It was well she did not, for the sight of them would have unnerved her cruelly.

But Clifford Standish was on the alert, and while posing as the magnificent Le Roy, scowled secretly at the occupants of that particular box.

When the first act was over, he intercepted Geraldine on her way to the dressing-room, and said:

"I have something very particular to tell you.

"Yes."

"Now call your pride to your aid, dear one, for you will be shocked, I know. But I thought it best to put you on your guard."

"Yes," she answered, paling suddenly, but with her small head proudly erect.

"Have you noticed the first box to the right?"

"No, I have not looked at the house at all. I heard it was crowded," wearily.

"It is, and we have made a hit. But—that box—there's a theatre party in it—all people that you know."

"Indeed," listlessly, pretending no interest.

"Yes, and I tell you about them now so you will not notice them when you go on again in the second part. They are the Stansburys; the bride and groom, Harry and Mrs. Hawthorne; the two single Odell girls, and Cissy Carroll, with three young men—their beaus, no doubt."

She clutched his arm with a trembling hand.

"I—I—wish you had not told me," she faltered. "I—shall—be nervous now—in my part, I fear."

"You do not mean that you can care for that fellow still—you, my promised bride, and he the husband of Daisy Odell?" reproachfully.

"Oh, no, no; do not accuse me of such weakness," wildly. "But there is—Cissy, you know—Cissy turned against me, and we were so fond once!"

Her voice was almost a wail.

"Do not think of her, my dearest love—she is not worthy of it, the jealous, envious creature! Call pride to help you appear indifferent. Do not even turn your head toward that box, and they need never know how they have wounded your fond heart," he persisted, anxiously.

"Yes, yes; I will obey you," she answered, faintly.

"And, Geraldine, my darling—my sweet, promised bride—you know how madly I love you, but you have denied all my prayers for an immediate marriage! Will you not relent and make me the happiest man on earth? Oh, let us be married to-night after the play! It can be managed easily enough. Say yes, dearest?"

A call-boy came through the corridor, chanting:

"Only five minutes till next act—only five minutes."

She broke away from him, panting, breathlessly:

"I cannot answer you now."

She fled to her dressing-room, glad to escape his importunities, yet feeling as if she did not do him justice by her lack of love.

"He is so patient, so tender, and so eager to spare me pain, that I ought to love him more than I do," she told herself.

Respect and esteem she could give him, for she believed that he was good and noble, so well had he acted the traitor's part; but love—oh, we cannot give love at will!

"Life's perfect June, Love's red, red rose,Have burned and bloomed for me.Though still youth's summer sunlight glows;Though thou art kind, dear friend, I findI have no heart for thee."

She stole to the wings one moment, to gaze by stealth at the theatre party, and by the merest accident Harry Hawthorne was leaning over the bride's chair, talking to her of some trifle, but the sight made Geraldine draw back all white and quivering, with a cruel pang at her heart.

"I hate him!" she moaned, to herself, in a passion of jealous despair.

But when she came upon the stage she did not look again at the box, or she would have seen that Harry Hawthorne sat apart from Daisy, by the side of Cissy. She acted her part well, for in it there was much of the tragic pain that suited well with her desperate mood.

At the close of the second act, Standish renewed his pleadings for a marriage that night, and in her bitter mood, Geraldine, like many others who exchange one pain for another in mad impatience, ceased to struggle against his importunities and yielded a passive consent to his ardent prayer.

CHAPTER XVII.

AT THE END OF THE PLAY.

"A love like ours was a challenge to fate;She rang down the curtain and shifted the scene;Yet sometimes now, when the day grows late,I can hear you calling for Little Queen.For a happy home and a busy lifeCan never wholly crowd out our past;In the twilight pauses that come from strifeYou will think of me while life shall last."

Yes, she had promised to marry Clifford Standish as soon as the last act of the play was over. The act would leave the heroine, Laurel, presumably "happy ever after" but must plunge poor Geraldine into deeper despair.

For though she admired Clifford Standish greatly, was proud of his love, and grateful for his kindness, she did not feel as if she could ever love him as she had loved another. Her poor heart seemed dead and cold in its numb misery of slighted love, and the thought of marriage was repugnant to every instinct of her nature.

But she owed Clifford Standish such a debt of gratitude that there seemed no way of paying it save by yielding to his importunate entreaties for an immediate marriage.

But how she shrank from the moment that would seal her fate, although she had failed in courage to defend herself from it.

It was a bitter pride that was pushing her into this unloving marriage.

She would let Harry Hawthorne, who had flirted with her so cruelly, see that she did not care for him at all; that she could marry a man who was his superior in position, in riches, and in everything that made up true and noble manhood.

Geraldine despised a male flirt. Whenever one of the creatures tried to catch her eyes in public, she always set him down beneath contempt, and one withering glance from her flashing eyes would make him shrink into himself, ashamed for once before the scornful eyes of a true woman.

And the thought that Harry Hawthorne was one of those contemptible wretches was inexpressibly bitter.

She had shed many secret tears over the dread that he had read in her frank brown eyes the tenderness he had awakened in her heart.

She thought when she was married to the actor, and Hawthorne heard of it, he would think she had only been flirting with him at Newburgh, and that she had been engaged to Standish all the while. In this fancy there was a kind of balm for her aching heart.

She could hardly keep the tears back from her eyes as she thought it over and over, wondering if, after all, Harry Hawthorne had not cared for her a wee bit, but had been bound to Daisy Odell beforehand.

She wondered if she should ever meet him again, after she was married, and if it would give him pain to know if she belonged to another man.

To save her life, Geraldine could not help half-believing in the ardent love that had looked at her out of those dark-blue eyes, and if she would but have looked up at the box where he sat, she would have seen that love shining on her still—a love as strong as death, although it was so hopeless.

But Geraldine did not look that way, tutored to proud indifference by the cunning arts of Standish. She seemed cold as ice, but her heart was burning with restless longings for her lost love-dream.

"Perhaps he may repent and love me some day when it is too late—too late!" she sighed, bitterly, thinking of the sweet

SONG OF MARGARET.

"Ay, I saw her; we have met;Married eyes, how sweet they be!Are you happier, Margaret,Than you might have been with me?Silence! make no more ado!Did she think I should forget?Matters nothing, though I knew,Margaret, Margaret!

"Once those eyes, full sweet, full shy,Told a certain thing to mine;What they told me I put by,Oh, so careless of the sign.Such an easy thing to take,And I did not want it then;Fool! I wish my heart would break;Scorn is hard on hearts of men!

"Scorn of self is bitter work;Each of us has felt it now;Bluest skies she counted mirk,Self-betrayed of eyes and brow.As for me, I went my way.And a better man drew nigh,Fain to earn, with long essay,What the winner's hand threw by.

"Matters not in deserts oldWhat was born, and waxed, and yearned,Year to year its meaning told,I am come—its deeps are learned.Come! but there is naught to say;Married eyes with mine have met.Silence! Oh, I had my day,Margaret! Margaret!"

Poor Geraldine wished that the hands of time could turn back and delay the moment of her marriage, now so speedily approaching.

But the second act was over, the third and last began.

She was so nervous, it was the greatest wonder in the world that she did not forget her lines, and call down the ridicule of the audience. But she threw herself with abandon into the part. It was so tragic she could feel every word of it.

And so the end came.

It was the moment before the curtain fell, when the whole company were grouped upon the stage in the final tableau, that—a startling interruption occurred.

A deputy sheriff, with his aids, strode upon the stage, and clapped his hand on the shoulder of Clifford Standish.

"You are my prisoner!" he said, sternly; and added: "I have a warrant for your arrest for deserting your wife."

It was like a thunder-clap, so sudden and so startling.

The actor, at that moment, was holding Geraldine's hand in a fervent clasp, and he felt it turn cold as ice as she drew it from him in trembling horror.

He grew lividly pale beneath his stage make-up, but he tried to brazen it out by saying:

"Officer, you have made a mistake. I am not the man."

"Oh, yes, you are, Clifford Standish, and you must come with me to the Tombs at once," returned the deputy sheriff, with a satirical smile.

"I tell you it is a mistake; I have no wife, and this is a base attempt to injure an innocent man. I will prove it in court to-morrow," exclaimed the actor, putting on an air of injured innocence.

The audience was in an uproar, cries of sympathy and jeers of execration blending together. The accusation of the deputy sheriff had been heard by all. Mrs. Stansbury's box party looked and listened with breathless interest, and Cissy whispered to Hawthorne.

"Oh, the grand villain! trying to brazen it out! but I am sure that he is guilty. And poor Geraldine, how white and stricken she looks. I'm going down to her to persuade her to come home with me to-night."

"You must come with me," repeated the deputy sheriff, sternly, to Standish, and he answered, sullenly:

"Very well; but first let me speak to Miss Harding."

And while they guarded him closely, he whispered to the dazed and shrinking girl:

"For God's sake, do not believe the falsehood that has been trumped up against me by some enemy just to injure me in your regards. It is not true, and if you will only believe in me till to-morrow, I will prove it."

"I—I—will try to trust in you," she faltered, gently, but in her heart she knew that she was glad of this interruption to her wedding—knew that she hoped the charge was true.

If he had a wife already, he would be proved a villain, and she—Geraldine—would be free of the promise so rashly made.

"One more promise, my angel! Do not have anything to say to—to—my enemies in the box. They will try to turn your heart against me," he pleaded, feverishly.

"Come, come! I cannot wait any longer," the deputy sheriff said, roughly, and pulled him away before she could reply.

And the next moment Cissy's soft hand clasped hers, and her gentle voice said:

"Let us be friends again, dear Geraldine."

"Oh, Cissy, darling," and the pretty actress, whom all had been praising for her genius, fell into the other's arms, sobbing like a weary child.

"You poor, dear child!" cooed Cissy, patting the golden head. Then—"You'll come home with me for to-night, dear, won't you? I have a cab waiting."

Geraldine was only too glad to go. She hurried her friend to the dressing-room to wait while she got ready.

Cissy chatted incessantly:

"You didn't see us all, so grand in that box to-night, did you? I tried to catch your eye, but you never looked once! And poor Harry Hawthorne, how disappointed he was at your indifference!"

"Cissy!" and the pretty actress stamped her tiny foot angrily.

"Good gracious! What is the matter, my dear?"

"Never mention that man to me again! I hate him!"

"Who—Clifford Standish? I don't blame you! I've hated him ever since he first became known to me."

"No, no; I mean Harry Hawthorne!"

"Why, what has he done to you, Geraldine?"

"Has—hasn't he—gone and married Daisy Odell?" with a stifled sob.

CHAPTER XVIII.

REUNION.

"Let us begin, dear love, where we left off;Tie up the broken threads of that old dream;And go on happy as before; and seemLovers again, though all the world may scoff.

"Let us forget the cold, malicious fateWho made our loving hearts her idle toys,And once more revel in the old sweet joysOf happy love. Nay, it is not too late."

Cissy Carroll made big eyes of surprise at Geraldine's charge.

"Married Daisy Odell? Harry Hawthorne? Why, certainly not! Whatever put such an idea into your dear little noddle?" she demanded, in wonder.

"Mr. Standish told me so before we came back to New York. He said he had an invitation to the wedding. And isn't Daisy married to him, after all? Oh, Cissy, don't try to deceive me, for I saw her—saw her in the box all in white—so bride-like—and Harry Hawthorne leaning over her chair," exclaimed Geraldine, clutching the other's arm with unconscious violence, her beautiful eyes dilated with doubt and entreaty.

"My darling Gerry, don't pinch me black and blue, please, and don't get so excited. Yes, Daisy Odell is certainly married."

"Oh-h-h!" groaned Geraldine, in anguish.

"She is married," pursued Cissy, "and married to one of the dearest fellows in the world, she says—Charlie Butler—but not to Harry Hawthorne. Why, I don't believe he wants to marry any one in the world but you!"

"Me—Cissy!" and Geraldine's face, so lugubrious a moment before, grew radiant with joy, while the girl continued:

"That wretch, Clifford Standish, has told you falsehoods about Mr. Hawthorne, dear, for he never thought of loving any one but you. Didn't you see him with me in the box to-night? I am the only girl he ever goes with, and that is just for your sake, dear, because I was your friend."

"Oh, Cissy!"

Such joy as there was in those two words, for new life came to Geraldine in the assurance that Hawthorne was free, and loved her still.

She put on her dress with trembling fingers, crying:

"Oh, help me, Cissy, I'm so nervous—and—and tired, you know."

"Poor child! no wonder. And troubled, too, perhaps, for maybe you—loved that Standish!"

"Oh, no, no—never, Cissy!"

"Oh, I'm so glad, for that would have broken poor Hawthorne's tender heart, he loves you so much. And you, dear—didn't you care for him a little, too?"

Geraldine was all blushing, blissful confusion.

"I—I—you know how that was, Cissy. I liked him—just a little—at first, but when he did not come that night, or after"—she broke down, sobbing under her breath.

"Oh, Geraldine, he could not—he was hurt you know—and Standish intercepted his letter of explanation. But I mustn't rattle on like this, or I'll leave nothing for Hawthorne to tell you himself."

Geraldine looked at her with a glorified face.

"Oh, Cissy! Shall I see him soon?"

"He's waiting at the cab, dear, so let us hurry."

She fastened the ribbons of Geraldine's cape, and, taking her hand, hurried her through the corridor to the stage door.

And there—oh, joy of joys! stood Harry Hawthorne, waiting, with an eager, expectant look.

How Geraldine's heart bounded at the sight of that handsome face!

She could scarcely restrain herself from springing into his arms.

But, instead, she demurely held out her little hand, and he clasped it closely, saying as he led her to the cab:

"I am so glad to find you again, and we must have a long talk to-night."

CHAPTER XIX.

MUTUAL LOVE.

"Oh, happy love! where love like this is found!Oh, heart-felt raptures! bliss beyond compare!I've paced much this weary mortal round,And sage experience bids me this declare:If Heaven a draught of heavenly pleasure spare,One cordial in this melancholy vale,'Tis when a youthful, loving modest pairIn other's arms breathe out love's tender taleBeneath the milk-white thorn that scents the evening gale."

It was a long distance from the theatre to Cissy's home, but the distance was short to Geraldine and her lover, as they sat side by side in the cab, almost wishing that the ride would never come to an end, it was so heavenly sweet to be together again.

Both of them were in secret ecstasies at the catastrophe to Clifford Standish that had seemed to remove him from their path forever.

The future seemed to stretch before them roseate, shining, love-crowned, blissful.

Cissy did her best to explain away all the shadows that had come between them all.

"Geraldine, I wrote you five letters. Why didn't you answer them, you cruel girl?"

"Five letters? Oh, Cissy, I never received one of them; and it almost broke my heart that you would not answer all the long ones I wrote to you."

"You wrote to me? How strange that I did not get a line from you, dear. And I was so grieved, so uneasy over you. I thought you were proud and stubborn. But, tell me—did you post them yourself?"

"No; I always gave them to Mr. Standish to send out with the company's mail."

"Ah! that accounts for all. The wretch intercepted our letters to each other, just as he did Mr. Hawthorne's letters to you."

"I do not understand," said Geraldine; so they told her the story of the actor's treachery.

Everything lay bare before her now, and she comprehended that all she had suffered since her parting with Harry Hawthorne had been brought about by a deep-laid plot, involving both her happiness and honor; for what if she had married Standish to-night—he, who already had a wife, whom he had deserted!

Her honor would have been trampled in the dust; her life wrecked, to gratify the base passion of this monster, whom she had mistakenly believed the embodiment of truth and goodness.

Trembling with horror at all that she had so narrowly escaped, Geraldine bowed her head in her hands and sobbed aloud.

And Harry Hawthorne longed to take her in his arms and comfort her, but he did not have the right yet, for only words of friendship had been spoken between them, and he feared and dreaded that she had given her young heart to the wretch who had succeeded so well in his vile plans for parting them in the first flush of their sweet love-dream.

But now they were at home, and, bidding the cabman wait, he went in with the girls, saying:

"I know it is rather late to make a call, but something impels me to have a talk with Miss Harding to-night, if she will permit me."

She gave a glad assent, seconded by Cissy, who said, cordially:

"Yes, indeed, come in and talk to Geraldine. You are very excusable under the circumstances."

And, lighting up the poor, but neat, little room, she left them and retired to the adjoining one, where she busied herself with little preparations for the morrow, so as not to embarrass the lovers by her presence.

As for them, when they were left alone, Hawthorne, still standing, took Geraldine's hand and drew her to him, gazing into her face with tender, questioning blue eyes.

The answering look in her sweet tearful eyes was so satisfactory that he said:

"I think everything is explained between us now, is it not, Geraldine? You must have known before we parted that fatal day that I loved you!"

She could not speak because of the happy sob in her throat, but her burning blushes seemed to answer yes, and he pressed her little hand tighter as he continued:

"Yes, even in the brief time I knew you, dearest, you had become the one love of my life, treasured in my heart as the most rare and radiant thing under heaven. And I—I—fancied I read in your sweet smiles that my love would not be given in vain—that I should win you for my own!"

It was like the sweetest music in her ears to hear him telling his love so ardently, with that eager look in his eyes, and such a quiver of hope and fear in his musical voice. It was so dear, so sweet, so thrilling, Geraldine could have listened unweariedly forever.

Oh, first love! what a glimpse through the open gates of heaven it is to the youthful heart! Nothing that comes after, even in the longest life, can compare with it in bliss.

It clothes the world in new beauty, makes the sky more blue, the flowers more fair, the sunlight more golden.

And, thank Heaven, it can gladden the hearts of the poor and humble as well as the rich and great. None are so poor that beautiful Love refuses to visit them, or abide in their hearts.

So to this pair of lovers, though their lot in life was but lowly, and the roof that sheltered them humble, came as pure and rich a joy as if they had dwelt in palace halls. Is it not a glorious provision of Providence that love is free for all? Not bought like diamonds, although it shines brighter; not purchased like luxuries, although it is sweeter, but free as the pure air of heaven, although the greatest luxury, so that if it had to be bought it would bring the greatest price of all.

"Oh, Geraldine," cried her lover, "I love you still, I shall love you always, even if my love prove hopeless, and changes from bliss to endless pain! But give me some little hope to feed on, dearest one. Tell me that that base wretch Standish did not win you with his wicked arts, did not turn your heart against me!"

"Oh, no, no, no!" she murmured, faintly, then paused, abashed, remembering how she had listened to and believed all the cruel falsehoods against her true lover.

"You believed in me, in spite of all! Oh, how can I thank you——" he began, but she interrupted.

"Oh, no, I was not so noble as you believe, for I thought he told the truth. But—but—it made me wretched, thinking you were what he said, for—I could not love him, though he begged me. I—I—loved you, in spite of all!"

"Geraldine—my own!" and he caught her to his breast, their lips meeting in Love's first kiss.

Oh, the happiness of that moment; its never-to-be-forgotten bliss! It paid for all they had suffered in the months that they had been so cruelly parted by the machinations of a villain.

At last they thought of sitting down, although Hawthorne said, happily:

"But it must be for only a moment; then I must tear myself away, and not keep you from your needful rest, my beloved one. To-morrow I will come again, and feast my eyes on the sight of you."

"Oh, it is not so late, and—I am not sleepy," she faltered.

"Darling!" and he kissed the sweet lips fondly again; then, holding her hand, and looking deep in her tender eyes, he continued: "I am going to ask you for one pledge of the love you have so sweetly confessed for me, Geraldine. Promise me that you will never go on the stage again."

"Oh, never, never! I hate it now, and I will never tread the boards again!" vowed Geraldine, in eager earnest, shuddering at thought of the pitfalls Clifford Standish had spread for her unwary feet, and thanking Heaven in her secret heart that she had escaped them.

She could not bring herself to confess to her lover that she had actually promised to marry Standish that night, and that only a fortunate accident had prevented the consummation of the horror. Why, even now, instead of this dear hand-clasp, instead of these dear kisses, she might have been trembling in silent disgust at the caresses of a man she could never love! Oh, how good Heaven had been to save her from the consequences of her own folly, and restore her to her love again!

She resolved never to tell Hawthorne of that broken engagement. She felt that she could almost die of shame to have him find it out.

"I must keep that secret from him, and I must never tell him, either, that I tried to throw away my life when I thought him married to another. I should not like him to know quite how fondly I love him!" she thought, with sensitive maiden pride.

Then Hawthorne had to tear himself away.

"To-morrow is Christmas, and I shall try to spend it with you," he said, fondly. "But I may be kept from your side by a fire, for there are always so many on Christmas Day. So, if I fail to come, don't let Standish create any misunderstandings between us again," he laughed, secure in the thought that his enemy was safe in prison.

Geraldine promised very sincerely to trust her love, in spite of a hundred plots against him, and then they called Cissy in, and told her happily of their betrothal.

"I am the happiest man in New York to-night," he said, as he bade them good-night, leaving them to their sweet, girlish confidences.

CHAPTER XX.

"LOVE IS THE BEST OF ALL."

This golden ring, love, take,And wear it for my sakeWhen I am far away;And nightly we will prayThe dear God's pity on our pain,That we may meet again,Our partings o'er, our sorrows past,You mine, I yours, at last!

MRS. ALEX. MCVEIGH MILLER.

How much the two happy girls had to say to each other, when Hawthorne was gone!

It was long past midnight when they retired, and the joyous Christmas sounds were already filling the air. Even then they could not sleep, they had so many things to tell of all that had happened since they were parted from each other.

"I am quite cured of my passion for the stage. It seems to me that all actors must be deceitful villains!" cried Geraldine, and Cissy agreed with her, glad of her disillusionment.

"Do you think, Cissy," pursued Geraldine, "that I could get back my place at O'Neill's with you? Oh, I would be so glad to get back again!"

"We will try to manage it," replied Cissy. "One of the girls is to be married soon after New Year's, and perhaps you can have her place. I'll see about it as soon as I go back to the store; but we have Christmas holiday to-morrow."

"Yes; what a happy Christmas it will be for me!" cried Geraldine, thinking of what might have been, with a shudder. She laughed, to choke back a sob, and continued: "Let's hang up our stockings to-morrow night, as it's too late now, and fill them for each other as we did last Christmas."

"Agreed, my dear; it will be great fun," laughed Cissy, and added: "I suppose your Christmas gift from Mr. Hawthorne will be—an engagement-ring."

"Oh, Cissy, how nice that would be! Do you think he can afford it? Firemen aren't very rich, are they?" naively.

"I guess not; but of course he will give you a ring, even if it's a plain gold band, that will do also for a marriage-ring when the wedding comes off."

"No matter how simple a ring he gives me, I shall love it, and be proud of it, for his sake—just as proud of it as if it were a splendid diamond!" cried pretty Geraldine, tenderly, and then she laughed and said, further: "I used to be such a silly little goose, thinking I would never love and marry any man who could not give me silks and diamonds; but love has changed my nature, and I prize Harry's love more than anything on earth. Of course, I still admire beautiful, costly things, but I would not give him in exchange for a millionaire."

"You are right, dear. Although it is well to have love and wealth, too, yet love is the best of all, and I would not barter it for anything on earth," answered Cissy, so earnestly that Geraldine put her arm around her neck and whispered, coaxingly:

"Dear, you have always spoken so sweetly of love—and yet you do not seem to care for lovers yourself. Why is it? Have you never loved any one?"

Geraldine felt her companion tremble a little, then she replied, lightly:

"That is a leading question—as the lawyers say—and I don't believe I will answer it just yet. Wait—I will tell you another time."

And her answer only confirmed Geraldine in the belief she had cherished for a long time that there was a romance in Cissy's past—some love-story that had somewhat saddened her life and made her lips and eyes so sweetly pensive. From her own happy heart swelled up a silent prayer that love and joy might come soon to Cissy's life, with the same rich blessings it brought to her own.

"Now cuddle your head on your pillow, dear, and go off to the land of Nod, or you will not look pretty for your sweetheart to-morrow," commanded Cissy; and soon they were both fast asleep and wandering in the land of dreams, from which they did not return until the light of day peeped in at the windows.

"Good gracious! it must be eight o'clock! I've overslept myself this blessed Christmas morning. A good thing I don't have to go to the store to-day!" Cissy cried, springing out of bed and running to the window, where she thrust aside the curtain and peered out into the street.

A beautiful sight presented itself—a great city clothed in a resplendent mantle of deep snow, that had come between the dark and the dawn, and overhead a clear, blue sky and brilliant sunshine.

"Oh, how grand! how beautiful! and what glorious sleighing there will be to-day! Wake up, Geraldine, and see the beautiful Christmas morn!" cried the young girl, who, although she had so little of this world's goods, and did not expect a single Christmas gift, was unselfishly happy in the prospect of pleasure for others.

But they had scarcely finished their simple breakfast, gayly prepared by both their hands, when there was a knock at the door, and several packages were handed in for both of them—a little feast of fruit and confectioneries, jewel-box, with a dainty pin for Cissy, and another for Geraldine, with a ring. The gifts bore the card of Harry Hawthorne.

"Oh, how lovely in him to remember me like this! I shall fall in love with him myself! This dear brooch! How I adore it! See the dear little enameled violets, with dewy centers like real diamonds! Oh, how generous he is!" Cissy cried, rapturously, while Geraldine paled with emotion as she slipped over her finger a beautiful ring, and held it up for inspection.

Cissy went almost dumb at the sight, for the stone was a pure diamond of good size, and worth more than either girl had any idea of in their ignorance of the value of gems.

"Oh, Cissy, it is a real diamond, is it not? See how it glitters!" cried Geraldine, tremulously, as she turned her hand about, admiring the sparkling rays of light.

She was fairly overwhelmed with joy at this beautiful gift from her lover, and continued, breathlessly:

"Oh, it is so beautiful! I am so proud to have it! But—but—wasn't he rather—extravagant, Cissy? I should not have thought he could afford it, for surely it must have cost a hundred dollars at least—don't you think so?"

"More than that, in my judgment," cried Cissy, finding breath after her rapturous amazement, and continuing: "But it is none too pretty or costly for you, my beautiful darling, if he can afford it; and of course he can, or he would not have sent it. Perhaps he is not as poor as we thought. He looks like a prince in disguise, anyway, he's so stately and handsome!"

She paused, for Geraldine had found a note in the box, and was reading it.

> "MY OWN DARLING:—I am disconsolate this morning because I could not get leave of absence to come to you," wrote Hawthorne, fondly, "but I couldn't get a man to take my place at the engine-house to-day, and I daren't desert my post, for there have been two fires already this morning, and I was out with my engine in the driving snow of dawn, while you, I hope, were wrapped in slumber and sweet dreams of your adoring sweetheart!

"Isn't the snow fine? I shall try my hardest to get off in time to take you and Cissy for a grand sleigh-ride before the day is ended.

"I send you both some bon-bons and fruits, with a brooch for Cissy, and a ring for you. You will be asking yourself how can a poor fireman afford to give diamonds to his betrothed and her dear friend! Well, darling, both trinkets were heir-looms from my dead mother, who was richer in worldly goods than her son. So the little mystery is explained.

"God bless you and keep you, my beloved, until we meet again, which I trust and hope may be this afternoon.

"Devotedly,

HARRY."

Geraldine gave her friend the note to read, then they discussed some of the dainties, while Cissy said, regretfully:

"If I had only known yesterday that I should have you with me to-day, I should have prepared a real little feast for our dinner, but I felt so lonely and sad I prepared nothing extra, and now I really must slip out and buy something good. What would you like, dear—a dear little chicken and some oysters? For a turkey would be too big for us two!"

"Oh, some oysters, please; I am so fond of them, and they are not so good out West, where I traveled so long," cried Geraldine, with real girlish delight, it seemed so jolly to be back with Cissy, playing at housekeeping again.

"I'll never leave my darling again until—I marry!" she thought, with kindling blushes, and while Cissy was gone she employed her time writing a very polite note to Mr. Cameron Clemens, the manager of the Clemens Company, resigning her situation, to take effect at once.

When she remembered Mr. Clemens, she felt a little remorseful over her denunciation of all actors last night, for she had found this one very kind and clever during her engagement with the company.

She went down stairs and engaged the landlady's son to take her note at once to the hotel where the manager was staying, and then tried to dismiss the matter from her mind, but she felt a little remorseful, for Laurel Vane was billed to appear again to-night, and she knew it could not go on, now that she and Standish had both withdrawn—that was, of course, unless the latter could get free from prison, which did not seem likely, considering the nature of the charge against him.

When Cissy came in, Geraldine said, happily:

"I feel as free as a bird, for I have sent in my resignation in the Clemens Company, and now I shall not have to leave you any more."

"Until Mr. Hawthorne steals you away from me," amended Cissy, kissing her rosy cheek before she hurried into the adjoining room to prepare her little Christmas dinner.

"Let me help you!" pleaded Geraldine.

"Oh, no, you shall be company come to dine to-day. And, besides, you must stay dressed up, to receive callers."

"But there's no one to call."

"Oh, yes, there is," and her words proved true, for before the day ended there came Mrs. Stansbury, with her three sisters, Carrie, Consuelo, and Mrs. Charles Butler, the lovely bride of whom Geraldine had been so horribly jealous.

How glad they all were to see her again; how they petted and made much of her, denouncing Clifford Standish for a real villain.

"And you're engaged to that splendid Hawthorne—how charming! Oh, you needn't blush! He told my husband this morning, and we all hurried off to wish you joy," cried volatile Mrs. Stansbury.

CHAPTER XXI.

"OH, GERALDINE, I'LL HAVE TO TELL YOU MY GUARDED SECRET!"

"I have a secret sorrow here—A grief I'll ne'er impart;It heaves no sigh, it sheds no tear,But it consumes my heart."

At last the Stansburys were gone, but then some of the girls from O'Neill's dropped in. It was a merry, happy day to Geraldine, with but one shadow on its brightness—the absence of Hawthorne.

At every knock she started up, all blissful, blushing confusion, thinking that surely this time it was he, but each time she was doomed to a sad disappointment.

But from the constant ringing of fire alarms through the day she easily guessed what kept him from her side.

But when the afternoon was far spent, and the sunlight grew pale and cold, there was a masculine step at the door that made her heart throb quickly again with eager hope as she sprang to open it, thinking:

"I cannot be mistaken. He is come at last!"

But the next moment she stood face to face with the handsome manager, Cameron Clemens.

And as he entered there was a soft little swish of skirts as Cissy fled to the next room.

"How she hates anybody connected with the stage!" thought Geraldine, amusedly.

The manager had come to entreat her to reconsider her resignation.

He could get some one else to take the place of Standish in the play, if she would only go on, he said.

But Geraldine was obdurate. She told the manager frankly that she was engaged, and her betrothed objected to her return to the stage.

"I am very sorry for your disappointment," she said; "I like you, and you have been very kind to me, but my betrothed objects, you see, and that settles the case with me."

Mr. Clemens did not fly into a rage, as many another would have done in his place. He wished Geraldine joy, told her that the stage had lost an ornament in her withdrawal from it, presented her with the amount of salary still due her, and took a courteous leave.

He knew that he could put on another play, in which the remainder of the company could do very well that night, but he sorely regretted the loss of Geraldine, who had certainly proved a drawing card.

But he could not help the turn of events, so he went his way, bitterly disappointed, while Geraldine called into the other room:

"You can come back now, Cissy, for Mr. Clemens is gone. But, you silly girl, why did you run away? I wished you to know him, he is so nice and handsome!"

There was no answer from her friend, and she went back into the room.

There was Cissy, on a low seat in the darkest corner, and presently there came a low, stifled sob.

Geraldine flung herself on her knees by her friend, in great surprise and alarm.

"Oh, my darling girl! what ails you? Are you sick? Did the bonbons disagree with you?"

"No-o-o!" sighed Cissy.

"Then what is it, dear? Are you in trouble? Or were you angry because the manager came here? But this shall be the last of any stage visitors, I assure you! Or do you want me to go away, Cissy?" plaintively.

"Oh, Gerry, you will drive me mad with your questions! I'll have to tell you my guarded secret!"

CHAPTER XXII.

"THAT WOMAN SHALL PAY DEARLY FOR THIS!"

From my hand I tore in angerThat dear pledge, the wedding ring—Swore
that I would learn to hate him,But it is so weak a thing,This poor woman's
heart, that, beatingHeavily within my breast,Aches with jealous grief and
anger,Tortured with a fierce unrest.

MRS. ALEX. MCVEIGH MILLER.

Most bitter were the reflections of the elegant villain, Clifford Standish,
during the long night in his prison-cell.

He knew too well that the charge against him was perfectly true, and that
his boast to Geraldine that he would clear himself at court was absolutely
false.

Two years before, he had secretly married a piquant variety actress, of
whom he had soon wearied, but from whose fetters he could not get free.

Her life was absolutely irreproachable, and he could find no flaw in it on
which to base an application for divorce.

And all of his flagrant violations of faith, although known too well to his
wife, did not goad her to seek release from him.

She loved him, poor creature, with that dog-like devotion seen in some
women of average intellect, who love the hand that smites them. She was
romantic, and called it constancy; other women called it lack of spirit.

She could not and did not comprehend the baseness of the man she loved.

The end and aim of her poor, wrecked life was to win him back to the
allegiance of which he had wearied so soon.

Although she dared not disregard his injunction not to reveal their
marriage, she followed him about as often as her engagements would
permit, trying to keep track of his movements.

When he was away from the city, she wrote him long love-letters, over
which he laughed in heartless amusement.

It was one of these letters that he had pretended to read to Geraldine on
the bridge at Alderson, claiming that it contained news of Hawthorne's
marriage.

It was this woman who had prevented him from accompanying Geraldine to Newburgh, by threatening to reveal his fatal secret.

At length, driven almost mad by his fiendish conduct, she had thrown caution to the winds, and caused his arrest on the stage that night for desertion.

But she would have trembled with fear could she have heard his threats against her that night as he raged up and down his prison-cell, execrating her as the cause of his losing pretty Geraldine forever.

"A few more hours and my peerless girl would have been mine, all mine! Oh, to miss happiness by so slight a chance, it is horrible, and dearly shall that woman pay for this!" he swore.

But he knew that his wrath was futile, for she would have all the proofs of his conduct ready to cover him with shame in the morning.

The morning found him sullen, bitter, desperate. The policemen said afterward that his eyes looked actually fiendish when he was placed in the Black Maria to be conveyed to the court-house in Chambers street.

That fiendish look was still in his eyes when they started to transfer him from the vehicle to the court-house, and—how it exactly happened they never could tell—but the seemingly quiet prisoner whom they had not thought it necessary to handcuff, suddenly struck out with two athletic fists, landing one startled policeman on the snowy pavement, and the other one flat in the gutter. Then he fled like a professional sprinter, and nobody tried to stop him, perhaps because they pitied the poor devil, and wished him his liberty this glorious Christmas morning.

CHAPTER XXIII.

CISSY'S SECRET.

Ay, but, darling, speak his name;Give to sorrow words and tears;This strange silence, proud and cold,Fills my heart with anxious fears.Curse him, bairnie, or forgive him,For I know Love's subtle art;The grief that's never spokenMay sometimes break the heart.

MRS. ALEX. MCVEIGH MILLER.

"I must tell you my guarded secret," sobbed Cissy, to Geraldine, and the latter put a loving arm around her, whispering, tenderly:

"Yes, tell me all, dear; for maybe it will ease your sore heart. You know the poet says:

"'Give sorrow words—the grief that does not speakWhispers the o'erfraught heart and bids it break.'"

The last rays of the setting sun stole in and rested like a blessing on the dark and golden heads close together, then faded out, and left the little room in gloom as Cissy sighed:

"Oh, I thought I was getting over it; I thought I was contented again until his voice and face brought back the cruel past!"

"Whose voice and face, dear Cissy? Oh, do you mean Mr. Clemens? Did he have anything to do with your secret sorrow?"

"Everything!"

"Oh, dear, and was that why you rushed away when he entered the room?"

"Ye-es," sobbed Cissy.

"Why, this grows very interesting," exclaimed Geraldine, who dearly loved a romance. "Why, I never even dreamed of your knowing Cameron Clemens! Why didn't you tell me?"

"Oh, I did not wish to do so. I did not mean to resurrect my sorrow from the grave where it has rested for years. Oh, why have I promised to tell it now?" began Cissy, suddenly repenting her weakness.

"Oh, darling, I'll never, never breathe it to a living soul, poor dear. Now go on, that's a sweet girl! Was Mr. Clemens your lover?"

But as the last word left her lips there came a loud, impatient double knock upon the door, making both spring up in surprise and alarm.

"Oh-h!" cried Geraldine.

"Oh-h!" echoed Cissy.

Then they smiled at each other in the deepening gloom, and Geraldine exclaimed:

"How that knock startled me! But, of course, it's Harry at last."

He was Harry to her now, her darling, and how sweet the name sounded from her rosy lips.

"Of course it is Harry. Run to the door, dear," returned Cissy, secretly glad of an interruption to the story she had promised to relate to her friend.

All in a moment she had repented it, and wished to keep the secret still.

So she was glad of the opportune interruption.

"Run to the door, dear. Do not keep him waiting," she urged, and Geraldine flew blithely to open the door for her lover, as she had done a dozen times before that day, meeting each time, as she did now—blank disappointment.

A man stood before her, to be sure, but he was an utter stranger—good-looking and well-dressed, with a bearded face and a hat pulled low over his eyebrows.

"Are you Miss Harding?" he asked, in a low, muffled voice.

"Yes."

He handed a note to her; and forgetting, in her wonder, to ask him in, she took it, and leaving him at the open door, crossed over to the window to read it by the dim and failing light of the waning day.

It ran simply:

> "My darling, there have been so many fires to-day I've been on a dead run, and am almost tired out; but I didn't forget my promise to take you for a sleigh-ride, and the thought of you has been singing in my fond heart all day. It's late, I know—past five now, and I can't get off duty at the engine-house until six o'clock; but I thought I would take time by the forelock and be ready to take you for a little spin, if you don't mind the hour. So my friend, Jem Rhodes volunteered to go to the livery stable and get a

sleigh for me, and bring you down to the engine-house by six o'clock, so I could take the reins the minute I'm free.

"Will you come with my good friend, Rhodes, dear? A clever fellow to do us this good turn, is he not?

"Hastily and fondly,

H. H."

In the dim light the writing looked the same as that she had received that morning from her lover. Not a doubt crossed her mind.

She hastily explained the case to her friend.

Cissy could see no objection to the plan, and she was rather relieved that Geraldine was going, so that she could not tease her for the love-story she was now reluctant to tell.

"It seems all right," she said, encouragingly.

Geraldine flew to get on her warmest wraps, and Cissy invited Mr. Rhodes to come in to the fire.

"I will light the gas," she said, hospitably, but he shrank back into the shadowy hall.

"No, thank you, I must go down and look after the horses. Please tell the young lady to hurry," he said, in that strange, muffled voice, retreating down the stair-way as he spoke.

Geraldine was ready in a minute, and Cissy went down with her to the sleigh, an elegant turn-out, with two horses.

"Don't stay too late, dear, or you may take cold," cautioned Cissy, tenderly; and then they kissed each other good-by, little dreaming how long it would be, poor dears, before they met and kissed again.

CHAPTER XXIV.

IN THE POWER OF A FIEND.

"The bard has sung: God never formed a soulWithout its own peculiar mate, to meetIts wandering half, when ripe to crown the wholeBright plan of bliss, most heavenly, most complete.

"But thousand evil things there are that hateTo look on happiness. These hurt, impede,And, leagued with time, space, circumstance, and fate,Keep kindred heart from heart, to pine and bleed."

Cissy went back to her lonely rooms, stirred up the fire to a brighter blaze in the tiny stove, then sat down to a dreary retrospection of past days, her small hands folded idly in her lap, her dark head bowed in sadness.

The sight of the handsome actor-manager, Cameron Clemens, had brought her memories from the past sweet and bitter in a breath, kindling old love and renewing old pain.

"How dared he come? He must have known that Geraldine was with me! Did he think I would ever willingly meet him again?" she murmured, bitterly; then started to her feet, for there was another masculine rap upon the door.

"Who is it this time?" she wondered, as she opened the door.

A cry of surprise came from her lips for there stood Harry Hawthorne, handsome as a picture, in citizen's dress, his fireman's uniform laid aside, his stately figure looking its best in a long fur-lined overcoat.

"Good-evening, Miss Carroll. May I come in?" he asked, gayly, with that ring of happiness in his musical voice one hears from a recently accepted lover.

"Come in," Cissy answered, mechanically, in her amazement, letting him enter and close the door ere she asked, uneasily:

"Where's Geraldine? Didn't she come back with you?"

"With me? I don't understand you. I've just got away from my duties at the engine-house, and I thought if you and Geraldine didn't mind going out at night, we could have our sleigh-ride yet. There will be moonlight after a while."

Cissy grasped the back of a chair to steady herself. Her face was pale, her dove-eyes dilated.

"But—didn't you send a sleigh here just now for Geraldine?" she gasped.

It was his turn now to look startled, and his eyes went from her face to the next room as he exclaimed:

"Isn't Geraldine here now?"

"No, no—of course not. Didn't I just tell you that she went away just now in a sleigh that you sent to bring her to the engine-house?" answered Cissy, turning up the light in a mechanical way, as women will attend to trifles even in trouble.

She saw that he was deadly pale and excited, and he said, in a strained voice:

"But I did not send any sleigh. There must be some mistake."

"There is treachery somewhere. Oh, why did I let her go, poor child?" cried Cissy, with a sudden awful presentiment of evil.

He sank into a chair, trembling with dread.

"Tell me quickly what you mean—give me every clew you can—for I must go in search of her," he exclaimed, anxiously.

And Cissy told him about the man, Jem Rhodes, and the note, and the elegant sleigh in which Geraldine had gone away so blithely, her rosy face radiant with joy, thinking to meet her lover.

"Why, there is the note now," she said, taking it up from the table where Geraldine had left it, and handing it to Hawthorne.

He ran over it hastily, his blue eyes flashing with anger and apprehension.

"I never wrote this note—it is not in my writing! How did Geraldine ever make such a mistake?" he cried, hoarsely.

"She read it hastily by a dim light," said Cissy.

"And there is just enough likeness to my hand to have deceived her that way," he cried, in anguish, for the conviction of something dreadful had come to him. "Oh, my darling, you are the victim of some cruel plot," he groaned, his handsome face blanching to a deathly hue.

Poor Cissy breathed, faintly:

"Oh, who could have planned this outrage? Clifford Standish is the only man I know likely to be guilty of it. But he is in prison."

"Have you not heard? The villain escaped from the officers at the door of the Chambers street court-house this morning, and is still at large. No doubt he wrote this fraudulent note; no doubt it was he who carried Geraldine off. Tell me what the wretch looked like."

Then Cissy remembered that the man Rhodes had refused to enter the lighted room, and had been strangely taciturn, speaking only when necessity required, and then in a low, muffled voice.

"Oh, I ought to have suspected him then. I was culpably careless and thoughtless, letting that poor child go with him," she thought, in an agony of distress.

When she had described the man to Hawthorne, he declared his belief that Standish himself, with but slight disguise, had personated the mythical Jem Rhodes.

"She is in the power of that fiend at this moment!" he exclaimed, starting up in a passion of grief and anguish that made poor Cissy burst out into hysterical weeping.

He was rushing to the door, and he looked back at the sound of her sobs, and said, gently:

"Don't take it so hard, Miss Carroll, for Heaven's sake. You are not to blame, neither was she, for that note was plausible enough to deceive any one. But I'll find her and bring her back to you, or I'll have that villain's cursed life!"

CHAPTER XXV.

UNDER SUSPICION.

"Through the blue and frosty heavensChristmas stars were shining bright;Glistening lamps throughout the cityAlmost matched their gleaming light;While the winter snow was lying,And the winter winds were sighing,Long ago one Christmas night."

We must follow Clifford Standish on his successful flight from justice that Christmas morning, when the spirit of the day was so much in every heart that no one who witnessed his escape cared to give chase to the fugitive. Perhaps, indeed, they thought that one who could outwit two stalwart policemen deserved his liberty.

Be that as it may, the actor made good his escape to a place of refuge, where he lay a while *perdu*, concocting new plans for retrieving last night's disaster.

The thought that he had lost pretty Geraldine forever was bitterness to his heart.

But he felt just as certain of it as if he had witnessed all that had transpired last night.

He knew well that when he was not by to guard Geraldine, that her friends in the box would swoop down upon her and carry her off in triumph.

There would be fond meetings, eager explanations, and all his treachery to her would be painted in its blackest colors. His only hold on her esteem, her touching belief in his truth and goodness, would be destroyed.

He would stand forth in his true colors before her horrified eyes—a black-hearted wretch, the husband of another woman, who had sought by the blackest lies and foulest arts to lure her—pretty Geraldine—to irrevocable ruin.

She would thank God that He had interfered in time to save her from him at almost the very last moment.

Standish gnashed his teeth as he thought of her joy over her escape, for he knew well how she had secretly shrunk from him, though out of her wounded pride she had promised him her hand.

He guessed well that all was explained between her and Hawthorne now, and that they were already betrothed lovers.

If hate could have killed this pair in their exquisite happiness, then Clifford Standish would have sent a bolt of it to strike both of them dead.

In his jealous fury he raged and swore almost constantly. The little room he occupied became stifling with the fumes of wine and tobacco that he used to solace him in his terrible defeat.

But he was careful not to drink too much. He did not wish to stupefy his brain.

He wished to keep it clear that he might plot new deviltry.

Almost any man in his place would have given up the game after being so signally worsted by fate.

Not so with Clifford Standish. The stroke of adversity only roused in him a devilish obstinacy, a determination to rule or ruin.

Hate for Harry Hawthorne, and a mad passion for Geraldine Harding, drove him on to new wickedness.

He spent a good part of the day in seclusion, laying his wicked plans, like a crafty spider weaving his web; then, disguising himself with a wig, beard, glasses, and cosmetics, dressed himself in a cheap new suit, and sallied forth to victory. No look of Clifford Standish remained except the stately walk, and even this he could change at will.

So, later on, he imposed on Geraldine and Cissy as Jem Rhodes, the trusty friend of the fireman.

But, before coming on his fatal mission, he had informed himself as to everything that was necessary to make the daring abduction he had planned an absolute success.

He knew that Harry Hawthorne had become engaged to Geraldine through eavesdropping at the door when the Stansburys called on her. He had also heard her tell them that she and Cissy were to have a grand sleigh-ride with Harry, although it might be late in the day when he got off duty.

The unsuspected listener smiled grimly to himself as he muttered:

"You shall certainly have your sleigh-ride, my little beauty, but not with your Harry and Cissy—no, indeed!"

Between the hours of five and six he sought a livery stable, and asked for a driver and sleigh to take himself and a lady to the Cortlandt street ferry.

As the stable keeper was a stranger to him, he did not think it necessary to disguise his voice; but spoke in his natural tone, and a youth who was lounging about the office started and gave him a keen, curious glance.

Standish did not notice the young man, or he would have perhaps recognized him as the messenger-boy from the hospital where Harry Hawthorne had been taken after the accident—the youth from whom he had taken the letter to Geraldine.

Robert had promised Hawthorne that he would at some time pay Standish for his treachery, but fate had been unkind to him so far in the continued absence of Standish from the city, and the youth had almost forgotten the incident until the clear, ringing voice of Standish, familiar to his ears from hearing it on the stage, broke on him, awakening remembrance like a flash of light.

He started and gave him a keen glance that quickly penetrated the actor's disguise, especially as he was off guard for the moment, and his square shoulders and erect bearing betrayed him to those suspicious eyes.

Robert shrank back into the shadow, thinking:

"So he's got back to town, that scamp! Now I wonder what he's up to in that disguise? But he can't fool me! I know his voice and his square shoulders too well. I wish I could do him up, the grand villain, for playing me that low trick!"

On the alert for something on which to base a plan of retaliation, he followed every word and movement, and, to his amazement, when Standish got into the elegant sleigh, he heard him give the address of Geraldine, where he had carried Hawthorne's note.

Now, Robert had left the hospital, and obtained a place with his cousin, the keeper of the livery stable, and a wild thought came into his mind.

"That fellow's up to some mischief, or he wouldn't be in that rig—whiskers and spectacles! Wonder if that girl's got back, anyway? S'pose I go and tell the fireman about it, and see if he can make anything out of this strange lark?"

Turning to his cousin, who was very fond of the quick-witted youth, he said, roguishly:

"Seems like that fellow's going to take his best girl for a jolly sleigh-ride. Puts me in mind to take mine, too. Can't I get off for an hour and have a little one-horse sleigh?"

"Who's to pay for it, Impudence?"

"I am, of course! You can keep my week's salary for it. Who minds a little extravagance like that for his best girl, I'd like to know?" and ten minutes later he was driving in style to the Ludlow street engine-house.

"Mr. Hawthorne in the house?" he hallooed to a fireman in front.

"Too late, sonny. He left fifteen minutes ago."

"Where to?"

"Don't know, really."

"Can't you form some idea, please?" the boy cried, dropping the jaunty air in some anxiety.

The blue-shirted fireman stuck his hands in his pocket, whistled, and answered:

"Oh, he's gone to see his best girl, I reckon."

"What's her name?" queried Robert, wondering if Hawthorne was off with the old love, and on with a new one.

"I don't know," and Robert was about to turn off in disgust at the good-natured levity of the other when Captain Stansbury, who was inside, overheard him, and came to the rescue.

"You want Hawthorne?" he said. "Well, he isn't here."

"I know, but I want him very particular. Can't you tell me where to find him?"

The genial captain laughed, and answered:

"I can tell you, but I can also tell you, young man, that he doesn't like to be bothered when he goes a-courting!"

"Has he gone to see Miss Harding?"

"Yes."

"At the old address?"

"Yes."

"Thank you," and Robert whirled his keen little cutter about, and was soon out of sight.

"A likely lad," laughed the fireman, and then he and the captain went indoors.

Five minutes later a double sleigh whirled around the nearest corner, and came to a sudden stop in front of the engine-house. A man got out in the snow, and waded over to the door, followed by the yearning eyes of a girl whose fair face glowed like a rose, it was so beautiful in its eager tenderness.

"Oh, my love, how long the day has been without you, but I shall see you at last!" she whispered to herself, fondly.

The man went inside the double-doors and looked at the splendid horses neighing in their stalls. No one was in sight. The men were back in the office amusing themselves with a game of cards. He could hear them laughing and bantering each other.

He remained there a moment out of sight of Geraldine, then, with a sigh of relief, hurried back to the sleigh.

"It's very strange, but Mr. Hawthorne has gone," he said, in that thick, muffled voice. "He left word for me to bring you to Cortlandt street ferry."

"That is so far. I think he might have waited for us," the girl said, half to herself, and pettishly.

"Oh, maybe there was a fire down that way," Jem Rhodes returned, plausibly. "Go on, driver."

As they started, Captain Stansbury, who fancied he had heard something stopping outside, came and looked out and Geraldine saw his portly figure framed there a moment in the glare of an electric light.

She looked back, but he did not recognize her as the sleigh whirled past. Alas! why did not some subtle voice in her heart warn her that she was in deadly peril, and make her cry out to him to follow and save her from the snare into which she had fallen?

The call at the engine-house was only a part of the actor's plan for lulling Geraldine's suspicions to rest.

It had succeeded splendidly, and, with an exultant heart, he resumed his place by her side, burning with the desire to take her fair form in his arms and crush it against his breast.

But the time for this was not yet. He must first carry out one of the most daring plans ever conceived by man to elope with an unwilling beauty and make her his by sheer force of fraud and impudence.

And the worst of it all lay before him.

He was succeeding well in his plan for getting her to the ferry, but after that, how was he to manage?

CHAPTER XXVI.

TOO LATE! TOO LATE.

"'What is life?'A battle, child,Where the strongest lance may fail,Where the weariest eye may be beguiled,And the stoutest heart may quail,Where foes are gathered on every hand,And rest not day or nightBut the angels of heaven are on thy side,And God is over all."

When Robert returned from the engine-house, he was in doubt whether he ought to follow Hawthorne or not.

"If he has gone to Miss Harding's house, everything must be all right between them. It must be some other lady in the same house that Standish is going to take away. It's a lodging-house, and he may be acquainted with a dozen ladies there, for all I know."

But still, in spite of these thoughts, he kept on driving to the house.

"I'll go past it anyway, and see if the fellow is there yet with his grand sleigh."

He threw himself back with an air of importance, for he was certainly enjoying his little outing. The road was gay with vehicles, and the air musical with the ring of sleigh-bells. New York was enjoying its Christmas.

Almost before he realized it, he found himself on the obscure street, and in front of the shabby house where Geraldine lived, a pure pearl in an uncouth setting.

He reined up in front of the house and cogitated:

"The sleigh isn't here. Mr. Standish must have got his girl and gone. Maybe I ought to go, too. I don't see that I have any business going in!"

Smiling to himself at his humorous play on the verb to go, he waited a minute, glancing curiously at the front of the four-story house that looked dark and still as though most of the people had gone out or retired.

He pictured to himself the handsome fireman within that tenement, sitting by the side of his sweet young love, Geraldine, perhaps holding her dainty hand and looking love into eyes that answered love again.

"No, I mustn't go in. I might interrupt a charming *tete-a-tete*," he decided, and was about to turn back to the livery stable, when the door before him opened suddenly, and a man appeared, reeling down the steps like one under the influence of liquor or some heart-breaking emotion.

Robert stared at the handsome figure a moment, then called, questioningly:

"Mr. Hawthorne?"

Hawthorne stopped, looked up, and asked, hoarsely:

"Who is that? Oh, Robert, is it you? What are you doing here?"

"I came to see you, Mr. Hawthorne."

"What can I do for you? Speak quickly, for I'm going—oh, God! where—for I know not where to turn!"

The words were a cry of agony, and as he came up to the side of the sleigh, the youth saw that his face was deathly pale, as if from terrible trouble.

His first fear that Hawthorne was intoxicated gave way to the conviction that something was wrong about Geraldine, and he said, quickly:

"You're in trouble, sir, and I think I can help you if you'll tell me all about it. Get in the sleigh, won't you, and let me drive you wherever you want to go."

"Thank you, Robert. I came on a car, and this is very welcome," said Hawthorne, getting in by the youth's side.

"Where to?" asked Robert, taking up the reins.

"Where? Oh, God, where!" groaned Hawthorne, despairingly. "Wait," he added, laying his hand on the boy's shoulder. "Ah, Robert, this is one of the darkest hours of a life that has had many shadows. I came here to see my betrothed bride, my heart full of joy that has turned to keenest pain, for I found her gone from me—lured away by a scheming villain that she hates—and what her terrible fate may be, God only knows, for I have not a single clew to follow."

"Oh, yes, you have—a clew to follow the villain himself. You mean Standish, don't you?" shouted Robert, wildly, in his excitement.

"Yes, he has lured her away by a cunning trick—" began Hawthorne again, but the youth interrupted:

"Yes, yes, I know; he has taken her to the Cortlandt street ferry—going to elope with her, I reckon. But we'll follow and outwit the villain," and chirping to his horse, Robert drove to the ferry as fast as he dared.

On the way he told Hawthorne all that he knew, and received his confidence in turn.

So the actor's plot was laid bare. No doubt existed as to his intentions to abduct Geraldine.

On their way, just half a block from the ferry, Robert exclaimed:

"There's our sleigh going back now to the stables. Hello, Pete!"

The driver drew rein, and he asked, anxiously:

"Where's the lady and gentleman you took down to the ferry?"

And the answer was like the trump of doom to Hawthorne's sore heart.

"The lady and gentleman, sir? Oh, they took the Pennsylvania Limited train to Chicago."

"Are you sure?" cried Robert.

"Oh, yes; I crossed the river with them, and saw them board the train. That is, the man carried her in his arms. She got sick, or fainted, maybe, just beforehand, and he grabbed her up and climbed on with her just as the whistle blew. Oh, they're off, for sure. Is anything wrong?" added the driver, curiously, scenting an elopement.

CHAPTER XXVII.

HAWTHORNE CLUNG TO HOPE, IN SPITE OF HIS TROUBLE.

"Has Fate o'erwhelmed thee with some sudden blow?Let thy tears flow.But know when storms are past the heavens appearMore pure, more clear;And hope, when farthest from their shining rays,For brighter days!"

The curious sleigh-driver got no answer to his question.

Robert touched up his horse, and it bounded toward the ferry.

"What now?" queried Hawthorne, in a dazed way, so crushed by the shock he had received that he was for the moment incapable of coherent thought.

The quick-witted youth answered, readily:

"Aren't we going to telegraph ahead to arrest Standish at the first station?"

"Yes—oh, yes, of course we are; but I was so dazed by this shock that it seemed impossible for the moment for me to think clearly. Thank you for suggesting something, Robert. Perhaps, after all, we may foil the villain!" exclaimed Hawthorne, gladly and gratefully.

The youth smiled, well pleased at this praise from Hawthorne, and they proceeded on their way.

The telegram to arrest Standish having been sent, the pair next drove to Police Headquarters, where they lodged information of the whereabouts of Standish, who was wanted now, not only on the warrant of wife desertion, but for knocking over the policemen in his escape that morning.

"What next?" queried Robert, when they were once more seated in the sleigh.

"My good fellow, are you not weary of my troubles yet?" cried the grateful Hawthorne.

"I want to help you in every way I can, Mr. Hawthorne, not only because I like you, sir, but because I'm interested in that sweet young girl, and I also have a grudge against that wretch, Standish, for the trick he played all of us once. So now there's three motives urging me on, and you may command my services just as long as you have need of them," returned the intelligent youth, so earnestly that Hawthorne wrung his hand gratefully, exclaiming:

"Believe me, I'll never, never, forget this kindness."

"Thank you, sir," returned the gratified youth, and added:

"But what can we do next?"

"You can drive me back to the ferry, Robert, for I shall follow Geraldine on the first train. Think how lonely and terrified she will be with that wretch, who has told her, God only knows what artful story, to get her aboard the train with him. I must go to her assistance as fast as I can."

"You are right, sir, for she must be frightened almost to death. By Jove, but I'd like to go with you and see that fellow's face when he meets you, but I must go back with the sleigh."

"And, besides, I have another task for you, my faithful Robert. It is to return to the engine-house when I am gone, and tell Captain Stansbury all that we have discovered. From the engine-house back to Geraldine's home, and tell the young lady, Miss Carroll, the same story," continued Hawthorne, mindful of Cissy's cruel anxiety, and anxious to relieve it by some certainty of what had really happened.

"Tell Miss Carroll to keep up her spirits—that I will certainly bring Miss Harding back by to-morrow," he added, hopefully.

It was a sad ending for the Christmas Day that had dawned so pleasantly for the just reunited lovers, but Hawthorne would not permit himself to dwell despairingly on it. He told himself that by this time to-morrow he would be sure to have Geraldine back again.

- 102 -

CHAPTER XXVIII.

THAT WORD WAS LIKE A DAGGER IN HER HEART.

"Words are mighty, words are living;Serpents with their venomous stings,Or bright angels crowding round us,With heaven's light upon their wings.

"Every word has its own spirit,True or false, that never dies;Every word man's lips have utteredEchoes in God's skies."

Pete, the driver of the sleigh in which Clifford Standish had so successfully accomplished the abduction of Geraldine, had told the truth about the affair.

Geraldine had indeed fainted at some words he had said to her, and while in this condition he had lifted her in his arms and carried her aboard the train.

Ere she recovered from her long spell of unconsciousness, the train was flying across the country in the gloom of the falling night, that, dark as it was, could not equal the blackness of the fate to which Clifford Standish had destined his hapless victim.

On reaching the station he had said, abruptly, to Geraldine:

"Kindly wait here for me while I go and find Hawthorne."

In reality he secured tickets for Chicago, and, returning to her, he said, still in that strange, muffled voice of his:

"The time has come for me to explain why Hawthorne trusted you to my care to bring you here."

"Did you not find him?" exclaimed Geraldine, uneasily.

"Yes."

"Is he not coming to me? This looks strange!" she said, with rising resentment.

"Be patient, Miss Harding, and let me explain," he said, wheedlingly.

They were standing at an obscure place on the platform, and very few people were about except the depot officials. No one noticed the tall, bearded man and his beautiful companion, with her great starry brown eyes and masses of sunshiny hair.

Standish proceeded, in an oily voice:

"Something shocking happened to my friend Hawthorne this afternoon, and he is compelled to flee the city on this train that you see them making up now. He is watched for at every station in the city, so he dare not come to you now, for his arrest is certain. His sending for you was a desperate expedient to see you once more and bid you farewell forever, or—to take you with him in his flight from justice."

With every word he uttered he saw her face grow paler and paler, her large eyes widening with nameless fear; but, without pausing for her to speak, he continued, rapidly:

"He is mad with remorse over the awful deed he has done, and wild with grief at the thought of leaving you. He says that you have promised to marry him, and why not now as well as later? He prays you to go with him now on his exile, and to become his bride as soon as his destination is reached."

Her pale lips parted, and she interrupted.

"Oh, let me see him, let me speak to him! This is so horrible, so sudden!"

"You will have to board the train to see him. He is in the rear car, having slipped on almost under the eyes of an officer watching for him. Come," and he attempted to take her hand and draw her forward.

But she shrank back in nameless terror, moaning:

"Oh, I—can't—go! I am afraid. Oh, tell me what it is that he has done!"

He bent closer, muttering one terrible word:

"Murder!"

The word struck her like a blow in the face, then pierced like a dagger to her heart.

"Oh-h-h!" she gasped, throwing out her white, agonized hands as if to ward off a stroke of fate.

The next moment her senses gave way before the shock.

She reeled blindly forward and fell like a log at the dastard's feet.

This was what Jem Rhodes had hoped and expected.

With a laugh of demoniac satisfaction he lifted Geraldine in his arms, and bore her to a second-class coach, having bought tickets for this with a distinct purpose.

To his joy he found that he and Geraldine would be the only passengers on this coach.

"The foul fiend helps me! I'll have a fair field for my love-making," he thought, exultantly, as the train steamed out from the station.

Presently Geraldine, whom he had lain back on her seat, stirred and opened her eyes with a dazed look.

"Oh, what does this mean? Where am I?" she gasped.

Standish bent over her, and said, soothingly:

"Don't you remember, Miss Harding? I brought you here to see Hawthorne. He will be here in a moment."

"But—but—the train is moving," she cried, in a frightened voice.

"Hush!" he hissed, and suddenly Geraldine felt the cold muzzle of a pistol pressed against her warm, white temple, and a hoarse voice continued:

"You are at the mercy of a desperate man! Do not move or speak, or I will blow your brains out and then leap from the train in the darkness. I swear it. I have much to say to you, and I shall say it with my finger on the trigger of this pistol, ready to kill you if you utter one word without my permission. Now the conductor is coming in to take up our tickets. Do not dare to speak to him or show one sign of excitement."

Life is sweet to the young and loving, and Geraldine dared not disobey that hoarse command. She crouched, trembling in her seat while the gruff conductor took up the tickets and passed on to the next car.

They were again alone, and in a whirlwind of conflicting emotions Geraldine waited for the next words of her companion.

In his hoarse voice, vibrant with passion, she had suddenly recognized Clifford Standish.

She comprehended that he had set a trap for her, and that she had fallen into it. The horror of her thoughts no pen could tell!

He bent toward her as he sat on the opposite seat, and though her heart swelled with a terrible hate, she dared not utter a word of remonstrance, for she saw that, half-hidden by his coat-sleeve, he carried his deadly weapon ready to wreak vengeance on her for the least disobedience.

But though she dared not speak, Geraldine could not restrain the indignation that flashed upon him from her contemptuous eyes, and surely that glance was enough to wither him with its burning scorn.

But, unmoved by her wrath, Clifford Standish asked, calmly:

"Have you recognized me yet, Geraldine?"

She nodded in silent, ineffable scorn, and he went on:

"I have much to tell you, and when I am done you will not despise me as you do now, for I have been cruelly wronged and defamed, just to gratify the spite of envious people."

The dark, scornful eyes looked at him in silent amazement as he went on:

"Geraldine, that arrest on the stage last night was simply for the purpose of turning your heart against me. Another man envied me, and concocted that villainous plot to make you believe I was married, that he might win you himself. I have no wife, nor ever shall have, unless you will keep your promise to be mine."

His voice sank to the low, tremulous cadence that he had found so effective on the stage, but the unchanging scorn of the bright eyes assured him that she was not moved by his ranting.

Heaving a deep sigh, he went on, passionately:

"It was a deep-laid scheme of that contemptible fireman, that low fellow, to turn you against me. And you know I had no time to explain anything to you. I was simply dragged away like a dog! Well, when my case came up in court this morning, the woman who had been hired to testify against me broke down in the witness chair, and owned that she did not even know me. Hawthorne had bribed her, she said, to claim me for her husband. I was discharged, as I told you last night that I would be to-day. Had you not heard, Geraldine, of my discharge, cleared of the foul imputation on my honor?" he demanded, anxiously, wondering if her knowledge of the truth would enable her to cast back the falsehood in his teeth.

But Geraldine had heard nothing, so, when he said again, "Speak Geraldine, did you not know I was free?" she answered, simply:

"No, I did not know it."

He breathed a sigh of relief at her ignorance of his escape, and resumed his falsehoods with more self-confidence:

"I was free, but half broken-hearted over the thought of the ignominy to which I had been subjected and the cruel impression it had made on my betrothed bride."

He saw her shudder at the last two words, but he was pitiless in his resolve to sacrifice her to his mad passion.

"Ah, Geraldine, was it not a fiendish act to turn your heart against me like that?" he cried. "I left the court-house and went to the hotel to see you. All the members of the company received me joyfully, but they had cruel news for me. They told me you had left them for Hawthorne—that you were betrothed to him, and he had demanded your retirement from the stage. Was this true, Geraldine?"

She bowed a cold, affirmative answer.

"It was true! I knew it, and I was in despair," ranted Standish. "Oh, how easily a woman's heart can turn against a man! You might have waited a day, Geraldine, and given me a chance to clear myself from that false charge. But, no! in your wounded pride you turned against me, and pledged yourself to the traitor who had plotted that vile outrage—my arrest on the stage—to further his own base ends."

She sat listening dumbly while the train rushed on and on, bearing her farther and farther away from New York and her own true lover—for she knew in her heart that he was true, and that the actor was telling her vile falsehoods—and her poor heart sank like a stone in her breast.

Oh, what would be her fate now, she wondered in anguish, hating herself because she had fallen so easily into this fatal trap.

Standish continued, in a pleading tone:

"What could I do in my despair, darling, but oppose cunning to cunning, and fraud to fraud? I knew that if I came to you in my own person, I should not even be allowed to see you. My enemies would separate us, keep us apart so that you should never know how cruelly I had been wronged. So I planned to get you away from them and into my power. I determined to have my promised bride if I had to steal her away from our enemies. I knew," eagerly, "that when you heard the truth, sweet Geraldine, you would forgive me for this bold move, and love me again. So—we are on our way now to Chicago, and there you shall become my bride!"

CHAPTER XXIX.

A LEAF OUT OF HIS OWN BOOK.

"As I came through the valley of Despair,As I came through the valley, on my sight,More awful than the darkness of the night,Shone glimpses of a past that had been fair,And memories of eyes that used to smile,And wafts of perfume from a vanished isle,And, like an arrow in my heart I heardThe last faint notes of Hope's expiring bird,As I came through the valley."

Poor Geraldine! poor Geraldine! What a cruel ending this was to the Christmas Day that had dawned so auspiciously upon her life.

She had had a few hours of exquisite happiness—the pure and perfect happiness of tender mutual love, that brings heaven down to earth for young, ardent hearts.

* * "That passionate love of youth,That comes but once in its perfect bliss—A love that, in spite of its trust and truth,Seems never to thrive in a world like this."

From bliss to despair—that was the story of Geraldine's one day.

But for the shining ring on her little hand she would have believed it all a dream, so swiftly had the brightness fled.

How she loathed and hated the smooth, smiling villain before her, who, while pretending to love her, had actually threatened her with death; who held at that moment, under his hand, a deadly weapon with which to compel her obedience.

The poor girl sat looking at him with angry tears in her large brown eyes, her cheeks alternately red and pale with the blood that rushed to and fro from her wildly throbbing heart. At one moment she would feel ill enough to faint, the next her burning indignation would drive away all weakness.

She did not believe one word of the smooth story he had related to her, hoping that her girlish credulity would accept it for truth.

And she was determined that she would die before she would marry the wretch.

But how was she to escape if he stood guard over her all the way to Chicago, with a deadly weapon in his hand?

If she shrieked out to the conductor for assistance, her abductor would kill her on the spot.

It was a situation to blanch the bravest cheek, and Geraldine was only a poor, weak girl. No wonder that the blood ran cold in her veins with despair.

She could see nothing before her but death—certain death at the hands of the desperate villain by her side.

For he was determined to marry her or kill her; and of the two calamities she resolved to choose the last.

But—and a faint spark of hope came to her—if she could only get him to leave her side a while, she might escape—might jump from the flying train in the darkness.

He was watching her changing face with eager anxiety as to what she was going to say to him now, and suddenly he saw it brighten with a thought he could not fathom.

There had flashed over Geraldine a remembrance of his last words:

"What could I do in my despair but oppose cunning to cunning, and fraud to fraud?"

Her sombre eyes brightened as she thought:

"He has taught me a lesson that I will profit by. Perhaps I can thus throw him off his guard."

Standish exclaimed, eagerly and curiously:

"What have you to say, Geraldine, to my story? Will you accept it for the truth, and renew your faith in my love and honor?"

Duplicity was a stranger to Geraldine's nature, and it was hard indeed to act the part she was planning, but her stage training enabled her to carry it off superbly.

Her lovely face softened inexpressibly, and she looked up at him with a shy yet tender glance that thrilled him with hope.

"Oh, what a strange story you have told me!" she twittered, sweetly, and added: "How can you forgive me for my unfaith?"

Clifford Standish started with blended surprise and joy, for he had not counted on such an easy victory.

He had expected that Geraldine would accuse him of falsehood, scorn him, flout him—do anything else but weaken in this simple way.

But his masculine vanity made the task of gulling him an easy one, for he thought instantly:

"How weak and silly women are! They will believe any garbled story a man chooses to tell them."

Aloud, he said, joyously:

"Then you believe me, Geraldine? They have not turned your heart against me?"

She answered, with seemingly pretty penitence:

"At first they did—for—for it all seemed so real on the stage last night— the arrest and all, you know. And I was wild with pain and humiliation; so I let them persuade me into anything. But, now that you have explained all to me, I see it in a different light, for of course you would not have wished to marry me if you had a wife already."

"Of course not," he echoed, smiling to himself at her innocent ignorance.

"So," continued Geraldine, smiling also, but at his gullibility, "you may put away your pistol, for it makes me very nervous to see it. And you do not need to stand guard over me, and I am ready to keep my promise to marry you."

"Geraldine," he cried, transported with joy at her sweetness, and bent to kiss her, but she repulsed him with shy grace.

"No, no—wait till we are married, sir!"

"Very well, darling; but—will you promise me not to speak to any one on the train but myself?" suspiciously.

"I promise you that," she answered, carelessly, hoping that he would leave her, but it seemed that he had no such amiable intention.

He removed the glasses under which he had posed as Jem Rhodes, the better to feast his eyes on her peerless beauty, and remained by her side, talking to her until she was wild with disgust.

Yet she had to wear her brightest smile, and answer him with seeming vivacity, to keep up the impression she had made of satisfaction with her fate.

Meanwhile the train rushed on to the first station and passed it without interruption. Hawthorne's telegram had not overtaken the fugitives. Poor Geraldine's fate was sealed, and Standish was triumphant.

"I wish something would happen," she thought, desperately. "I wish the train would get off the track and hurt him, and nobody else, so that I might escape!"

How strangely our impetuous wishes are answered sometimes.

Something did happen to Geraldine the very next moment.

The conductor came back from the Pullman coach, and, pausing at her seat, said, respectfully:

"I beg your pardon, miss, but there is a lady back in the Pullman whose husband has just died suddenly from a frightful hemorrhage. In her distress there is not a woman to comfort her except an unfeeling negro maid, who is too busy flirting with the porter to attend to her duties. Could you—would you go back in there and speak a word of comfort to the poor soul?"

His gruff voice was very kindly now that his sympathies were awakened, and he gazed almost pleadingly at the girl who looked, in turn, questioningly at Standish.

He hesitated a moment, as if about to refuse, then answered, quietly:

"Yes, go, and I will accompany you," and, like a jailer guarding a prisoner, he followed her to the Pullman coach.

CHAPTER XXX.

A STARTLING DECLARATION.

"Eyes that are closed to earthly sight,Can never wake to weep;Nor pain, nor woe, nor grief, nor blight,Can move that slumber deep.

"So hearts of dust all griefs forsake,They never break nor bleed;The living hearts that throb and acheOur tender pity need."

The newly made widow leaned against the berth where the dead man lay with his face hidden beneath the sheet, her face in her hands, sobbing in a subdued but heart-broken way. None of the other berths had been made up yet, and the few men in the car looked solemn and ill at ease. A gayly dressed mulatto woman, evidently the lady's maid, was whispering to the smart yellow porter.

Geraldine paused by the weeping woman with a timid glance that took in every detail of her appearance—the elegant curves of the stately figure in a fine cloth traveling gown, the glint of golden hair beneath the dark, close hat, the glittering rings on the hands that held the handkerchief to her face.

She whispered, shyly, to Standish:

"She is one of those grand aristocrats that I used to see at O'Neill's store. I'm afraid to speak to her. Some of them are so proud, so haughty, they can wither you with a look."

"Suppose we go back, then, to our seats," he returned, eagerly.

But something held Geraldine by the mourner's side, in spite of her terror of proud, rich women; and as a sudden low sob broke on the air, she started hurriedly forward with a gentle touch on the lady's arm, bending her face down to whisper, brokenly, out of the wealth of her sympathy:

"Oh, I am so sorry for you, I am so sorry for you! May God help you to bear it!"

The mourner lifted up a lovely face framed in golden hair—the face of a woman somewhere between thirty and forty—and met the glance of those sweet brown eyes swimming in sympathetic tears, and her heart seemed to answer the girl's words. With another heart-breaking sob, she dropped her face against Geraldine's shoulder, and let the girlish arms infold her like a daughter's clasp.

"Come away to a seat," she whispered, and led her away some distance from the berth.

Sitting side by side, they mingled their tears together, for it seemed to Geraldine as if she could feel, by some divine instinct, all the force of the other woman's grief.

"For what, if I were married to my darling Harry, and Death took him—oh, it would break my heart!" she thought, wildly.

Standish had followed and taken a seat just behind her, where he could listen to every word that passed.

Oh, how she hated him for his dastardly espionage, but she dared not openly revolt. She bided her time.

She felt with a keen thrill of pleasure how the strange lady clung to her in the abandonment of her grief, nestling her weary head so confidingly against her shoulder, and letting her arm rest around the girl's waist.

"Tell me if there is anything I can do for you," she whispered, kindly, and the mourner hushed her sobs and murmured:

"Tell the conductor to make arrangements to take—take—my poor husband through to Chicago, our home."

Standish beckoned the conductor back to the seat, and there was a colloquy for some time over mournful details. When he went away, the lady who had grown calmer, lifted her tearful face, and looked at Geraldine, eagerly, tenderly.

"Who are you, child, with that voice and face from the haunting past? What is your name?"

"I am Geraldine Harding!"

"Geraldine Harding! Oh, Heaven!" springing to her feet in strange excitement, her blue eyes glittering through their tears.

Geraldine did not know what to make of her strange excitement, so she waited, mutely, while the lady went on, breathlessly:

"Where did you live?—oh, I mean, tell me all about yourself! Oh, I am in such trouble that I cannot express myself clearly! I mean no impertinence, but I am terribly interested in you and in your past."

"There is not much in my past that could interest you, dear madame—only the simple story of a poor country girl who came to New York, with another girl, to earn her own living," Geraldine said, modestly.

"So young, so lovely! Yet thrown on the world to earn her bread!" murmured the lady, tearfully. She caught the girl's hand, holding it tightly as she continued: "Your parents, dear? Why did they let you leave them?"

"I was an orphan, madame."

"An orphan! Where was your home?"

"I lived in the country near New York, with a farmer, to whom my father took me when I was a delicate child. The farmer's name was Newell, and his wife, Malinda, had formerly been a servant to my mother. She gave me tender, motherly care, and raised me from a frail child to a robust girl. My father sent money for a while, then he died, and left me dependent on those people. They were poor and had a hard struggle to get along with their large brood of children, so I—I—wearied of the life, and ran away to seek my fortune in the great city."

"And your mother, Geraldine?"

"My father said that she was dead," she replied, simply.

"It was false! He, your cruel father, took you from me! I am your own mother, darling!" cried the lady, extending imploring arms.

CHAPTER XXXI.

FROM WANT TO WEALTH.

"At sea—we're all at sea upon life's ocean,And none can boast a never-failing chart;Sail as we may, we'll meet with dread commotion,And hidden shoals to terrify the heart.We're all at sea; some favored ones, enchanted,Float peacefully upon the placid tide,While others with sad doubts and fears are haunted,And ever on the roughest billows ride."

FRANCIS S. SMITH.

Clifford Standish watched the scene before him with eager interest.

It was like the plot of a play, this touching union of a long parted mother and child.

In watching the interesting scene he forgot for a moment how it might affect his own interests.

The beautiful, sorrowful widow, with tears streaming down her pale cheeks, extended her arms to Geraldine, exclaiming:

"I am your own mother, my darling!"

Startling and surprising as this statement was to Geraldine, not a doubt of its truth entered the girl's mind.

On the contrary, her heart leaped with joy, for she had already felt herself drawn with inexplicable tenderness to the speaker.

And the moment that she held out her arms to Geraldine the girl sprang into them gladly, and the next moment they were embracing each other with ineffable tenderness, the grief of the widow comforted in a measure by the restoration of her daughter.

Clifford Standish looking on, suddenly felt a touch of uneasiness, and muttered, under his breath:

"Confound the luck! I wish she had not met this woman until after we were married."

And thinking it was time for him to assert his claim, he waited until the mother and daughter withdrew from each other's arms, and said, respectfully:

"Accept my congratulations, madame, on the finding of your beautiful daughter, my promised wife!"

The lady, with a quick start of surprise, as if she had but that moment become aware of his presence, turned and looked at the speaker.

His words had fallen like hail-stones on her heart.

She was one of the proudest women on earth, and her large dark eyes scanned Clifford Standish with cold inquiry.

He had just announced himself as the betrothed of her daughter, and the cold glance of her eyes asked distinctly if he were worthy of that honor.

There was a moment of breathless silence, and the actor looked at Geraldine with eyes whose veiled menace defied her to deny his claim. She, remembering his deadly threats, paled and shuddered.

She could not afford to anger him yet. She realized that fully.

The lady, after transfixing the daring actor with one steely glance, looked at her daughter.

"Is this true?" she asked, in displeased surprise.

"It is true," faltered Geraldine, without daring to look up; and again Standish, encouraged by success, interposed:

"Let me explain the case to you, madame. We have been engaged to marry for some time, and we are now on our wedding journey—that is, we are to be married as soon as we reach Chicago."

The lady, still icily ignoring her daughter's suitor, exclaimed:

"Can this be true, Geraldine?"

The young girl answered again, dejectedly.

"It is true."

Standish beamed upon her gratefully, joyously, hoping from her acquiescence that he had indeed made some impression on her heart.

But the mother was wearing her most frigid air as she remarked:

"This is a rather unusual proceeding. Should not the marriage have preceded instead of following the wedding journey?"

Standish answered, quickly:

"That is the usual way, certainly, but this was an elopement."

"An elopement?" cried the lady, with rising indignation; but Geraldine laid a pleading hand upon her arm, crying:

"Mother, dear mother, let us discuss this question later. At present let me present Mr. Standish to you."

The mother bowed with cold courtesy. She evidently did not approve of her daughter's suitor.

Standish read her mind like an open book.

He comprehended that she was proud and rich, and would scout the idea of her daughter's marriage with one beneath her in social position.

Yet he was all the more determined to make her his own.

Bending down to Geraldine, he whispered, hoarsely:

"Let me speak to you alone."

She withdrew with him to a little distance, and he whispered, sternly:

"Do not forgot that I have sworn that you shall marry me, or become the bride of Death."

"I will remember," she faltered, and he added:

"The discovery of your mother makes no difference in your promise to me. She must not refuse your hand to me."

Geraldine saw that he was in a desperate mood, and she did not care to offend him; but her heart was throbbing joyfully in her breast, for she knew that heaven itself would come to her aid, and that she would surely outwit him at last.

But she said, with quiet dignity:

"Mr. Standish, it would seem as if common decency required the postponement of this subject until after my mother has buried her dead."

"You are trying to escape me!" he exclaimed, warningly; but he saw by her indignant look that he was presuming too far, for she said, quickly:

"This harshness will not further your cause with me, sir. You cannot marry me by brute force."

"That is true; but I have your promise."

"Extorted from me under menace of death!" she returned, indignation getting the better of her calmness.

"Oh, Geraldine, cannot you forgive the madness of a love like mine that dares anything rather than lose you?" he implored, with theatrical fervor.

"Geraldine, dear," called her mother, softly, and she darted back to her side.

The lady said, quickly:

"My dear daughter, I can never give my consent to your marriage with that person."

Geraldine threw her arms about the lady, and whispered, thrillingly:

"Dear mother, I do not wish to marry him; but—let us wait until after we reach Chicago before we repudiate my promise. I fear his anger, for he is a desperate man. Let us temporize with him until we are out of his power."

By that time Standish had returned to his seat, and seeing that the proud mother of Geraldine was determined to ignore him, his anger made him say, sullenly:

"Madame, you have asserted a claim to Miss Harding, as your daughter, but you have presented no proofs to substantiate your claim. As her present guardian and her betrothed husband, I must request the production of those proofs."

She gazed at him in cold astonishment at this audacity, but answered, frigidly:

"Your solicitude does you credit, but I can satisfy all your doubts."

Beckoning the conductor, who was passing through the car, she said, quietly:

"Kindly tell this person my name and standing."

Standish winced under the contemptuous epithet, "person," and glared at the conductor, who turned to him and said:

"Mrs. A. T. Fitzgerald, formerly of New York, now of Chicago, was the wife, now the widow, of A. T. Fitzgerald, the foremost banker and capitalist of Chicago."

Standish bowed without a word. He saw the impassable gulf of wealth and social position yawning between him and pretty Geraldine, but he swore to himself that he would not give her up.

Mrs. Fitzgerald thanked the conductor, and added:

"No doubt you are familiar with the circumstances of my first marriage, and—divorce. Kindly tell him these also."

The conductor looked embarrassed, but she smiled at him encouragingly, and said:

"Do as I ask you, please. It is indeed a favor."

"Mrs. Fitzgerald's first husband was Howard Harding, of New York, from whom she obtained a divorce ten or eleven years ago."

"State the cause," broke in Mrs. Fitzgerald's clear voice, and the conductor, who was fully conversant with this scandal in high life, added:

"Howard Harding led a gay life, and deserted Mrs. Harding for a notorious Parisian of the demi-monde. His wife secured a divorce, and in about two years married Mr. Fitzgerald, of Chicago."

"And the custody of their only child, little Geraldine, was given——" she began.

"To the mother, of course," ended the conductor.

"Yes, and within a year she was stolen from her by the guilty father and hidden from her so securely that she never found her again until to-night," cried the lady, her eyes resting tenderly on the face of her lovely child.

"Is it so indeed? Let me congratulate you most heartily, madame," exclaimed the conductor, his eyes resting admiringly on Geraldine, while he added: "The likeness between you is most startling."

"And, oh, mother, dear mother, it was this kind gentleman who came to me in another coach and begged me to come and comfort you in your sorrow. But for him we might never have found each other," cried Geraldine, in boundless gratitude, for she felt that not only had he restored her to her mother's arms, but he had also delivered her from the power of her desperate lover.

Mrs. Fitzgerald, who had been so frigid to Standish, unbent from her haughty mien and wept tears of gratitude as she wrung the hand of the conductor.

"Oh, Captain Stevens, as kind as you have always been to me on my journeys on your train, I never knew your true worth till now, but ere long you shall receive ample evidence of my gratitude," she assured him.

The conductor was very proud and happy over his agency in restoring Geraldine to her mother's arms, but while he was declining her promised reward, he was called away, and then Mrs. Fitzgerald turned again to her daughter's suitor.

"Are you satisfied with my proofs?" she demanded, icily.

"Perfectly, madame, and I hope you will permit me to express my joy at your reunion with your daughter."

"I thank you, and I have a request to make of you. I wish to be left alone with my daughter at present. Will you kindly respect this desire, and call on me later in Chicago, where I will consider your claims for my Geraldine's hand?" said Mrs. Fitzgerald, presenting him with a card on which was engraved her address on Prairie avenue.

Thus coolly dismissed, and not daring to protest against the authority of the haughty lady, Standish bowed and withdrew to another seat in the same coach, where he covertly watched them without daring to intrude his hated presence on them.

"Ah my darling, how strangely all this has happened!" cried the lady.

"How strangely and how fortunately!" echoed Geraldine, gladly.

"But, oh, how sad that it did not happen sooner—before my darling husband died! Oh, how he would have loved you for my sake, Geraldine; for he was so good to me, he made me so happy, that no grief remained in my heart for that false one who deserted me for a wicked woman, and then stole you away from me!" cried her mother, her mournful thoughts reverting to that loved lost one whose pulseless form had now been conveyed to another coach to be made ready for its last long sleep.

"Oh, my mother, how can I comfort you for your sad loss?" cried Geraldine, tenderly.

"You can love me, darling, and try to fill the void left by his loss. Oh, I hope that his kind spirit hovers near and knows that I have found you, my dear, for we have wished for this so often, and he has spent many thousands of dollars trying to trace you for me, but all in vain. For all our efforts were made abroad, in the belief that your father had taken you away with him. I could not conceive of his taking you away and then deserting you so heartlessly. But doubtless that wicked woman induced him to do it. Such women have great influence over weak-minded men. But let us try to forgive him the wrongs we suffered at his hands now that he is dead," ended Mrs. Fitzgerald.

CHAPTER XXXII.

"YOU WILL SOON FORGET YOUR POOR LOVER IN THE NEW SPHERE THAT YOU WILL FILL."

"She has a suitor rich, and I am poor,And love 'gainst money has no armor sure;For it is said when poverty appears,Love through the window straight his pathway steers.She's only human; it may be that sheWill barter love for wealth and misery."

FRANCIS S. SMITH.

How bitter was the disappointment of Harry Hawthorne on reaching the first station on his route in following the fugitives to find that his telegram had not been received until the Pennsylvania Limited had thundered past with the triumphant actor and his helpless victim.

His heart sank at the first moment with a terrible despair, but hope quickly reasserted itself.

"I will follow them!" he exclaimed, determined to leave no effort untried to rescue his heart's darling.

But the train with the fugitives was two hours ahead of the desperate lover, and long ere he reached Chicago the objects of his pursuit were at their destination—Standish in a second-rate lodging-house, Geraldine, with her mother, at her magnificent home on Prairie avenue, which holds to Chicago the rank of Fifth avenue to New York.

To Geraldine it was a wonderful transition, this change from the simple life of a working-girl in New York to this palatial home, where obsequious servants sprang to gratify her slightest wish, and where a devoted mother found time even in the anguish of widowhood to lavish on her the fondest love and care.

And in that home she had found another charming surprise—a dear little half-brother and sister, the children of her mother's second marriage—Earl, a beautiful, manly boy of ten, and Claire, a lovely fairy of seven years.

These two children had been left at home with their governess while their parents made a hurried business trip to New York—the trip that had ended so disastrously to the father, who had been in declining health for several years.

Bitter was the grief of the little ones when called to gaze for the last time on his beloved face, and Geraldine's tears mingled with theirs, for she knew that had he lived he must have proved to her a tenderer parent than the heartless father who had deserted her mother and then stolen her child and left her to grow up in poverty and heart-loneliness.

The second day after their arrival in Chicago the sacred remains of the beloved dead were taken to a crematory, and reduced to ashes, in accordance with the will of the deceased.

But the wife to whom he had been so kind and devoted could not bear to consign his remains to kindred dust.

She had the precious ashes sealed in a beautiful box of wrought silver and gold studded with precious jewels, and kept this box in her own apartments, a sacred treasure, dear to her for its precious memories.

When all these solemn ceremonies were over, the mother was ready to hear the story that Geraldine was waiting to pour into her ears.

A note from Clifford Standish arrived the morning after Mr. Fitzgerald's cremation, asking when he might call on Geraldine.

She went with the note to her mother and begged pardon for intruding on her sacred grief with her own troubles.

"Sit down, my darling, and tell me all," was the gentle reply.

When she had learned the story of Geraldine's persecution by the actor, her indignation was beyond measure.

"He shall be sent to prison for this outrage!" she exclaimed.

"Is that necessary?" Geraldine asked, timidly.

"Is it possible that you wish to spare him, darling?"

"Yes, if we can get rid of his pretensions to my hand without resorting to extreme measures."

"You shrink from notoriety. I understand, and will try to indulge your wishes, although the wretch ought to be punished to the full extent of the law for his villainous conduct," exclaimed the lady, adding, fearfully:

"Only think what might have been your fate, dear, but for the accident that threw us together on the train."

Geraldine shuddered as she recalled the peril from which she had been delivered, then said, with infinite relief:

"But I am out of his power now, and I need not even see him again, I hope."

"No, it will not be necessary; for although you may grant him liberty to call this evening, I will be the one to receive him and settle his pretensions," replied the lady, decidedly.

While she was speaking her eyes fell on the dimpled white hands of Geraldine, and she saw for the first time that the young girl was wearing a superb diamond ring.

"If that is Mr. Standish's property, you had better let me return it to him," she remarked.

She was surprised at the warm blush that overspread the fair young face.

"It—it—is my engagement-ring, mamma," she said, shyly.

"Given to you by that wretch! Then of course you do not wish to keep it. You shall have all the diamonds you wish now, my dear one."

"Thank you, my precious mamma, for your generous promise. I adore diamonds, and shall enjoy possessing plenty of them, but with this one I would not part for a queen's ransom!" exclaimed pretty Geraldine, pressing her lips fondly to the shining ring on her fair hand.

Mrs. Fitzgerald could not repress her rising displeasure.

"Indeed, my dear, I am surprised at you. I shall have to insist on your returning that person's ring," she said, gravely.

Geraldine looked up with a lovely smile.

"Oh, mamma, you cannot think this ring was given to me by Clifford Standish? Oh, no; it was the gift of a lover I left behind me in New York— my promised husband, the noblest lover any girl ever had!" she breathed, enthusiastically.

"Geraldine!"

Surprise and disapproval breathed in the lady's voice.

"May I tell you all about him, mamma?"

"Yes; I'm anxious to hear. And, by the way, are these two the only ones to whom you have promised your hand, or have you any more disclosures to make in that line?"

"Oh, mamma, are you offended with me?" exclaimed Geraldine, alarmed at the sarcastic coldness of her mother's voice.

"I am only surprised, my dear. Go on with your story," Mrs. Fitzgerald returned, quietly.

And, curbing her impatience and disapproval under a mask of calmness, she listened eagerly to Geraldine's story of her love for Harry Hawthorne.

And she thought she had never realized how radiantly lovely her daughter was until now, when her praises of her handsome betrothed brought the bright blushes to her cheeks, and the softened brightness to her starry brown eyes.

She did not interrupt her story by a word, but she listened in the deepest gravity until Geraldine had finished; then she kissed her tenderly and said:

"My dear, I can never consent to your marriage with Mr. Hawthorne."

"Mamma!" in alarm.

"It was well enough, my child, for the poor shop-girl of New York to be engaged to the brave young fireman, of course. But circumstances alter cases. Do you not understand that, Geraldine?"

Geraldine was terribly alarmed and frightened by the words and looks of her proud, rich mother.

She faltered, imploringly:

"Mamma, I am afraid to try to understand you, for—it would kill me to give up my love, Harry."

"Oh, no, it would not, dear, for you will soon forget your poor lover in the new sphere of life you will now fill. He is no longer a proper mate for you. Let him marry your sweet friend, Cissy, who is more suited to him in social station than my daughter an heiress."

"Mamma, you are surely jesting with me! You do not really believe that I would throw over my noble lover! Why, it would break my heart to lose him, and if he married Cissy I should hate her till my dying day!"

"Nonsense, my dear! you will soon forget him, and the match must surely be broken off, for I may as well tell you now that almost in your cradle you were betrothed to another—the son of a very dear friend of mine. So now that I have found you, dear, you will belong to that other one."

"Mamma, you are cruel, heartless! I cannot yield to you in this, fondly as I love you."

"You would not surely defy my authority, Geraldine, when I command you to write to Mr. Hawthorne, returning his ring, and breaking the engagement!"

They gazed fixedly at each other, and Geraldine said, imploringly:

"Mamma, I wrote to Harry yesterday, telling him all that had happened to me, and promising to be true to him through everything."

"You were a rash girl to act without consulting me in the matter. But we will not discuss the subject any further at present. Go now, and send the note to Standish, giving him permission to call this evening," Mrs. Fitzgerald answered, with an air of bitter displeasure.

CHAPTER XXXIII.

CLIFFORD STANDISH TRIES TO CREATE A GRAND IMPRESSION.

"When you see a vain pretenderRushing aimlessly along,Boasting of his wealth and splendorTo the giddy, thoughtless throng,Pity him, and while you pityIn your mind this adage keep:Though he may be *fast* and *witty*,Rapid streams are seldom deep."

FRANCIS S. SMITH.

Geraldine hastened to her room and scrawled a hasty line to Clifford Standish:

"You may call at eight o'clock this evening."

When she had dispatched the note by a servant, she threw herself, weeping, on a sofa.

Her fond heart was almost broken by her mother's command to give up her lover.

"I will not obey her, for she has no right to demand such a sacrifice from me!" she sobbed, resentfully.

It was true that she had already written to Hawthorne, telling him all that had happened to her since she had seen him last, and adding that no change of fortune could turn her heart from its love. She had begged him to answer her letter as soon as received, and added a postscript to ask him to go and tell Cissy Carroll what she had written.

But an adverse fate seemed always to come between Geraldine and her heart's choice.

Hawthorne, who was in Chicago by this time, vainly seeking his lost love, was fated not to receive the letter.

But Clifford Standish, writhing with impatience over the uncertainty that attended his love affair, was elated at the reception of Geraldine's note permitting him to call.

When the time approached, he laid aside the clumsy disguise he had assumed, and clothed himself in "purple and fine linen," as the saying goes, hoping to make some impression on the girl's proud mother by his handsome person and stately manners. He remembered how contemptuously she had called him "that person," and flattered himself that she could not deny him the title of a gentleman now.

Promptly at the time appointed he presented himself at the splendid Fitzgerald mansion, and was ushered into a luxurious little reception-room, where he waited in solitude some time after sending his card to the ladies.

He smiled to himself, as he thought:

"Geraldine is probably adorning herself in all the splendors of her newly acquired wealth to startle me with her beauty. She will burst upon me presently in gorgeous array, rustling in silk, and loaded with jewels, with all the purse-proud vulgarity of the *nouveaux riche.*"

And he did not reflect that he himself, following the "loud" taste of many actors, was almost too stunningly dressed for gentlemanly effect.

But just as he began to grow decidedly impatient at the long delay, a handsome young woman came softly through the draped door, and, advancing toward him, said, courteously:

"Mrs. Fitzgerald desires that you will excuse her delay in coming in. She has been detained by an unexpected caller, but will be with you in a few minutes now."

He sprang excitedly to his feet.

"Azuba!" burst from his lips.

The handsome young woman, who had scarcely looked at him before, turned her eyes toward him at that cry, and recoiled with a stifled shriek of unutterable dismay.

Clifford Standish came close up to her, muttering:

"Azuba, what are you doing here?"

The woman's face became death-white with sudden fear, and lifting her hand warningly, she almost, hissed:

"Hush! breathe not that name beneath this roof! It is not my name now!"

"Another alias, then," he muttered. "What is it now?"

Her reply came with a groan:

"What does that matter to you? I am done with you and the past forever—I am trying to lead an honest life and earn an honest, respectable living. For Heaven's sake, do not betray me to these people!"

"What are you doing here?"

"I am governess to Mrs. Fitzgerald's children. I am trusted and liked by the whole family, and I try to deserve it. Will you go away, and leave me in peace to my new life?" she prayed, with clasped hands, her large blue eyes swimming in frightened, beseeching tears.

"I have no wish to trouble you, Azuba—— Oh, pardon, that name was a slip of the tongue! What do you call yourself now?"

"Simply Kate Erroll—Miss Erroll to all. I have a right to that name. It was my mother's before she was married. But I cannot stay to talk to you now. I must go; but keep my secret, will you, Clifford Standish?"

"What if I refuse?" he demanded, and she answered, quickly:

"You could not injure me without bringing down harm upon yourself;" and with that vague threat the handsome governess fled by another door just as Mrs. Fitzgerald entered, a sombre object in the long, trailing black robes of widowhood.

She bowed to him with a sort of cold expectancy. Calling all his native effrontery to his aid, he rose, and said, theatrically:

"Mrs. Fitzgerald, I have come to plead with you to sanction my engagement to your daughter, Geraldine. We love each other devotedly, and it would break our loving hearts to be separated. You may think, perhaps, that I am no mate for your daughter, because you are rich; but that is a great mistake. I am an actor, I own, but I am paid a magnificent salary. My mother is very rich, and makes me a handsome allowance. At her death—and she cannot live much longer, being quite old and frail—I shall inherit her large fortune and can support my wife in grand style."

CHAPTER XXXIV.

ENEMIES AT BAY.

"Punishment o'ertakes the transgression,In time;Fate compels a full confession,In time.None can safely sin forever—Conscience leaves the bosom never—It will crush guilt's best endeavor,In time."

FRANCIS S. SMITH.

Clifford Standish paused to note the effect of his boasting on Mrs. Fitzgerald.

Every statement he had made was a falsehood, but he knew that she could not disprove a single one.

The magnificent salary of which he boasted was only fifty dollars a week, and as for his rich mother who made him such a handsome allowance, and would leave him a fortune when she died, the old woman was as poor as poverty itself, and took in washing. But as she lived away off in Colorado, he was not afraid that she would ever appear to contradict his statement. In fact, he had told the same story to every new acquaintance, until he had almost come to believe it himself.

He judged that Mrs. Fitzgerald was proud and arrogant, and would prefer her daughter to marry rich; so, after telling his boastful story, he waited with some confidence for her reply.

She drew herself erect to her stateliest height, and if scorn could have killed, the lightnings of her dark eyes would have stretched him dead at her aristocratic feet.

"You contemptible villain!" she exclaimed, angrily.

"Madame!"

"You perjured wretch! You cowardly wife-deserter! You escaped criminal! You persecutor of innocence! You—you—fiend!" concluded Mrs. Fitzgerald, losing her temper in her righteous indignation and piling opprobrious epithets one upon another in the white heat of her wrath.

Startled, cowed by this most unexpected onslaught, the wretch could only cower in pallid amazement before the lady as she continued her scathing denunciation.

"How dare you intrude yourself here after your vile persecutions of Geraldine? Your audacity is startling, and I should do quite right to hand you over to the police on the charge of abducting and intimidating an innocent young girl! But I abhor scandal, and for this reason I shall not have you punished, unless—you dare to annoy us again!"

Recovering his hardihood, he muttered, sullenly:

"Madame, I deny the truth of your statements. Your daughter promised to marry me!"

"At the point of a revolver, yes, when, fearing for her life, she determined to temporize with you, hoping to throw you off your guard that she might escape your cowardly persecution. She has told me her story from beginning to end, and I shudder to think what might have been my dear girl's fate but for our meeting on the train!" exclaimed Mrs. Fitzgerald, flashing on him the scornful lightnings of her reproachful eyes.

Realizing for the first time that Geraldine had duped him in her apparent acquiescence to his will, and feeling himself beaten for the time in the dangerous game he had played, he cowered sullenly before her as she pointed to the door, saying, authoritatively:

"Now go, you hound! and never let me see your craven face again!"

Defeated, humiliated, writhing under her womanly scorn, he slunk out of the room and from her presence, into the wintry streets whose chill he could not feel, so hotly was he raging in his inmost heart against the two women who had scorned him for his wickedness.

"So you were playing on my credulity, laughing at me in your sleeve, pretty Geraldine!" he muttered, with a stifled oath. "Very well. You defeated me this time, but—look to yourself in the future!"

So muttering, he turned toward the sleigh that he had left waiting for him, but, to his surprise, it was gone.

For some unknown reason the driver had proved false to his engagement, and deserted his post.

Cursing the man's stupidity, he walked some distance along the snowy streets in the piercing cold of the western air before he boarded a car to take him to his boarding-house on State street.

Leaving the car, however, at an obscure side street with the intention of seeking a near-by saloon and concert hall, he crossed the street, and was proceeding on his way when suddenly he heard hurried footsteps behind, and then a hand clutched his arm whirling him fiercely around.

"Wretch!" hissed a man's voice, vibrant with hate. "Wretch! So I have caught you at last! Where is she? Where is my Geraldine?"

Under the glare of the electric lights that shone with ghastly whiteness on the snowy pavement, he found himself looking into the stern blue eyes of Harry Hawthorne.

For two days the young man had been on his track, without one clew to reward his efforts, for the villain, hiding his identity under an assumed name, had been swallowed up, like a wave breaking on the shore, in the vast city of Chicago.

Now, by chance, they were face to face, on an obscure street, almost deserted by reason of the piercing cold, and they looked at each other with mortal hate in their flashing eyes.

"Where is she? Where is my Geraldine?" demanded Hawthorne, hoarsely, tightening his grip on his enemy's arm so that he vainly tried to throw it off.

Standish looked at him a moment in fear and indecision then a devilish thought came to him, and he laughed aloud, mockingly.

"Your Geraldine, ha! ha! Your Geraldine!"

Something in his voice and laughter seemed to freeze the blood in Hawthorne's veins, but he said, in deadly wrath:

"You stole her from me by a vile trick. I saw the forged note you sent to her, and I know that you have betrayed her to some terrible fate; but by the God above us, if she has suffered wrong at your hands, Standish, your vile life shall pay the forfeit!"

"Bah! Hawthorne, this ranting is useless. She is alive, she is well, she is happy, and I have just come from keeping an appointment with the charming little beauty."

"Liar!"

"Do not bandy epithets so generously, Hawthorne. We really have no quarrel with each other—for she isn't worth it!"

"Liar! Hound!" and Hawthorne looked as if he could barely restrain himself from throttling his defiant foe.

But Standish kept his temper well in check, knowing that he could gain more thus than by losing it.

He smiled mockingly, and said:

"Those are hard words, but I think you will offer an apology for them presently. See! here is Geraldine's note to me. It is yours if you wish to keep it."

He thrust a crumpled sheet of paper into Hawthorne's hand, and by the glaring electric light he read:

> "MR. STANDISH:—You may call at eight o'clock this evening.
>
> GERALDINE HARDING.
>
> "Dec. 29th, 1894."

How the words glared up at him, for he knew the writing well, and a groan burst from his lips as he flung it from him, crying:

"Where is she? I must see her! I must have an explanation!"

"I cannot tell you where she is. She would not wish it. You may as well give up the game, Hawthorne, for I have won!"

The triumph in his voice was hateful.

Hawthorne did not speak for a moment, and his opponent continued:

"Let us understand each other. We have been rivals for Geraldine Harding's love, and she has coquetted with us both, promised her hand to both. Well, all is fair in love or war. My little scheme succeeded, and she is satisfied!"

"You have married her, Standish?"

"How could I when I have a wife living in New York, and Geraldine knows it? But I tell you she loves me and is satisfied. We stage people are not at all prudish, you know."

The next moment Hawthorne's strong fingers were about his throat.

"You have lied, you miserable dastard! Geraldine is as pure as snow, and unless you take back your falsehoods I will strangle them in your throat!"

A hoarse, gurgling laugh issued from the convulsed throat of Standish, and the next moment they closed in deadly combat.

Both were strong and athletic men, both brave, both desperate, and for a few minutes the contest they waged was an equal one.

But suddenly Hawthorne began to get the advantage.

He had his foe down and his knee on his breast.

"Will you take back your foul lie, hound?" he hissed, fiercely.

Standish made no answer in words.

He had been struggling all the while to get at his hip-pocket, and now he succeeded in drawing out a dagger and plunging it in Hawthorne's breast. There was a horrible ripping sound, and he rolled over bleeding in the snow.

CHAPTER XXXV.

GERALDINE'S CHOICE.

"Howe'er it be, it seems to me,'Tis only noble to be good;Kind hearts are more than coronets,And simple faith than Norman blood."

TENNYSON.

"Fair maiden, let me say to you,Mark well the man who comes to woo;Select the one as true as steel,With brain to think and heart to feel."

FRANCIS S. SMITH.

When Mrs. Fitzgerald had dismissed Standish, she returned to her daughter and recounted all that had passed.

She was vastly amused at the actor's boastfulness, and said:

"It is only low-bred people, 'beggars on horseback,' as the saying goes, who brag of their possessions or their expectations. Really high-toned people— and they may be high-toned even if poor—can never tolerate purse-proud vulgarity."

Geraldine laughed and said:

"Clifford Standish's story of his rich mother has always been his trump card in social life. I have often been secretly disgusted at hearing him tell it to new acquaintances."

"He probably sets a very low estimate on his own merits when he has to resort to such silly boasting to curry favor," returned her mother, adding: "I have met people of his stamp before, and, as a rule, their statements were untruthful. I dare say, if the facts were known, the fellow's mother takes in washing or goes out scrubbing."

"Thank Heaven, I am rid of him at last! I do not believe he will ever dare to cross my path again since finding out that I have such a strong defender in my noble mother," declared Geraldine, gladly, for she did not yet comprehend with what an evil nature she had to deal.

Believing herself rid of Clifford Standish forever, her longing thoughts returned to the true lover from whom she had been so cruelly torn.

"Oh, my love! my love! I cannot give you up," she thought, tenderly, and after a moment's hesitancy she cried:

"Oh, mamma, you said just now that a person may be high-toned even though poor, and it made me think of my lover Harry. If you should meet him, mamma, not knowing his obscure station, you would think him not less than princely. He has the bearing, the speech, and the heart of a gentleman—of one of nature's noblemen. Then why should you despise him for his poverty?"

Mrs. Fitzgerald's fair brow clouded with annoyance at her daughter's words and she said, quickly:

"I do not despise him for his poverty—I do not despise him at all. I said that you could not marry him because almost from your cradle you have been promised to another."

"What nonsense!" said the girl, petulantly, to herself but she asked, with seeming calmness:

"To whom, mamma?"

"To a splendid young gentleman of wealth and rank in England."

"How romantic! Tell me all about it, dear mamma!" cried Geraldine, anxious to know the worst.

"You are laughing at me, Geraldine," her mother cried, doubtfully.

"No, no, mamma; I was only smiling at my transformation. Such a little while ago I was simply a poor shop-girl in a New York dry-goods store, and engaged to marry a fireman, who was considered an exceedingly good match for me. Now I find myself a rich young heiress, betrothed to an English nobleman. It is quite startling."

"I believe you regret your good fortune!" cried the lady.

Geraldine answered with a burst of tears.

For a few moments she sobbed vehemently; then calming herself, she sighed.

"Dear mamma, I can never regret that I have found you, but I can never cease to deplore your hardness of heart that would part me from my heart's chosen one!"

"Hardness of heart," echoed the mother, reproachfully.

"Oh, mamma, you do not know how fondly I love him!" sobbed the daughter, and for a little while there was a painful silence.

Mrs. Fitzgerald was a woman of strong will and high ambition.

She could not forego her plans for Geraldine.

So presently she said, soothingly:

"My darling girl, I know you would not wish to have me break my plighted word. When I was in Europe, at the time when you were two years old, I spent two months at the home of a New York cousin of mine who had married a rich lord. They had a son seven years old—a bright, manly little lad—who fairly worshiped you; and one day his mother said, gayly: 'Leland, why don't you ask little Geraldine to be your wife when she grows up?'

"The pretty blue-eyed boy laughed and knelt down by your side, repeating the question his mother had prompted, and you kissed him and lisped 'yes.'"

"But I was only a baby, mamma. Of course, such a betrothal was not binding," remonstrated Geraldine, though she was touched at the pretty, childish betrothal.

"Wait till I have finished, darling. Lady Putnam, my cousin, smiled at me with tears in her eyes, and said that she hoped that the childish love would endure till they were grown, and that they might indeed marry. I agreed to this, and we solemnly betrothed the children next day, buying a tiny diamond ring on purpose to fit your finger. Little Leland was delighted with his promised bride, and grieved bitterly when we left him and returned to New York."

Geraldine was about to speak, but her mother interrupted:

"Wait, dear, till I have finished the story I began. Then I will listen to your objections."

CHAPTER XXXVI.

GERALDINE'S DEFIANCE.

"There are some sweet affectionsThat wealth cannot buy,That cling but still closerWhen sorrow draws nigh;As the mistletoe clingsTo the oak, not in part,But with leaves closely round it,The root in its heart."

CHARLES SWAIN.

Mrs. Fitzgerald sighed, and continued:

"I must touch briefly now on a subject painful to us both—your father's faithlessness."

"Oh, mamma, how could he be false to one like you—so noble, so beautiful?" cried Geraldine, in wonder.

"He was weak and easily flattered by a designing woman—that is all I will say, Geraldine, for how can I disparage an erring father to his child? Well, while I remained at my cousin's in Devonshire, my husband kept running back and forth to Paris, seeming infatuated by its charms. At length a rumor reached me that he was lavishing money and attention on a notorious woman who had caught his fancy. I wrote to him, begging that he would deny it, but he treated my letter with disdain, plunging more recklessly into dissipation, and even appearing in public by the side of the woman who had lured him from me, seated in a magnificent vehicle he had purchased for her use. To be brief, Geraldine, his vile conduct killed every spark of love I ever had for him. I returned to my home in New York and secured a divorce as soon as possible, encouraged by my father, who was then living. But he died in a few months, and afterward I was very lonely, having no near relatives to cheer me except you, my pet and darling. At a watering-place I met Mr. Fitzgerald, and a mutual fascination for each other was followed by an early marriage. Soon after our return from our bridal tour, your father—enraged, perhaps that I could find happiness with another—came to Chicago and stole you away. A cruel fate foiled all my efforts to trace you, until that day when chance brought us face to face."

"Do not call it chance, mamma; it was Providence, surely, that saved me from that wretch!" cried pretty Geraldine, fervently.

"We will call it Providence, then," agreed her mother, and continued: "Until the last few years, when my heart and thoughts were all occupied by your step-father's failing health, I kept up a regular correspondence with my cousin, Lady Putnam, and her letters were filled with praises of her noble son, Leland. She had a sweet little daughter also, called Amy, but her pride seemed to centre in the boy who would inherit his father's rank and wealth."

She paused, sighed, then added:

"Now, Geraldine, you see how I had planned your future before you were so cruelly stolen from me. And now that you have been restored to my heart, all my old ambitions for you have revived. Can you wonder that I prefer for you to marry noble Leland Putnam, whom I have known and loved ever since his childhood, rather than a stranger, who, however worthy, is poor and obscure, and could not elevate you to the position your beauty merits?"

Geraldine had listened silently and earnestly. The romantic story of her childish betrothal pleased her, but it could not turn her true heart from its firm allegiance.

She said, gently:

"You have told me a deeply touching story, dear mamma. I grieve that my own father proved so false and unworthy, and I rejoice that I did not inherit his fickleness, for my heart is true as steel to the first object of its choice. I can never cease to love Harry Hawthorne, and as for the betrothal you speak of, it was simply a childish affair, forgotten, no doubt by all but yourself."

"You are mistaken, my dear; for my cousin often mentioned it in her letters after you were lost to us, as we feared, forever. I shall write to her this very day, and tell her you are found again."

"But not one word of that childish engagement, please, mamma! I will not be offered to any man!" remonstrated Geraldine, in alarm.

"Certainly not, Geraldine. Of course, I know what is due to you. But if Leland revives it of himself, if he still claims you, you cannot refuse to marry him!"

Geraldine felt as if she were choking.

A cruel fate seemed to destine her to a loveless marriage.

Oh, how could her mother be so cruel, so heartless, wrapped up in sordid ambition, reckless of a young heart's misery!

Filled with fear and anger at her threatening fate, she sprang to her feet, crying, passionately:

"Mamma, I do not wish to offend you, but—but—I will not be forced into a loveless marriage. I will be true to Harry, though the whole world oppose me! Why, I would rather have remained a poor salesgirl forever than have lost him, my own true love, by finding myself an heiress!"

The passionate defiance was out, and the mother knew that all her ambitions were likely to be defeated by a girl's perversity.

She called it perversity in her mind. She would not own that it was love—constant, faithful love, that has been the theme of poets since first they struck the sounding lyre.

She did not want to excite the girl any further now, though she determined that in the end she should yield to her mother's will.

Rising from her seat, she quitted the room like a skillful general, though casting one single glance backward that rankled reproachfully in Geraldine's heart.

CHAPTER XXXVII.

"A WOMAN'S HONOR IS INVOLVED, AND MY SILENCE IS ITS ONLY SAFEGUARD."

"Woman's honor is nice as ermine—Will not bear a soil."

"Her maiden pride, her haughty name,My dumb devotion shall not shame;The love that no return doth crave,To knightly levels lifts the slave."

When Clifford Standish plunged the dagger into Hawthorne's breast, and heard the groan of the victim, felt the hot blood spurting over his hands as he rolled over in the snow, he thought he had killed him.

But no pang of remorse touched his cruel heart.

He exulted in the deed that he had done.

Springing to his feet, he glanced hurriedly around, and seeing no one near, coolly wiped his bloody hands on Hawthorne's overcoat, and hastened away, exclaiming:

"I am rid of my dangerous rival at last!"

But there had been an unsuspected witness of the deadly crime he had committed.

From a window above a young man had been looking down just as the rivals closed in mortal combat.

He had come to the place to call on a friend who roomed there, and learned that he was out, but was told that he would be in directly.

Without removing his hat and overcoat, he walked restlessly up and down the room, and at last became so impatient that he pushed up the window and looked out to see if his friend was yet in sight.

But the narrow street, its snowy expanse lighted by the flaring electric lights, was deserted, save by two men, who hurled themselves with tremendous force against each other in deadly conflict.

Mr. Hill was not alarmed at first. He smiled, and murmured, whimsically:

"Whew! A prize-fight! I bet on the one that whips!"

Oblivious of the cold air that rushed through the open window into his friend's warm steam-heated apartment, he leaned out and watched the contest, adding:

"I don't suppose they would thank me for spoiling their sport, so I won't interfere. It's the blue-coat's business to break it up, but they're never in place when needed."

The battle went on, and the unseen witness gazed admiringly at the well-pitted antagonists.

He was a jovial young fellow, and he really felt inclined to cheer the gallant athletes, so cleverly did they handle each other.

But he restrained his inclination, and continued his watching, and wondering who the combatants were and which would gain the mastery.

But all at once he uttered a startled cry:

"Heavens! that was murder!"

He had heard the ripping sound of the dagger pressed upward into the victim's breast, and his dying groan as he rolled over in the snow.

Starting away from the window, he ran away from the room into the hall, eager to make his way into the street.

In the lower hall he blundered against another man, who caught him by the arm, saying, roughly:

"Hello! what are you running away like this for, eh?"

"Don't you know me, Doctor Rowe? Come with me, for God's sake, into the street. I was looking out of the window, and saw a murder being done."

They rushed into the street, but the little delay had enabled the murderer to make his escape.

Nothing was to be seen of any human creature but that still form lying there in a drift of snow that had turned crimson with the blood that was spurting from his breast.

With exclamations of pity and horror, they bent over him, the physician quickly feeling for his heart.

"Is he dead?" asked Leroy Hill, his laughing dark eyes growing soft with pity.

"Not yet; his heart beats faintly, but this flow of blood must be stopped at once. It is very fortunate we came to him so quickly," returned the old physician, tearing open Hawthorne's shirt-bosom and preparing to stanch the flow of blood.

Several people came out of the house and joined them, and a crowd collected quickly, a policeman coming at last around the corner.

Those who could assist the doctor did so, others plied each other with questions.

"Who is he?"

"Who killed him?"

No one could answer either question.

No cards nor letters were found on the stranger's person to prove his identity, and no one present recognized him.

Leroy Hill could only tell that he had seen the encounter from an upper window, and that the assassin had escaped before he reached the street.

Doctor Rowe looked up, asking: "Has any one 'phoned for an ambulance to take him to the hospital? His last chance of life will soon be gone if he has to lie here in the street."

A bystander interposed, sarcastically:

"And he won't have much chance of life among some of those brutal nurses at the hospital, neither."

Mr. Hill's absent friend had come up a moment before, and the young man turned to him, saying, kindly:

"Let's give the poor devil a chance for his life, Ralph. Can't we get a room in the house and hire a nurse for him?"

"Why, certainly, Lee. Glad you thought of it! We will put him in my bedroom and I can sleep on the lounge in my study," returned Ralph Washburn who was an author, and had the kindest heart in the world.

And so Harry Hawthorne found true friends among those jolly, big-hearted Westerners, and, under their faithful ministrations, he came back to the life that had used him so hardly.

And then they found that he was inclined to throw a bit of a mystery around himself, for he was unwilling to answer questions about anything.

"Don't think me ungrateful, boys," he said to Ralph and Lee, as they sat by his bed. "God only knows how grateful I am for your goodness, and I hope to prove it to you some day. I'm from the North; I don't belong in Chicago—I'll own that. I won't tell my name yet—call me Jack Daly; that will do as well as anything until the time comes when I can safely confess all."

They liked him in spite of his mysterious ways, for there was too much nobility in his face to lead any one astray. They felt sure that he was worthy of honor and respect.

"But, Jack Daly," began Leroy Hill, smiling as he ran his white hand through his clustering auburn curls, "I'm going to ask you one question. Do you mean to shield the man who tried to murder you?"

"To shield him? Was he not a stranger?"

"I do not believe he was a stranger to you. You did not meet as strangers. You had a terrible quarrel. Perhaps it was about a woman. Listen: I found a bloody glove in the snow that night, and it belonged either to you or to him. I deciphered in it a name—Clifford Standish!"

"Heavens!" exclaimed the patient.

"Then that is your name?"

"No."

"Then it was your assailant's, and I am bound to put the police in possession of this important clew."

The patient raised himself on his elbow, crying, feverishly:

"For God's sake! spare that villain, Mr. Hill; not for his sake, no, no—but for a woman's sake! Listen: there is a tragedy behind what you know. A woman's honor is involved, and my silence is its only safeguard!"

CHAPTER XXXVIII.

"STOP THE CARRIAGE!"

"Come love! Until thy face I see,All things seem valueless to me;Nor singing birds nor blooming flowersCan make less sad the weary hours.Friends cannot cheer, mirth cannot move,While thou art absent, dearest love.Dejection holds my heart in thrallTill thou art here, my all-in-all."

FRANCIS S. SMITH.

"How strange, oh, how strange, that Harry does not answer my letter!" cried Geraldine, impatiently.

About ten days had passed since she had posted the letter with her own hands to Hawthorne, and for days she had been waiting in silent anxiety for his reply.

But, as we know that he had left New York suddenly, without leaving directions to forward his mail, we can understand the cause of the silence that was torturing her tender heart. Since the day when Geraldine had impulsively defied her mother to turn her heart from her betrothed, a slight reserve had grown up between them that nothing seemed to bridge. Mrs. Fitzgerald never brought up again the subject of her daughter's lover. She was bitterly and unreasonably offended at the stand the girl had taken.

So she became more chary of showing affection to Geraldine, and lavished caresses on her two younger children, the charming Earl and Claire.

Geraldine, who was as loving as she was proud and willful, suffered sorely from her mother's coldness. She began to feel like an alien in the great, splendid mansion. In secret she pined for Cissy and her old happy life among the girls at O'Neill's before her own mad ambition for the stage had cut her off from those pleasant days forever.

"I have a great mind to run away from my grand home and ambitious mother and go back to Cissy," she sobbed one night to her lonely pillow.

But she did not have the heart to carry out her threat, for Mrs. Fitzgerald was kind in spite of her reserve, lavishing beautiful gowns and jewels upon her, as if to make up to her for her heart-loneliness. Dressmakers and milliners had *carte blanche*, and Geraldine had an outfit fine enough for a young princess.

These beautiful gowns, these flashing jewels, and the luxury of her home would have made the lovely girl very happy, but for the cruel separation from her lover. Without him there was a blank in everything.

"Where I am the halls are gilded,Stored with pictures bright and rare;Strains of deep, melodious musicFloat upon the perfumed air.Slowly, heavily, and sadlyTime with weary wings must flee,Marked by pain and toil and sorrow,Where I fain must be."

One day a sudden thought came into her mind.

"Why not have Cissy come and make me a visit?"

She spoke to her mother about it the same day, asking timidly for the privilege of inviting Cissy to spend a month with her in Chicago.

Mrs. Fitzgerald readily acquiesced, and gave Geraldine a liberal check for her friend's traveling expenses.

Geraldine flew to her room to write to her friend, and she did not fail to inquire of Cissy what had become of Harry Hawthorne.

"Tell him I have written to him and received no reply," she added, naively, in her keen anxiety.

She felt a little happier when the letter had been dispatched to Cissy. It would be a comfort to have her old friend with her, in spite of the fact that many of her mother's rich, fashionable friends had called and offered their friendship in affectionate terms.

But they were strange and new to Geraldine, and they could not make her happy yet. The transplanted flower had not taken root in this new, rich soil. It pined for its old habitation. It was strange to be a greenhouse exotic instead of a fresh wild-flower nodding to its mates beneath the free blue sky.

"But if I only had those I love with me, I should be supremely happy," she sighed, wistfully.

"There is no friend like an old friend,Whose life-path mates our own,Whose dawn and noon, whose even and endHave known that we have known. It may be when we read her faceWe note a trace of care;'Tis well that friends in life's last graceShare sighs as smiles they share."

More than a week had passed since Clifford Standish's visit, and they saw and heard no more of him.

Both mother and daughter supposed that he had passed out of their lives forever.

But the handsome governess, Miss Erroll, might have told them a different story had she dared.

She had received several letters from him, and she knew from them that the actor was weaving a spider's web to entrap poor Geraldine.

But she dared not speak, dared not warn the beautiful unconscious victim.

She was in the villain's power, through his knowledge of her past, and her terror for her own safety commanded her silence.

She was a weak woman, who had erred and repented; and now that she had begun to live a better life, she had a terror of losing her situation. She could not betray Clifford Standish, although she would have rejoiced in doing so with safety to herself.

So the days went by, and it was almost a week since Geraldine had written to Miss Carroll. She began to look eagerly for an answer.

Mrs. Fitzgerald proposed a shopping tour the next day.

"You have not made the tour of the Chicago shops yet, but I assure you they compare favorably with those of New York. We will drive to State street, and go through Marshall Field's immense establishment, which is one of the finest here. Then, too, we must visit Stevens & Brothers' magnificent silk store. We may find something to please us there. How sorry I am that I cannot introduce you formally to society yet, because of my mourning. You would be a vision of beauty in an evening dress."

Geraldine's thoughts flew back to the only time she had ever worn an evening dress—the night of the firemen's ball at Newburgh, when she had been so happy because Harry Hawthorne's eyes had told her over and over of her beauty. Ah, she would never be quite so happy again, she feared.

They entered the elegant liveried carriage and were driven to State street.

It was Geraldine's first shopping tour with her mother, and she found a great deal of zest in it, in spite of the sorrow that ached at her loving heart.

How delightful it was to be buying beautiful fabrics instead of selling them; to have a purse full of money to spend on whatever she liked!

How different from the days of the shabby black serge gown and the waiting on customers from morning till night, with weary feet and oft-times aching back. She looked at the pretty salesgirls of Chicago with kind, pitying eyes, and was careful to give as little trouble as possible when making her purchases. They looked at the rich young beauty in her sealskin cloak enviously, little dreaming that but a short while ago she had been a simple working-girl like themselves, with no prospect of the good fortune that had come to her so suddenly and strangely.

They re-entered the carriage, and Mrs. Fitzgerald gave the address of an artist.

"I must have some picture of you in your carriage suit, and this is such a bright, sunny day, just suited to a sitting," she said.

It pleased her to have her beautiful daughter photographed in several graceful styles, then they left Stevens' and proceeded home.

"You have had fatigue enough for one day, but we will come out again to-morrow and see more of the city," said Mrs. Fitzgerald, kindly.

The carriage drove away, and neither of them noticed three men who had been walking slowly toward them as they entered the carriage, and who had paused to gaze admiringly at Geraldine as she crossed the pavement.

They were Ralph Washburn, Leroy Hill, and Harry Hawthorne. The two former had brought their patient out for the first time for a short walk.

He had convalesced very fast, the wound not being as deep as at first supposed.

But the keen stroke of Standish had only missed a fatal ending because it had been blunted by passing through a cigar case in Hawthorne's breast-pocket.

His high health and vitality had enabled him to pull through fast, and to-day he was out for the first time, looking pale and thin, his restless glances roving from side to side, seeking ever for one beautiful face so deeply loved, so cruelly lost.

And suddenly he encountered it—where least expected—in the garb and the trappings of wealth.

He gave a gasp like one dying, and clutched young Hill's arm in icy fingers.

The latter looked around, exclaiming:

"What is it, Jack, eh? Have we brought you too far in your weak state? Oh, I see, you're looking at the beauty! You're hard hit, aren't you? So am I! She's a stunner!"

At that moment the footman closed the door on Geraldine, and the carriage rolled away.

She did not look out of the window, or she would have seen Hawthorne—the lover over whom her fond heart was yearning—start forward with outstretched arms toward the carriage, crying, wildly:

"It is she! it is she! Stop the carriage, I say! I must speak to her one moment!"

But his friends restrained him on either side. They feared that he had suddenly gone daft.

Weak as he was, he struggled with them, broke their hold, and ran a few paces after the carriage.

Then he dropped, exhausted, to the pavement.

They overtook him and raised him up between them.

He looked at them pleadingly.

"You think I am crazy, I know. But let me explain. I know that girl in the carriage. I came to Chicago to find her, and now, she has escaped me!" he groaned.

"What! you know the beautiful Miss Fitzgerald, of Prairie avenue?" exclaimed Ralph Washburn, in surprise.

"That is not her name!" cried Hawthorne.

"Oh, yes, it is Miss Fitzgerald, certainly. You have made a mistake," returned the young author, who had seen Mrs. Fitzgerald often, and had read in the society newspapers that her lovely daughter, Miss Fitzgerald, who had been educated abroad, had just been called home by her father's death.

But to make assurance doubly sure, he ran up to the photographer's studio to inquire. They assured him that their late sitters were Mrs. and Miss Fitzgerald.

Hawthorne was so unnerved by the discovery of his mistake that a cab had to be called to take him home.

CHAPTER XXXIX.

IT IS NOT POSSIBLE FOR TRUE LOVE TO FORGET.

"Have you seen the full moonDrift behind a cloud,Hiding all of natureIn a dusky shroud?

"Have you seen the light snowChange to sudden rain,And the virgin streets growBlack as ink again?

"Have you seen the ashesWhen the flame is spent,And the cheerless hearth-stoneGrim and eloquent?

"Have you seen the ball-roomWhen the dance is done,And its tawdry splendorMeets the morning sun?

"Dearest, all these picturesCannot half portrayHow my life has alteredSince you've gone away!"

HARRY ROMAINE.

It was impossible for Hawthorne to sleep that night after the sight of the beautiful stranger, Miss Fitzgerald, whose startling likeness to his lost darling had awakened in his heart a fresh agony of love and pain.

He tossed and turned restlessly all night upon his pillow, thinking of Geraldine until his heart was on fire with its agony.

Could it be true what that dastard Standish had told him?

Had he indeed won the girl from the path of truth and honor, to make shipwreck of her life for the sake of a guilty love?

No, no, no! He could not, would not believe it!

She was pure as snow, his lovely Geraldine.

But where was she, what had been her fate since she left New York in company with the arch-villain, Standish?

"I cannot find her by myself. I must put a detective on the case to-morrow," he decided.

The young author, who was burning the midnight oil over a charming poem, was disturbed by his groans, and came in to see about him.

"I fear you are worse. That little outing was too much for you," he exclaimed.

"No, it is not that. I am restless; it is a trouble of the heart," confessed the patient, frankly.

"Ah!" exclaimed Ralph, sympathetically, adding: "Can I help you?"

"No one can help me," sighed Hawthorne, hopelessly.

"Is it a love affair?"

"Yes."

"It is hopeless, I judge, from your expressions. Then why not throw it from your mind? Forget the cruel fair one?"

"Have you ever loved, Ralph?"

"Never," laughed the handsome young author, who only worshiped at the shrine of the muses.

"I thought not, or you would not use that hackneyed word forget. It is impossible to real love—a poet's dream, but an impossibility."

"Have you loved so deeply?"

"With all my heart, with all my soul, and with all my mind!" groaned Hawthorne, adding: "My dear friend, may God keep you from ever knowing such love and pain and grief as fill my heart to bursting."

Ralph was silent. He saw that here was a grief beyond comfort.

He wondered what was the mysterious nature of Hawthorne's sad love-story, but he was too generous to ask such a question.

He could only gaze at him in tender, silent sympathy.

Hawthorne continued, passionately:

"It is not my way to dwell on my own troubles, but to-night my sorrow overwhelms me! To love and to lose—oh, Ralph, that is the bitterest thing of life!"

"Is she dead, your loved one?"

"Ah! no, she is not dead! I could almost wish that she were, in my dread that she is dead to me forever! And if she is, oh, if she is, how can I bear the gloom of my life henceforward?—the blank darkness of a night of storm following on the sunshine of a perfect day. Oh, God!" groaned Hawthorne, tossing his arms above his pillow in anguish.

The young poet gazed at him in deepest sympathy and pity. He had not loved yet, but he could understand and pity, for to the poet's soul all the secrets of life are felt and known through the subtle occultism of genius.

"The poet in a golden clime was born,With golden stars above;Dowered with the hate of hate, the scorn of scorn,The love of love.

"He saw through life and death, through good and ill,saw through his own soul."

As Ralph gazed at the handsome face of the unhappy lover, he felt that here was the material for a novelist's pen to frame a most bewitching love-story, and he hoped that some day Hawthorne would confide in him.

Suddenly the young man looked up at him, saying, abruptly:

"Ralph, I want you to take me to the best detective in Chicago to-morrow morning."

"Very well," replied Ralph, going to a table and mixing a sedative that had been used under Doctor Rowe's orders. He presented it to the patient, saying:

"Drink this, or you won't be able to stir to-morrow morning."

Hawthorne complied readily, for he was, indeed, weary of the tumult of his mind and heart.

He closed his eyes wearily, and Ralph dimmed the light and returned to his study, and the last verse of the pretty poem he was composing.

When he had written the last line he heard Hawthorne breathing gently in a saving sleep, and he, too, retired to his bed.

Both slept late the next morning, and breakfast and the morning papers were brought up together for Hawthorne.

Ralph saw that his charge was comfortable, and went out to a neighboring *cafe* where he was wont to meet his friend Mr. Hill at the morning meal.

Hawthorne made a very light meal in bed, dismissed the servant with the tray, and then turned his attention to the newspapers—the Chicago *Herald* first.

And as he skimmed over the telegraphic news from abroad, he came across a paragraph that worked a curious change in him.

His face grew pale with emotion, and sinking back on his pillow, he sighed to himself:

"I must go home."

When Ralph returned with Mr. Hill, who always made a morning call on his *protege*, as he humorously termed Hawthorne, they found the patient dressing in feverish haste.

"Boys, I must return to New York to-day," he exclaimed.

While they gazed at him in surprise, he continued:

"Business of a very important nature obliges me to cross the ocean as soon as possible; and—in brief—I owe you both a debt of gratitude that I wish to repay you by asking you to accompany me on my trip to Europe as my guests. Will you come? I am not poor, as you supposed, in the kindness of your hearts, when you took me in, a stranger, and nursed and cared for me, and a cordial welcome will meet you in my English home!"

They were startled and surprised at his generosity, but Hawthorne would not listen to their refusals.

"I love you both like brothers, and I will not be refused. You shall come with me," he declared, and his cordiality won their consent.

Arrangements were speedily made, and after a visit to a detective, the three friends left for New York.

CHAPTER XL.

"IT IS LIKE SUICIDE!"

"Round the post-office window are pressingA motley and turbulent
throng.All eagerly bent on possessingThe letter they've looked for so
long.To some come dark tidings of sorrow,To others come tidings of
bliss;Uncertain is every to-morrow,And the world like the post-office is."

FRANCIS S. SMITH.

All unconscious of the fact that she had been so near to the lover for
whom she mourned, Geraldine returned home with her mother, and even
as they went up the steps the postman followed on his afternoon round
and placed two letters in her hand.

She glanced at them, and a cry of joy broke from her lips as she saw that
one bore the New York postmark and was in Cissy's familiar hand.

The other one was postmarked Chicago, and was addressed to the
governess, Miss Erroll.

And if Geraldine could have guessed how fatally that letter concerned
herself, she would have been justified in tearing it to fragments and
scattering it in wrath to the four winds of heaven.

If some saving hypnotic power had but impelled her to this course, what
suffering she would have been spared. But in her joy over Cissy's letter, she
scarcely gave a thought to Miss Erroll.

Going up stairs to her own apartments, she passed the school-room and
tapped lightly on the door.

"A letter for you," she said, courteously, to the governess, not noticing how
the woman's hand trembled, when she took it.

But the face of Miss Erroll grew ashy pale when, alone with her pupils, she
opened and read her letter from Clifford Standish.

"To think that she should have this letter in her hands; that she should have
brought it to me, it is a mockery of fate! It is like—suicide!" she muttered,
through her writhing lips, and a bitter sigh heaved her breast.

Geraldine hurried to her own rooms and read Cissy's letter before she
removed her wraps, so eager was her fond heart for news from New York.

"She will be here to-morrow, to-morrow, the dear girl!" she cried, joyfully, kissing the letter in the exuberance of her gladness.

But the letter contained other news that was very puzzling.

"Harry followed me to Chicago on the next train, the darling boy! But how strange that he has never come to me! Does he know where I am? Is he in the same city with me?" were questions that repeated themselves over and over in her bewildered brain.

She could understand now why he had never answered her letter. Of course, he had never received it, since he was on her trail following her abductor and his victim in their flight from New York.

"But why, oh, why does he not come to me? Is it possible he cannot find me, my dear, dear, love? Ah, I have it now! He is following Clifford Standish up, and of course he can find no trace of me," she decided, and immediately resolved to insert personals in the prominent newspapers of the next day in the hope of reaching him.

When she had exchanged her carriage dress for a lovely house robe, fluttering with lace and ribbons, she sought her mother, with Cissy's letter.

Mrs. Fitzgerald rejoiced with her daughter over the coming of her friend, but she said not a word about Harry Hawthorne.

She was secretly annoyed at learning that he had followed Geraldine to Chicago. She thought, in dismay:

"He may be turning up here at any moment, claiming my daughter, and she is so headstrong, she will never consent to give him up. What shall I do?"

But her woman's wit could suggest no answer to the question.

She was honorable and high-minded, and shrank from using harsh or underhand means to break off Geraldine's engagement.

Geraldine saw the lack of sympathy in her mother's mobile face, and thought, sadly:

"She is still unrelenting. I shall have no sympathy in my sorrow until Cissy comes. Then I can whisper all my grief to her faithful heart."

And she longed all the more anxiously for to-morrow's sun that would shine on the coming of her beloved friend.

And, to lighten her suspense, she spent some time superintending the arrangement of the beautiful room next to her own that was being prepared for Miss Carroll's occupancy. Some of her own favorite books were carried in—Cissy was inordinately fond of reading—flowers were lavished here and there. When it was all ready, the pretty room in pink and silver was dainty enough for a princess.

"Cissy will enjoy it so much. She likes pretty things. And I shall buy her some dainty gowns, and—lots of things! She shall see how I love her!" the girl whispered to herself, with tears of joy in her beautiful brown eyes.

Then she went to her desk and wrote out and sent the personals she had thought of to the newspapers for to-morrow.

"Mamma would not approve, I know, but perhaps she will never find out what I have done. But, at any risk, I would have done it. I cannot give up my own true love! I believe God made us for each other," she thought, tenderly.

She spent a restless night, thinking of Cissy's coming to-morrow, and wondering where her lover was to-night in this great Western city, little dreaming that he was speeding from it in the deepening night.

CHAPTER XLI.

GERALDINE'S SUSPENSE.

"Half the night I waste in sighs,Half in dreams, I sorrow afterThe delight of early skies;In a wakeful doze I sorrowFor the hand, the lips, the eyes,For the meeting of the morrow,The delight of happy laughter,The delight of low replies."

TENNYSON.

The long winter night was over, and with the morning's sunshine Geraldine's heart began to beat with eager expectancy.

A few hours more and sweet Cissy would be here! Cissy, her old friend, who would sympathize with her in all her trials, and perhaps help her to a way out of them.

After breakfast she hastened to her room, leaving Mrs. Fitzgerald intent on the morning papers.

She did not wish to be present should her mother chance to peruse the personal column.

"Conscience makes cowards of us all," she quoted, nervously to herself, fancying her proud parent's indignation when she should read, staring her in the face:

> TO HARRY HAWTHORNE—I am safe and well, and wondering what has become of you. Do you wish to see me? If so, answer this personal to-morrow, giving your address, and I will write to you, with instructions how to find me.
>
> Anxiously yours,
>
> G. H.

Oh, how happy it would have made her lover's heart if he had chanced on that message in the papers he read that morning.

But, by one of the terrible blunders of fate, he had read, as always, the telegraphic news first, and then thrown the papers from him, in that wild excitement that had determined him to return to New York at once.

Soon the broad, illimitable ocean would roll between their yearning hearts.

Suddenly she heard her mother's step at the door, and sprang up in nervous alarm.

"She has discovered it already, and is coming to reproach me," thought the hapless girl, bracing herself to meet the storm.

Mrs. Fitzgerald came in excitedly, clutching the newspaper in her hand.

"Mamma!" cried Geraldine, tremulously, entreatingly, as if to pray for mercy in advance.

"Geraldine, I have found a startling paragraph in this paper," cried the lady, without noticing her daughter's agitation.

"Yes, mamma," Geraldine answered, forlornly, pushing forward a seat.

Mrs. Fitzgerald sat down, the paper rustling nervously in her hand. She cleared her throat and began.

"You remember the story I told you about my cousin, Lady Putnam, and her son?"

"Yes, mamma," Geraldine replied, again, meekly, and the lady continued:

"I have not heard from my cousin for several years, and I have just read in the telegraphic news from abroad that her husband, Lord Randolph Putnam, is dead."

"I am very sorry," Geraldine answered, gravely.

"Oh, as to him, it doesn't matter much. He was an old man, gouty and disagreeable," replied Mrs. Fitzgerald, frankly, adding: "The interest of the matter centres in his son and heir—Leland, now Lord Putnam—your betrothed! I was surprised to read here that several years ago the old lord and his son had a bitter quarrel—so bitter that the heir was driven from home, and vowed that he would never return while his father lived. He went to America, and all trace of him was lost. Now there is a great hue and cry for him everywhere, for he is wanted to return and assume his rank and estate. But, of course, he will be found, as missing people always come back when they inherit money."

CHAPTER XLII.

"YOU DON'T KNOW HOW I HATE TO RAKE UP THE ASHES OF THE PAST."

"Vast the empire Love rules over—Held in bonds his subjects are—Firmly shackled is each loverBy the boy-god everywhere.Yet we could not live without him,So, young tyrant, let him rove,Though by turns we doubt and fear him,Still we cling to Love, sweet Love."

FRANCIS S. SMITH.

Geraldine was so relieved that her mother had not come to upbraid her about the personals to Hawthorne that she affected a great interest in what she had just heard.

"Do let me read it myself, mamma," she exclaimed, eager to get possession of the newspaper before the lady should find any more startling paragraphs in it.

Mrs. Fitzgerald readily gave up the paper, her excitement over the news she had just read having destroyed all interest in anything else.

"I shall write to my cousin at once, to condole with her on her bereavement," she said, rising to go, and adding: "It is quite a coincidence that both of us should be widowed almost at the same time."

When she was gone, Geraldine glanced over the personal, and hastily destroyed the paper, though she sighed:

"I feel mean over keeping this from my dear mother, but what can I do? I must not forsake my true-hearted lover for the sake of a mere prejudice."

And believing that she would be sure to hear from the personal very soon, her heart grew light with joy.

Soon it was time to go and meet Cissy.

Mrs. Fitzgerald accompanied her daughter to the station to meet her friend, and when she saw Miss Carroll, she liked her at once.

She had been dreading to see a very ordinary girl indeed; but Cissy's beauty and style, above all her lady-like manners, won their way at once to her proud heart.

And she was so glad, too, over Geraldine's happy looks that she felt almost grateful to Cissy for accepting her invitation.

What a happy day the girls spent together!

They had so much to tell each other that the hours passed like minutes.

Cissy was rejoiced when she heard of the discomfiture of Clifford Standish, whom she had always disliked and distrusted.

"You know I warned you against him, but you would not listen," she said.

"I was a silly, stage-struck little goose, that was the reason; but I have been well punished for my ambition," Geraldine replied, frankly.

"Then you have no further desire for a stage career?"

"No, indeed, dear. My experience on the road quite cured me of that. Why, I was never so hard worked and unhappy in my life. Besides, after all, I don't think I had any great talent for acting. I had some triumphs, it is true, but I believe it was only because I was rather pretty," Geraldine owned, candidly, and then the conversation drifted to other subjects.

"You have not seen my little half-brother and sister yet. They are beautiful and charming little children, and love me dearly already," she said. "Their governess, Miss Erroll, is one of the handsomest women I ever saw—fair and stately, and with that look in her face, somehow, as of one who has an interesting story in her past."

"And do you know the story?"

"Oh, no; she came to mamma from New York, I believe, with very good recommendations. That is all we know; but the children get on well with her, and she seems to study to please every one."

They were alone in Cissy's dainty room, lounging at ease in their pretty dressing-gowns. It was bedtime and past, but Geraldine could not tear herself away.

"Are you tired of me? Do you want me to go?" she queried.

"I could talk to you all night, darling!" cried Cissy, brightly, without guessing to what the confession would lead.

But Geraldine came over and put a coaxing arm around her neck.

"I'm so glad you aren't tired, for, Cissy, I'm just dying to take up our conversation where we left it off, you know, that Christmas evening when we were parted so suddenly."

"Oh!" cried Cissy, remembrance rushing over her in a burning wave.

"You were about to tell me a delightful love-story, and I was all impatience to hear it. It was about Cameron Clemens, you know. You owned that he was once your lover. Now please go on with the story, that's a dear!"

"Oh, Geraldine, how you like to listen to love-stories!" sighed Miss Carroll, with a far-away look in her soft gray eyes.

"Of course. All girls are fond of love-stories!" laughed Geraldine, and she added: "You know all about my love affairs, Cissy; now you must tell me about yours."

And she kept up her entreaties until Cissy sighed and yielded, saying:

"You don't know how I hate to rake up the ashes of the past, dear, and go over all my trouble again, but I will do it for your sake, although I dare say you will not find it very interesting."

"Were you ever engaged to Mr. Clemens, Cissy?" exclaimed Geraldine, plunging at once into the subject.

"Yes," acknowledged Cissy.

"Tell me how it came about, dear?"

"Oh, in the usual way—we fell in love."

"But how?—where?—when?" persisted Geraldine, with charming eagerness.

CHAPTER XLIII.

CISSY'S PATHETIC LOVE STORY.

"Oh, would I knew thy heart! Thine eye seems truthful!Thy smile is bright, thy voice is low and sweet;Thou seemst the very counterpart of honorWhen thou art kneeling suppliant at my feet.But eyes we may not trust with truth implicit,And smiles are oft but false lights to allure;A man may smile, and smile, and be a villain;Fair fruit is often rotten at the core."

FRANCIS S. SMITH.

Miss Carroll saw that there was no escaping the importunities of the charming little tease, so she answered, with pretending carelessness:

"Taking your last question first, I met him five years ago. As to where, it was at the sea-shore. We used to go there every summer before dear grandpa failed in business, and had to move out to the country, to the only home left him, the little farm where I first knew you."

"Yes, go on," breathed Geraldine, eagerly, and with a pensive little sigh, Miss Carroll continued:

"We met at the sea-shore, as I have told you—at that gay resort, Atlantic City. We danced together in the evenings, flirted on the sands and in the water, rode, boated, watched the sea by moonlight, and he taught me how to swim and to row. I was very happy."

"I know just how it was," sighed Geraldine.

"We became engaged," continued Cissy. "My grandfather was opposed to actors, and was not pleased with my engagement, but he relented, and gave his consent when he saw how my heart was set on it. Cameron pleaded for an early marriage, and before I returned to New York the wedding-day was set for the first of December. My trousseau was bought and in the hands of the dressmakers."

Cissy's voice faltered, and she brushed away some pearly tears that had brimmed over on her cheeks.

"Poor darling," murmured Geraldine, caressingly.

"Don't pity me, dear. I—I—can't bear it. Let me finish," cried Cissy, and she hurried on:

"Just a few weeks before the wedding-day, an actress in his company came to see me. She was a great beauty, and she told me that Mr. Clemens had been her lover, betrothed to her before he ever saw me. She declared that if I did not give him up it would kill her, and raved so wildly that I sent for Cameron. He came, and was very angry when he saw her, but she raged like a tigress, and claimed him passionately. He admitted that he had promised to marry her, but after seeing me, repented his engagement, and tried to get free, but she would not release him, so he was going to marry me anyway. Geraldine, you can fancy my feelings, perhaps. Although I knew it would break my heart, I dismissed my lover, bidding him return to his old love, who had cruelly wounded me by hinting that it was grandpa's money he wanted, not me."

"Well?" breathed Geraldine, eagerly.

"Well, I declined all his overtures toward reconciliation, and a few months after he married Azuba Aylesford, the actress. The marriage was not a happy one, and within two years she deserted him, going off with some Western actor, whose name I never heard. Cameron secured a divorce— but that is all, really. Grandpa died in the meantime, and when the mortgage was paid off on the farm, there was so little left that I came to New York to earn my bread. So, there, it was not so much of a love story after all," sadly.

"Oh, yes, it was very interesting, and it may have a happy ending yet. I rather pity poor Mr. Clemens."

"You should not, for he does not deserve it—false to two women, as he was!" flashed Cissy. Then she kissed Geraldine, saying: "Good-night, dear one, and don't let us refer to this painful subject again."

CHAPTER XLIV.

"HOW CAN I REPAY THEIR BOUNTY WITH SUCH TREACHERY?"

"Last night I was weeping, dear mother,Last night I was weeping alone;The world was so dark and so drearyMy heart it grew heavy as stone;I thought of the lonely and loveless—All lonely and loveless was I;I scarce could tell how it was, mother,But, oh, I was wishing to die."

While Geraldine and Cissy were exchanging confidences, Miss Erroll, the governess, was keeping an unhappy vigil in her own room.

In her hand she held the letter that Geraldine had brought to her the day before, and as often as she read it she groaned in anguish.

The letter was from Clifford Standish, the actor. It ran, curtly:

> "You have begged me not to betray you, to let you keep the position you hold in Mrs. Fitzgerald's family unmolested. Of course, you expect to pay a price for my charitable silence.
>
> "Very well. Here are my conditions:
>
> "I love Geraldine Harding, and her scorn has made me reckless, desperate.
>
> "I am determined to get her into my power, and humble her towering pride.
>
> "You must help me to carry out my designs.
>
> "In brief, I am determined to kidnap her and conceal her in a safe place, where she cannot escape my attentions. She came very near to loving me once, and I think if I am given a good opportunity, I may win her heart again.
>
> "I am arranging a place for her, and by to-morrow I shall have everything ready for my pretty bird.
>
> "Some plan must be perfected then by which to get possession of the girl.
>
> "As you are in the same house with her, and know all her comings and goings, your woman's wit ought to be able to

suggest some plan of procedure without drawing suspicion on yourself.

"Set your wits to work, and write to me to-morrow what you can do to help me.

"And remember that the penalty of refusal will be exposure of your past to the girl's mother, and expulsion in disgrace from your comfortable situation.

C. S."

"The man is a fiend!" groaned Miss Erroll, rising from her seat, and pacing up and down the luxurious apartment, her crimson dressing-gown trailing far behind her on the soundless velvet carpet.

She loved luxury, this woman, and she had sinned to attain it, but everything seemed to go wrong in her life. Punishment for her sins seemed to follow on her footsteps.

So she had put the past behind her, and tried to reform her life.

But ghosts from the dead past would rise up and haunt her, troubling her repose.

"The man is a fiend!" she groaned again. "Why cannot he leave that beautiful, innocent girl in peace? I have done wrong in my life, I know, but nothing so bad as what he asks of me, to lend myself to a vile plot against the peace of a girl who has never harmed me, a girl who has won my liking by her high-bred courtesy, as freely given to me as if I were her equal, instead of a paid dependent. How kind and good they all are to me, and how can I repay their bounty by such treachery?"

All the good in her nature rose to the surface, and did battle against the wrong she was asked to do.

And yet she dared not refuse; dared not risk what her tempter threatened.

Cruel had been her battle with poverty before she obtained this situation.

And if she lost it the dire struggle would begin again.

She might not be able to get honest work; she might be tossed into the terrible maelstrom of women who had to sin for bread.

Yet how could she, who was trying to redeem her own life from a hideous stain, how could she vilely plan to wreck another's life?

It was a terrible struggle that was going on in her breast as she kept her lonely vigil there.

She had not answered the letter yet, although he had commanded her to send a reply to-day. She waited in terror, silent, yet hoping that something would interpose to save her—praying that ere the morrow dawned her persecutor would fall down dead.

"It is no harm, no sin, to wish him dead, that fiend who only lives to plan ruin for the innocent," she cried, in anguish, crumpling the fatal letter in her writhing hands.

Then she gave a violent start, and looked toward the door, her hair seeming to rise on her head with terror.

Did she really hear a low rat-tat upon her door there in the dead waste and middle of the night?

She stood motionless, with her handsome head turned toward the door in an attitude of startled expectancy.

The low knocking came again, and then a low, sweet voice called, softly:

"Are you asleep? It's only me! Please let me in, dear?"

The voice sounded like that of Claire, her sweet little girl pupil.

With a sigh of relief she moved to the door and cautiously opened it.

The next moment she started back with a shuddering cry of fear that was echoed by the figure on the threshold.

The intruder was Cissy Carroll, with her long, dark hair flying loose over her white dressing gown.

With startled outcries, they gazed at each other, and then Miss Carroll demanded, shrilly:

"Do my eyes deceive me? What are you doing here, Azuba Aylesford?"

The woman in the scarlet robe darted forward, and dragged the white-clad girl into the room, whispering, in terrified tones:

"Hush-h! for sweet pity's sake! Do not breathe that name beneath this roof!"

She closed the door softly, and they stood looking at each other in wonder and dismay, while Cissy, recovering her wits, retorted, sharply:

"By what name shall I call you, then, since your divorce from Mr. Clemens?"

"Call me Miss Erroll. Azuba Aylesford and Mrs. Clemens are both dead. From her ashes rises Kate Erroll, governess."

"Ah-h!" and Cissy remembered what Geraldine had told her about the governess with a history in her face. She understood it now.

Light was also dawning on the other, and she asked:

"Is it possible that you, Miss Carroll, are the guest who arrived to-day from New York?"

"Yes, but I did not dream of finding you here, Miss—Erroll. When I knocked at the door, I supposed this was Miss Harding's room. My head ached, and I wished to ask for some camphor."

"You were mistaken. Her room is on one side of yours, mine on the other, hence the mistake."

"I am sorry I disturbed you. I will withdraw now," said Cissy, in her coldest tone, moving toward the door.

But suddenly she was prevented from going by Miss Erroll falling madly at her feet.

"You shall not go yet—not till—not till—you promise not to betray me to your friends, not to tell them of my wicked past!" she exclaimed.

Cissy Carroll drew back her robe from contact with the kneeling suppliant. Her face was very pale, and her eyes flashed with scorn.

"Why should I spare you, woman? You did not spare me—nor him!" she answered, bitterly.

"That is true—oh, how true! But I have been bitterly punished for my sins—so bitterly that even those I have wronged might pity me. I sinned, but I have suffered!" moaned the kneeling woman, lifting despairing eyes to her accuser.

"The way of the transgressor is hard," answered Cissy, with the harshness of woman to woman.

"Do I not know it! Alas! alas!" moaned Kate Erroll, and she continued: "Now that I have repented my sins, and am trying to be good, my past rises up to menace me on every hand with danger!"

Cissy Carroll did not answer, and she could not pity, for had not this woman robbed her life of happiness?

Suddenly Kate Erroll asked, eagerly:

"Have you never forgiven Cameron Clemens yet?"

"He has never asked me," Cissy returned, evasively.

"He would not dare after the scorn with which you dismissed him when I put in my claim to him. Ah, Miss Carroll, you did wrong, and you made my victory an easy one. If you had clung to him he would never have turned to me."

Cissy did not answer, save by the curl of a disdainful lip.

"Oh, I wronged you both most bitterly," Kate Erroll added, with keen, though late remorse. "Listen: I never loved Cameron Clemens—never; I only angled for him because he was a good catch, and I, a poor actress, loved luxury, and wanted to make a good marriage. He was not in love with me, but I pushed the flirtation so far that he could not avoid the proposal. I am sure he scarcely regarded our flirtation seriously. Before it was a week old he went away for his summer outing. He met you, and fell in love in earnest. He wrote to me, and asked release. I was furious, and would not reply. I waited—waited until just before the marriage. Then I swooped down on you, enraged you with hints that he was after your grandfather's money. You dismissed him with furious scorn—just what I wanted; and I—oh, shame to my womanhood, for I did not love him!—I pursued him till he made me his wife!"

"You did not love him? Oh, Heaven! yet you wrecked both our lives for selfish gain!" groaned Cissy, appalled at the woman's confession.

"It was cruel, oh, I know it now, but I did not then, for I had never loved, and could not realize the anguish of your loss. But I have been punished for my sins, I tell you. Of course, we led a wretched life, hating each other after a short time most bitterly. Then the tempter came in the person of a handsome young actor who taught me the meaning of love. He begged me to elope with him, promising to marry me as soon as my husband secured a divorce. Well, I fled with him, and Mr. Clemens lost no time in applying to the courts for a dissolution of his marriage bonds. Soon I was free; but did my betrayer keep his promise to me? Ah, no; he laughed me to scorn, and told me he already had a wife. All my love turned to hate, and I fled from him as from the presence of a leper. All my life since has been a struggle for honest bread. I could not return to the stage, for I could not live down the awful notoriety of my sin. Fortunately, I had a good education, and after months of wretchedness, during which I buried a nameless child, I secured this situation with these noble people. Will you let me keep it, or will you take your just revenge?"

Her tremulous voice wavered and broke; then silence fell.

She remained kneeling in a suppliant position at the feet of the woman she had wronged so bitterly, her large blue eyes upraised in passionate appeal.

Cissy Carroll stood like a statue in front of the kneeling woman, her face death-white, her eyes sombre, with painful thought.

It was her hour of triumph.

Her enemy was delivered into her hand.

Her vengeance was assured, if she chose to take it.

Why should she not? she thought, in the first bitterness of the meeting with the woman who had wronged her so deeply.

Then something else came to her mind.

"'Vengeance is mine; I will repay,' saith the Lord."

Looking at the humble suppliant there, she felt that punishment had already been meted out to her in fullest measure.

She could almost pity now instead of spurning the wretched creature who, having dashed love's brimming cup from the thirsty lips of another, had been forced to drink its bitter lees herself.

She moved back a pace, and said, quietly:

"Rise. You are safe from vengeance of mine."

"You will forgive me?" faltered the governess, gratefully.

Cissy answered, coldly:

"I did not say I would forgive you, for I do not think I ever can. But I will not betray your secret. To-morrow we may meet as strangers, who have no interest in each other."

She moved toward the door, followed by protestations of undying gratitude to which she made no reply.

It seemed to her that she could not breathe freely in the presence of this woman, to whom she owed all her misery. She fled to her own room to weep in solitude.

CHAPTER XLV.

"IF I WERE A KING I WOULD RAISE HER TO MY THRONE!"

"As shines the moon in cloudless skies,She in her poor attire was seen,One praised her ankles, one her eyes,One her dark hair, and lovesome mien,So sweet a face, such angel grace,In all that land had never been;Cophetua swore a royal oath,'This beggar maid shall be my queen!'"

TENNYSON.

But, leaving our interests in the Garden City temporarily, we must journey across the dark-blue sea, to follow the fortunes of our noble hero, Harry Hawthorne.

As the intelligent reader has doubtless surmised already, he was the hero of the newspaper paragraph Mrs. Fitzgerald had read to her daughter, and he had crossed the seas to claim his own.

Young blood is often too hot, and an angry quarrel with his old father had made the heir of a noble name and fine estate a voluntary exile from home under distant skies, where he was not too proud to earn his bread by honest toil.

But all that was changed now.

In the English county of Devonshire, at the grand old castle home of Raneleigh, the old lord lay dead, and my lord, his son, must lay aside his masquerading and come home to wear the honors and the title that were his by ancestral right.

His two Chicago friends were charmed with his romance when he told it to them, one day on the steamer, just before they landed on the bonny shore of England.

"I only borrowed the name of Jack Daly," he laughed. "The one that belongs to me is Harry Leland, and my title will be Lord Putnam."

They congratulated him warmly. It was a romance in real life, they said, and Ralph Washburn declared he should weave it into a novel.

"But you do not know the most romantic part of it yet," said the young man, with a sigh. He debated the question with himself a moment, then decided it could do no harm to confide in his two noble friends.

So, sadly enough, he told them the story of the love affair that had brought him to Chicago, keeping back nothing.

"So now you know how I came by the wound that made you two my stanch friends for life, and you can understand why I let my enemy alone, rather than bring into publicity the name of a woman I loved," he ended.

"But you left the case in the hands of a detective?" said Leroy Hill.

"Yes, he is to find Clifford Standish and shadow him until it is found out whether he lied to me about Miss Harding. He has full instructions to act in my place during my absence."

"And this beautiful girl that you loved when you were simply Harry Hawthorne, the New York fireman, do you mean that if she is found and proved innocent that you will stoop to her now that you have come into your ancestral honors?" inquired the romantic young author, with interest.

"If I were a king I would raise her to my throne!" replied the ardent lover, proudly.

They applauded his faithful love, but they thought that the prospect of his happiness looked very dismal.

The actor's story seemed so plausible that they feared it might be true that he had won the vacillating heart of pretty Geraldine.

They looked at each other significantly, but they did not have the heart to breathe their doubts aloud. They saw that he was already unhappy enough.

But they felt sure in their hearts that if the detective ever traced the movements of the persons in whom Hawthorne was interested, he would report Standish's story as true.

When they had been in England a week, having witnessed the joy of the mother over the truant's return, and had been the recipients of the most charming hospitalities from the family, a letter came from the Chicago detective to Lord Putnam.

But the information it contained was very meagre.

He had traced Clifford Standish through a very clever disguise, but the whereabouts of Miss Harding remained a mystery.

In fact, the detective was inclined to believe that the actor had lost interest in the girl he had brought to Chicago. Perhaps he had wearied of her, and left her to despair. At any rate, he was conducting a correspondence, perhaps a flirtation with a handsome governess, Miss Erroll, employed by Mrs. Fitzgerald, a wealthy widow, on Prairie avenue.

The pride of Geraldine's mother and her repugnance to the name of her first husband had induced her, on bringing the girl to Chicago, to give out to the newspapers the paragraphs for publication stating that her daughter, Miss Fitzgerald, had been called home from school by the death of her father. Even in the household Geraldine bore the same name, and thus the clever detective was baffled by the simple substitution of another name; and while he had traced Clifford Standish up to his very entrance to the Prairie avenue mansion, he had no suspicion that the actor was interested in any one of the family besides the handsome governess.

But the same mail had brought Lady Putnam also a letter from Chicago, and when she had read it she called her son into her boudoir, where she sat alone, saying, in a flutter of excitement:

"I have a letter from America, dear Leland, and as you are so fond of everything American, perhaps you can remember the beautiful little American girl to whom you were betrothed when she was only about two years old?"

CHAPTER XLVI.

"I WILL TEST MY DARLING'S LOVE."

"I have heard or dreamt, it may be—What love is when true;How to test it—how to try it—It the gift of few.Only a true heart can find itTrue as it is true;Only eyes as clear and tenderLook it through and through."

The handsome young lord looked at his mother in surprise when she uttered those words: "Perhaps you remember the beautiful little American girl to whom you were betrothed when she was barely two years old?"

That episode of his childish days had almost escaped the young man's memory, so he said, carelessly:

"Indeed, I have almost forgotten it, dear mother."

"Then I must refresh your memory, Leland, for you are old enough now to redeem your pledge."

Lord Putnam looked startled, and said, hastily:

"Of course, you would not consider a trifle like that binding on a grown man."

The stately mother looked somewhat disappointed, and answered, slowly:

"I had hoped it might be, especially as you have no other entanglement."

"Why are you so sure of that, my dear mother?"

She started, and gave him a frightened look.

"Oh, I—I—hope there is none," she said, vaguely.

For a moment it came to him to tell her this love story.

"A mother's sympathy would be very sweet," he thought.

But a sudden impulse of pride restrained him.

"For what if it be proved that Geraldine is unworthy? How could I bear to be pitied?" he thought, with the sensitive pride of true manhood.

So he answered, evasively:

"I was only teasing you, dear mother. Go on with the story you have to tell me."

With a quick sigh of relief, she plunged into the subject:

"As I was saying, when you were a manly little lad of seven, a cousin of mine, from New York, paid me a long visit here, and she had with her a lovely little daughter of two years. You and the little girl were almost inseparable, so much so that my cousin Florence and myself began to look forward to a possible future that might unite your destinies in one. In brief, we solemnly betrothed you to each other."

"I begin to remember it all now, only the little one's name, which escapes my memory," smiled the young man, as a vision of a tiny golden-haired beauty returned to his mind from the past.

"But you were parted soon after that," continued Lady Putnam. "My cousin returned to her American home, and suffered a series of misfortunes. Her husband proved unfaithful, and a divorce followed. She married within two years a splendid gentleman—a Western millionaire—but the happiness of her second union was destroyed by a terrible trial. Her first husband stole away her lovely daughter, little Geraldine, and all these years the most rigid search has failed to find her, so that——"

"Mother, mother, I beg your pardon for interrupting—but—but—you said the girl's name was Geraldine," exclaimed the young man, starting to his feet and betraying for the first time an interest in the subject.

The utterance of that dear and beloved name—Geraldine—had touched a vibrating chord in his sore heart, and he waited in breathless eagerness for her reply.

Lady Putnam, not understanding his fiery impatience, replied, placidly:

"Had you, indeed, forgotten the very name of your dainty little American sweetheart, Leland? Yes, it was Geraldine—Geraldine Harding."

"Oh, Heaven!" and Lord Putnam sank back to his seat the picture of surprise.

Here was a romance indeed!

It was, it must be, his own loved Geraldine of whom his mother was telling him.

They had been betrothed from their very childhood, he and pretty Geraldine. How sweet was the thought!

No wonder their hearts had leaped to greet each other the first moment of their meeting in New York.

But the thought of the mystery that surrounded her fate now forced a hollow groan from his lips.

"What is it, my son? You are not ill?" exclaimed Lady Putnam, in alarm.

"No, no; it was only a passing twinge of pain. Do not mind me, but go on, if you have any more to tell. But perhaps your story is finished."

"No, indeed, for the best part is to come," smiled the lady.

"The best part," he repeated, incredulously.

"Yes, for I have a letter from Florence Fitzgerald, my cousin—the first letter in several years. I told you, did I not, that since her second marriage she has lived in Chicago—that great Western city where they held that wonderful World's Fair, you know, Leland."

"Yes, I know. I was there."

"Well, this letter from Chicago contains both good and bad news. Florence has lost her good and kind husband, and found her missing daughter."

"Found her daughter! Found Geraldine Harding!" cried the young man, springing to his feet, in wild excitement.

"Yes, or Geraldine Fitzgerald, as she calls her now. And, Leland, she will be a great heiress, for her mother's large private fortune will be given to her eldest daughter, as her second husband left her millions of money and a perfect palace of a home on Prairie avenue, the grandest location in the city."

She paused again in alarm, for this time her son had fallen back in his chair, his face death-white, his eyes half-closed.

Her words had been such a revelation to him that the joy of it all overcame him.

He remembered instantly the day he had seen the beautiful girl getting into the carriage before the artist's studio.

He had cried out that he knew her, but Ralph Washburn had said it was Miss Fitzgerald, a great heiress.

So he supposed himself mistaken, and the cruel disappointment had made him actually ill.

But now he knew that it was no mistake.

It was Geraldine herself that he had seen—dear, beautiful Geraldine, his own betrothed, his heart's darling.

He cared nothing for what his mother had said about her being a great heiress.

He loved her for herself alone, and he was rich enough for both.

He would rather have had her remain poor, so that he could have bestowed everything upon her himself.

But, oh, the joy of knowing that she was safe under her mother's roof, safe where he could find her again—it made him dizzy with such a rapture of joy and relief that his face paled with emotion, and his eyes nearly closed, startling Lady Putnam so that she sprang to his side, exclaiming, in alarm:

"You are indeed ill, my dear boy, and I must send for a physician. Please tell me in what way you are affected."

"It is my heart, dear mother!" he groaned, then caught her around the waist, laughing: "Forgive me for alarming you, dearest mother. I am not in the least ill; only overcome with joy at hearing that my darling betrothed is found again."

"Do you really mean it, Leland?" she inquired, dubiously.

"Indeed I do mean it, and I can hardly wait for the time when I shall return to America to claim my bonny bride."

She saw that a curious transformation had come over him.

His cheeks were flushed, and his dark-blue eyes flashed with joy.

She had never seen him look so radiantly happy.

But a sigh heaved her breast as she replied to his words:

"But I fear that I may never see her your bride, Leland, for her mother owns in the letter that the girl has formed an attachment for a poor young man she knew in New York when she was only a poor salesgirl at O'Neill's store. She clings stubbornly to this poor fireman, although she has been told all about her betrothal to you."

"She repudiates my claim, eh?" he laughed, gayly.

"It seems so," she answered.

"Let me see the letter, please, mother."

She gave it to him, and although it covered many pages, he read it with the deepest interest.

And no wonder, for he found there the story of all that had happened to Geraldine since she had boarded the train for Chicago with Clifford Standish. Mrs. Fitzgerald had not failed to relate the discomfiture of the villain who had kidnaped her daughter. Oh, the gladness of his heart when he found how Geraldine had been saved from the villain's power and restored to her mother's arms.

He knew that he could tell all his story to his mother now, for Geraldine was proved pure and faithful; but a moment's reflection decided him not to do so yet a while.

He had a romantic fancy to prove Geraldine's love to the utmost, now that she had come into fortune and position. Not as the Lord of Raneleigh would he woo her, but as Harry Hawthorne, the fireman. Then he would know the true value of her heart.

His first impulse was to return to America at once, his impatience to see her was so great; but he remembered that it would be almost impossible to do so now.

It was not yet two weeks since his father had been buried, and his mother and sister were very sad and lonely. They would be loath to have him leave them so soon. Besides, as the new lord, there were matters to be seen to that could scarcely admit of delay.

He remembered, too, that he had guests for whom he had planned a tour to London and Paris. It would not look well to desert them now. Business and hospitable duties would detain him here at least two weeks longer before he could return to America.

In the meantime, Geraldine was safe with her mother.

Standish, having received such a rebuff from Mrs. Fitzgerald would naturally relinquish his pursuit as hopeless. Indeed, the detective's news that the actor was engaged in a flirtation with the governess had seemed to be proof that he had given over his persecution of Geraldine. He was off with the old love and on with the new.

So our hero, believing that everything was working together for his happiness, permitted himself to indulge in a delightful conviction of security—a very mistaken one, as the sequel will show.

Smiling fondly on his anxious mother, he said:

"Mother, I have a very romantic plan for winning my pretty betrothed from her fireman lover, and I will explain it to you soon. But you must not reply to Mrs. Fitzgerald's letter until I give you leave."

CHAPTER XLVII.

LADY AMY'S LOVERS.

"Her ruby lips hiding teeth of pearlThat dazzle me when she speaks,Her nut-brown hair in riotous curl,Her laugh, which sets all my senses awhirl,And the damask of her cheeks;Her Venus form, like a flower arrayed,In the garb of the blushing May,All bid me rejoice, and undismayed,Swear my heart shall ever lie true to this maid."

Lady Putnam was delighted to find that her son was not averse to the union with his fair American cousin.

Being an American herself, she had a fondness for her old home and her old friends, especially her kinswoman, Mrs. Fitzgerald.

So she heard with delight her son's avowal that he would cut out the humble fireman in the regard of pretty Geraldine.

She readily acceded to every condition he imposed on her in the furtherance of his plans.

Their conference over, he went to seek his friends, whom he found playing a game of billiards with his pretty sister, Lady Amy.

The young Americans were both charmed with the dainty beauty whose dark, curly tresses and laughing blue eyes were so like those of her brother that they showed their near kinship very plainly indeed.

The young lady herself was delighted with her brother's friends. She could not have decided which one she liked better.

When Leroy Hill, who was of a joyous, rollicking disposition, would entertain her with witty anecdotes of people he had seen, she would almost decide after all he was the more interesting of the two, and perhaps the handsomer, for his hazel eyes, with that twinkle of fun in them, were irresistibly fascinating.

But, then, Ralph Washburn, who was of a more thoughtful turn than his friend, and had large, serious, dark-gray eyes, would read to her selections from favorite poets, or sing to her in his rich, clear tenor, and the words would sink deep into her heart, and she would find herself musing:

"I almost like him better than Mr. Hill; but—I dare say they are both sad flirts."

To-day Ralph had been quoting to her some verses from a favorite poet of his own land, and as they gayly knocked the balls about the table, they seemed to sing themselves over persistently in her memory:

"Those dazzling dark-blue eyes!Laughing under shady lashes,Dusky fringed, like clouds of night,And with sudden rainbow flashes,They can hold your heart in thrallWith one sudden radiant glance;They can realize all visionsAnd all dreams of old romance.

"Those dazzling dark-blue eyes!How they haunt me in my dreams!With their glancing and their dancing,And their shy, coquettish gleams;They can soften as with love,They can flash with sudden scorn,They can droop like purple flowersMisty with the dews of dawn.

"Those dazzling dark-blue eyes,They grow sad at touch of sorrow;They grow radiant with joy,From her tender heart they borrowEvery feeling and emotionThat beneath the surface lies,And her very soul is speakingIn those dazzling dark-blue eyes.

"Those dazzling dark-blue eyes!I am captive to their charms!They are bright as stars at night,They are like the sun that warms.They are soft as velvet pansiesSparkling in the morning dew,They are all things under heaven,That are beautiful and true."

Since Ralph Washburn had repeated those lines to piquant Lady Amy her eyes had been very shy when they met his glance, hiding their light under the long-fringed lashes, and he smiled when he saw that he had the power to bring that bashful color to her cheek.

It took Lord Putnam but a few minutes to decide that he would not confide to his friends yet the fact that Geraldine was found. He did not want to jeopardize his plans for winning her as simple Harry Hawthorne.

But at heart he was exceedingly anxious to return to America, so he made his plans to begin to-morrow the sight-seeing tour he had planned for Ralph and Leroy. In a few weeks they could see and enjoy a great deal; then he would be free to pursue his courtship of Geraldine. In the meanwhile she would be safe with her mother, and if her heart were disturbed by suspense over his fate, it would only make it grow fonder, so that when they met again it would only be to find a joyous welcome awaiting him.

"'Tis said that absence conquers love,But, oh, believe it not;I've tried, alas, its power to prove,But thou art not forgot.Lady, though fate has bid us part,Yet still thou art so dear,As fixed in this devoted heartAs when I clasped thee here.

"I plunge into the busy crowdAnd smile to hear thy name,And yet as if I thought aloud,They know me still the same.And when the wine-cup passes round,I toast some other fair—But when I ask my heart the sound,Thy name is echoed there.

"E'en as the wounded bird will seekIts favorite bower to die,So, lady, I would hear thee speak,And yield my parting sigh.'Tis said that absence conquers love,But, oh, believe it not;I've tried, alas, its power to prove,But thou art not forgot."

When her brother and his friends had gone up to London it seemed very lonely to Lady Amy at Raneleigh.

"Mamma, I hope you will take me to America some time for a long visit; I like Americans so much!" she cried, artlessly.

"So do I," returned her mother, and then she sighed softly to herself.

Who can tell what memories stirred her heart of days of bellehood in New York, when, for plain ambition's sake, she had put aside a plain, untitled lover to wed Lord Putnam and reign at Castle Raneleigh? They had told her, her maneuvering relatives, that love would be sure to come after marriage.

"But what if I already love another?" the beautiful belle had said, pale with anxiety.

"You will soon forget him on the other side of the ocean, and Lord Putnam will have all your heart," they answered.

They were old in experience, and she was young, so she took their advice, and married her titled lover. Perhaps their assurances proved true, perhaps not. At any rate, she was a faithful wife.

But she was not by any means a disconsolate widow.

And at her daughter's praise of Americans, the proud woman's heart echoed every word, and her thoughts flew across the sea to the old home, and the old days, and the old love.

Perhaps he was dead now. She had not heard of him for many years.

Or if he were not dead, he was probably married to another, to some true-hearted girl who prized love above all else.

There was a sting in the thought, and Lady Putnam sighed and turned away without promising her daughter to take her to America. She had no desire to return to the scene of her old triumphs. She wanted sleeping memories to keep still in the grave where they were buried.

CHAPTER XLVIII.

EVERY WOMANLY IMPULSE IN HER NATURE CRIED OUT AGAINST SUCH A CRUEL WRONG.

"The villain who foully abused her,Though the husband to whom she was wed,After pledging his heart and his hand,Like a monster reviled and abused her,And she died in a far away land."

FRANCIS S. SMITH.

"You are in luck, my boy," chuckled Clifford Standish, to himself.

He had just read in a New York newspaper of the death of his deserted wife.

No pity stirred his cruel heart as his eye ran over the few paragraphs that told him in a sensational manner of the cause of her death.

Deserted by her husband, in ill-health, and unable to work, penniless, friendless, the unhappy woman had frozen to death in a miserable attic-room during the prevalence of a terrible blizzard.

He was guilty of her death, he knew, yet not one twinge of remorse tore his cruel heart for the fate to which he had consigned that true and tender wife.

She was out of his path forever, leaving him free to carry out his wicked designs, and he rejoiced exceedingly.

Fate seemed to favor him, although for a while things had looked exceedingly dark.

But that was when he had discovered that his murderous knife-thrust had not killed Harry Hawthorne.

He had been terribly alarmed at first, fearing that Hawthorne would set the authorities on his track, and that he would have to fly the city.

But, for some unknown reason, his victim had stayed his hand in vengeance, and by careful reconnoitering he found that he had left the city.

Standish could not comprehend why his rival had thrown up the game like this; but he finally concluded that Geraldine's altered position in life had caused her to break off her engagement with the young fireman.

But, whatever the cause, he rejoiced at the issue, and prepared to take advantage of it by getting Geraldine again into his power.

His passion for the beautiful girl and his determination to possess her grew and strengthened from hour to hour and from day to day. All he had felt for others in the past compared to this grand passion, was

"As moonlight unto sunlight,And as water unto wine."

And now he swore to himself that he would possess her by a tie none could dispute. He would marry pretty Geraldine, the dainty heiress, and teach her to love him. Surely, he said to himself, out of his measureless conceit, she could not find it hard to love him. She had been very near to it once.

But in this fancy he was quite mistaken. His attentions had simply flattered her girlish vanity. Her heart had not been touched.

He waited impatiently for the letter from Miss Errol, planning the kidnaping but it did not come.

The miserable woman, although distracted by fears for her own safety, had not yet brought herself to the point of consenting to become a party to Geraldine's ruin.

Every impulse in her woman's nature cried out against doing such a cruel wrong to the fair young girl she admired so much.

So she delayed replying to his letter, until, angered by her delay, he wrote again:

> "You have not replied to my letter. Of course you know the terrible risk you run by your silence. But I will give you one more chance.

> "Meet me at the nearest corner just after dark this evening, and I will unfold to you my plans, in which you must co-operate.

> C. S."

CHAPTER XLIX.

ONLY PRIDE.

"I have loved thee—fondly loved thee!No one but God can knowThe struggle and the agonyIt cost to let thee go.But woman's pride usurps my heart,And surges to my brow.To see thy cold indifference!We must be strangers now."

FRANCIS S. SMITH.

"Will no answer ever come?" sighed Geraldine, as she watched the papers, day after day, for an answer to her personal.

"Hope deferred maketh the heart sick," it is said, and her suspense was cruel and torturing. Not even Cissy's presence could assuage her pain, although it was borne in torturing silence.

One morning, while she was searching the newspaper columns, as usual, her eyes gleamed with a sudden light of pleasure, and she looked up at Cissy, exclaiming:

"Only think, dear—the Clemens Company will begin a week's engagement in Chicago to-morrow evening."

The quick color flew to Cissy's face, but she nodded with apparent indifference.

Geraldine continued:

"They will play 'Laurel Vane.' Oh, do you remember the night in New York when I played it, Cissy, and our terrible interruption by the appearance of the men who arrested Mr. Standish? I was very unhappy that night, for I believed that Harry Hawthorne had married Daisy Odell, as that wretch declared. Oh! how it all comes back to me now—my jealous misery when I stood at the wings watching you all in Mrs. Stansbury's box! But, oh, the happiness that came to me later, when I learned the real truth!"

She leaned her fair head down on Cissy's shoulder, and sighed:

"No girl ever loved a man as fondly as I love my darling Harry, and the mystery of his fate is breaking my heart."

Mrs. Fitzgerald entered the library at that moment, and Geraldine looked up quickly, saying:

"Mamma, cannot we have a box at the theatre to-morrow night? There is a play that I specially wish to see."

"Certainly, my dear, if I can find you some lady to chaperon you and Cissy. You know I cannot accompany you, because of my deep mourning."

The box was secured, and a chaperon found in the person of a very old lady, a distant relative of the Fitzgeralds, who had fallen into comparative poverty, but who would enjoy the outing all the more since she could not well afford to give herself the pleasure of a box, and was too proud to use a low-priced seat.

The next evening found the three in their box at the Columbia—Mrs. Germyn, the old lady, looking the chaperon to the life in her black velvet and point lace, set off by her silvery puffs of hair. The two young girls—Geraldine in silvery-blue brocade and pearls, Cissy in white, with gold ornaments and flowers—were the cynosure of all eyes. Not a face in the crowded and fashionable audience could compare with theirs in beauty.

When the curtain rose on the first act, it was not long before the company discovered Geraldine and Cissy in the nearest box. They were surprised and mystified, for no whisper of Geraldine's good fortune had reached her old associates. It had been whispered about that she had eloped with the missing actor, Clifford Standish, and some had pitied and others condemned.

So many and curious were the glances that went from the stage to the box where beautiful Geraldine was sitting, robed like some princess, in all the trappings of wealth and state.

The young girl enjoyed it thoroughly, and presently she whispered to her friend:

"I'm going to send a message to Cameron Clemens to come to our box at the first wait. You won't mind, will you?"

Cissy's heart leaped quickly under the lace and flowers of her corsage.

"Oh, Geraldine, you know I do not wish to meet him," she whispered back, while the half-deaf old chaperon lent both her ears to the play.

"Cissy, you are the proudest girl I ever saw! How can you be so cruel to poor Mr. Clemens? You are as much in fault as ever he was, for I am sure that nothing stands between your hearts now but your own abominable pride."

"Oh, Geraldine, how can you jump at things so? I dare say he has forgotten me now, and is in love with some other lady—that beautiful leading lady, Miss Mills, for instance."

"Why, Miss Mills has a husband whom she fairly adores. You needn't be jealous of her, darling. So I'm going to invite Mr. Clemens into our box to talk to us. You needn't be friendly with him if you don't choose. I'll introduce you as the veriest stranger, if you wish."

"Very well," answered Cissy, for she knew that the willful beauty would have her own way.

Geraldine's romantic heart was set on the reconciliation of the two long estranged lovers; so she sent the message at once, and Mr. Clemens came to the box at the end of the first act.

"Aren't you surprised to see me here, Mr. Clemens?" cried Geraldine, shaking hands with him cordially, then presenting her friends: "Mrs. Germyn, and my friend from New York. Miss Carroll, Mr. Clemens."

The estranged lovers, both pale as ashes, bowed to each other like strangers, without a sign that they had met before to-night.

CHAPTER L.

"LOVE MAKES FOOLS OF US ALL!"

"How lovely she looked as she stoodIn a robe of pink gossamer
dressed,Her curls waving in the night air,And the jessamine flowers on her
breast.Those dark eyes, so tender and sweet,That red mouth so temptingly
small,Those bright, perfumed ringlets—heigho!What fools such things
make of us all!"

MAY AGNES FLEMING.

Geraldine watched the meeting between the estranged lovers with a
knowing little smile.

Their sudden pallor and emotion, even the constraint of their meeting,
assured her that love was not dead in their hearts.

The ashes still smoldered, and needed but a breath to blow them into flame
again.

Geraldine loved Cissy so dearly that she longed to help the girl to happiness
again, and she determined to leave nothing undone to reconcile her to her
lover.

When they were seated again, she said, brightly:

"You must promise to call on me to-morrow, for I have dozens of
questions to ask you, and much to tell you, and I know you will not have
time to listen to it now."

"I will come with the greatest pleasure," he replied, his handsome face
glowing with delight, for he guessed that at her home he should meet Cissy
again.

Geraldine understood his thought, and said, quickly:

"Miss Carroll is staying with me for an indefinite period, and I mean to give
her a good time in Chicago. Perhaps you remember that we roomed
together in New York when we were both working-girls?"

He smiled affirmatively, and she continued:

"Perhaps you have not heard that I have found my lost mother since I left
New York?"

"No; is it true? Let me congratulate you," he cried, warmly, and then Geraldine ran over her adventures briefly, for she knew that he must soon leave her to return to his duties.

"But I shall come back at the end of the second act," he said, as he hurried away.

He was with them every minute he could spare, and Cissy was very angry with herself, for the traitorous throbbing of her heart told her so plainly how dear he was to her yet, in spite of the years in which she had been teaching her heart to forget him.

He was amazed when he heard the story of Clifford Standish's wickedness.

"I knew the man had a bad heart—his desertion of his wife proved that—but I did not dream he would go to such lengths as you tell me. What must have been your fate had you not met your mother so opportunely?" he exclaimed to Geraldine.

"What, indeed!" she shuddered, and then a low cry from Cissy made her turn her head.

"Look! there is the wretch now!" cried Cissy, excitedly.

They followed her glance, and saw the face of Clifford Standish peering at them from behind a pillar in the orchestra circle.

When their indignant eyes turned on him, he realized that he was being observed, and hastily dodged from sight.

They saw him no more that evening, but when they left the theatre he was near enough to have touched Geraldine with his hand.

He had come to the theatre from his interview with Miss Erroll, and had triumphed over her bitterest prejudices by representing that his wife was dead, and that he really meant to marry Geraldine once he got her into his power.

"I will teach her to love me after marriage," he boasted; and the poor governess, who had once loved him madly, and was still somewhat under the glamour of that old passion, did not doubt his power to win Geraldine's heart. She knew how fascinating he could be when he chose.

For one moment, indeed, a jealous pang tore her heart, and she said, pleadingly:

"If your wife is dead, as you say, Clifford, you ought to marry me. You owe it to me, after all I gave up for your sake. You know I trusted in your promises."

"You were a fool for your pains," he replied, with brutal frankness. "You had knowledge enough of the world to be sure that a silly married woman who deserts her husband for another man will surely reap what she has sown."

"You swore you would marry me when Cameron Clemens secured a divorce."

"You were very silly to believe me, Azuba. I was only amusing myself with your credulity. A man never means the vows he makes in an affair of that kind. The time is sure to come when he will meet some pure young girl, and give her the best of his heart. Then he despises the weak victims of his past passions."

"As you despise me?" she demanded, bitterly.

"It would not be polite to say so," he replied, indifferently, and hearing her stifled sob, he added, impatiently: "Bah, Azuba! I have quite got over my old fancy for you, and your sniveling cannot warm over the old coals. I never really loved you—never knew the power of love until I met pretty Geraldine, and the only way for you to get a kind thought from me is to help me to win the little beauty."

Crushed and humiliated by his scorn, she would have defied him if she had dared, but she was in his power, and dared not do it; so, ere they parted, the plot for Geraldine's abduction was made, and nothing remained but to carry it out that night.

"Do not dare to fail me, or the weight of my vengeance will crush you," he said, threateningly, and with a shudder she promised to obey.

They parted, and he hurried to the theatre, where she had told him Geraldine had gone.

Securing a seat in the orchestra circle, in the desirable concealment of a pillar, he alternately watched the heiress and the play.

An angry sneer curled his lips as he saw the new leading man in the play was even superior to himself in the role of the hero.

"So I can never get back my position in that company," he mused. "Well, no matter! I shall marry the heiress, and if the old woman cuts up rough and won't give us any of her daughter's money, we can go on the stage, and the elopement will be an advertisement for us."

As he watched Geraldine in all her beauty, sitting with her friends, his passion for her grew deeper, and he mentally hugged himself at the thought of how soon he would have her in his power.

When her carriage rolled away, and he noted the lingering glance sent after it by Cameron Clemens, he sneered, grimly:

"Bah! what fools love makes of us all! There is Clemens as madly in love with that hateful Cissy Carroll as I am with pretty Geraldine. He has been in love with her ever since Azuba Aylesford forced them apart, to marry him herself. Egad! I did them a good turn when I flattered Mrs. Clemens into eloping with me; and if the Carroll girl ever gets him back she may thank me for ridding him of his incumbrance, though she hates me like poison!"

He turned away with a harsh laugh, and went his way through the gloomy shadows of the winter night, like a thing of evil omen.

And in all that vast city of Chicago where crime stalks abroad under the cover of darkness, there was not a soul more lost to goodness than that of this man.

CHAPTER LI.

STARTLING NEWS.

"Say an encouraging word to the weary,They to whom life seems all darksome and dreary;One kindly sentence the sad heart will lighten,One smile of love the existence will brighten.

"Say an encouraging word to the erring;Sin-blasted, hunted down, crushed, and despairing;Even when vice his worst form is revealing,One word in season may wake better feeling."

FRANCIS S. SMITH.

Cameron Clemens had indeed gazed with longing eyes after the carriage that bore Miss Carroll away from his sight.

The old love, stifled so long by hopeless pain and absence, had leaped to life again full-grown within his fond heart.

And although Cissy had been painfully shy, seldom speaking to him, and then only in her role of a new acquaintance, he had read in her glance that she did not despise him now. Something had come over her that looked almost like forgiveness of his fault. He began to have a little hope of winning her after all.

"I will try my fate once more, if she is as gentle when we meet again as she was to-night," he resolved, joyously.

He could not sleep that night for thinking of Cissy's looks and words, and wondering if he should see her to-morrow when he called on Geraldine.

"I shall ask for her also, and then she can have no excuse for not seeing me," he resolved, firmly.

The next afternoon, at the earliest permissible hour, he presented himself at the door of Mrs. Fitzgerald's magnificent house, and sent in his cards for the two young ladies.

He was ushered into a dainty reception-room, fitted in blue, and waited with what patience he could for their appearance.

Presently the heavy portieres were swept aside by a plump, dimpled white hand, and Miss Carroll entered the room alone.

Cameron Clemens sprang to meet her, thinking that she had never looked more lovely in her becoming house gown of delicate blue, with lace and ribbons fluttering about it.

He offered his hand, and as she placed hers in it he saw a delicate pinkness about her eyelids that betrayed recent tears.

Pointing to a seat, she exclaimed:

"Isn't it surprising? Or—have you not heard?"

"I have heard nothing, Miss Carroll. Pray enlighten me."

"It is about Geraldine, you know."

"You do not mean that she is ill?"

"Oh, no, no—not ill. You remember how well she was last night. Well, after we came home Geraldine eloped," and the last word was almost a sob, for Cissy was terribly agitated.

A terrible fear came to him, and he faltered:

"Not with Standish?"

Cissy flashed her adorer a reproachful glance, exclaiming:

"Certainly not. Didn't Geraldine tell you last night how she hated and despised that wretch? She ran away to marry Harry Hawthorne, her betrothed, you know."

"Oh, yes, I've heard of him—fine fellow, they say. Tell me all about it."

"There isn't much to tell. Geraldine's mother was opposed to the match, because Mr. Hawthorne was poor. So this morning Geraldine was missing, and there was a note on her pillow, saying that she had gone away with her darling Harry, and they would be married right away. She hoped her mother would forgive her, as she (Geraldine) could not live without her dear boy."

"Plucky girl!" was Mr. Clemens' comment, and Cissy continued:

"Mrs. Fitzgerald is almost heart-broken, and very angry, too. She declares that she will never forgive her daughter."

"Is she so proud?" he asked, drawing his chair a little closer.

Cissy noticed the movement, and blushed prettily as she replied:

"As proud as a queen. But yet she is a magnificent woman, and I sympathize with her in her sorrow."

Before he could reply, there was an interruption, the cause of which we must explain.

Little Miss Claire, the pet and darling of the household, had run away from her governess in a willful mood and hidden herself where she could not be found. Miss Erroll, searching every room in turn for her naughty pupil, blundered suddenly upon the pair of lovers in the blue reception-room.

Cameron Clemens heard the sweep of her robe, and glanced hurriedly up.

The next moment he was upon his feet.

"You! You!" he burst out, with instant recognition, and in a tone of defiant hate.

It seemed to him in that startling moment, that Azuba Aylesford, the imperious actress, had come again, as she did years ago, to part him from his love, sweet Cissy.

She, on her own part, was so dazed by this unexpected rencontre, that for a moment she stood motionless, rooted to the ground by fear.

Cameron Clemens, gazing at her with eyes full of loathing, continued:

"How dared you follow me here? You have no claim on me now, nor ever can have again. I loathe you!"

His words assured both listeners that he thought the woman had followed him here to work evil to him, and with this explanation Miss Erroll's trance of terror gave way. She sprang to Cissy's side, pleading:

"Oh, for Heaven's sake! explain it all to him! He would not listen to me, I know, but he loves you. He will listen if you tell him the truth, and beg him not to betray me."

Cissy was paling and flushing alternately, as she sprang up, and said, tremblingly, to her lover:

"She did not follow you here. She is a member of this household— governess to Miss Fitzgerald's children. She is living an honest life, and would not wish her antecedents to be brought up against her now."

He answered, angrily:

"Why should either of us spare her now? She wronged us both, most bitterly, in the past, and did not scruple afterward to throw a blighting disgrace on my life."

"But I left you free to seek happiness with the woman you loved, so I did you a good turn after all, Cameron Clemens. You never loved me, and you did not grieve for me. You have even been friendly with the man who lured me from you!" Miss Erroll cried, eagerly.

He knew that much of her charge was true. He could deny only the last of it.

"Not friendly," he said, "for we had a bitter quarrel once. But he told me you had fled from him, refusing to become his wife, after I obtained my divorce. You were untrue to both of us. So why should we become enemies for the sake of a worthless woman?"

How she shivered with shame under the stinging contempt of his tones, for some womanhood lurked in her still, and she knew that she was not quite so black as she was painted.

But as she quailed before his righteous wrath, Cissy came generously to the rescue, her gray eyes dark with emotion, her cheeks suffused with blushes.

"Hush! do not utterly crush her with your scorn!" she cried. "Clifford Standish lied to you, the perjured villain! She did not refuse to marry him. He told her he had a wife already, and was tired of his liaison, so she fled from him in horror at her terrible position. She has been trying to lead a good life ever since, and we must not throw her back into temptation. I have forgiven her, and promised to keep her secret, and so must you."

CHAPTER LII.

FOR CISSY'S SAKE.

"The burden of my heart, dear,There's little need to tell;There's little need to say, dear,I've loved you long and well.

"And you will be my wife, dear,So may you ever blessThrough all your sunny life, dear,The day you answered yes."

Cissy paused for breath, and her lover looked at her adoringly.

Never had she looked so beautiful, never had she seemed so truly noble as at this moment when so generously pleading the cause of the woman who had brought such bitter sorrow into her life.

He forgot for a moment the tall, fair, beautiful woman who hung breathlessly on his fiat of fate, and exclaimed, rapturously:

"Cissy, you are an angel!"

"Yes, she is an angel!" cried the governess, eagerly. "She is an angel, and she will forgive you all your faults and make you happy yet—so happy that you might afford to spare the poor wretch whose sins have all recoiled upon her own head with crushing weight!"

"Spare her!" pleaded Cissy, with humid eyes.

He looked back at her tenderly, and answered:

"For your sake!"

With a sob of joy, the governess fled from the room.

And with her going the last shadow that her wicked influence had cast upon their lives faded into the past.

He moved closer to Cissy, catching both her trembling hands in his, and looking deep into her tearful eyes, saying, tremulously:

"My darling, the events of to-day have thrown down the last barriers of restraint between us, and we are back again where we left off that bitter day when you cast me off for the sake of the woman who declared she had a better claim to me. Cannot we go back to that past?"

Her face was downcast, her eyes drooped from his, she trembled, and did not speak.

But he was not repulsed, for she let him keep the little trembling hands in his, and he was thus encouraged to go on in a low voice, hoarse from passionate love:

"Cissy, I love you more devotedly than ever, and I should have sought you long ago but that I feared a repulse. I knew so well your willful pride, you see. But now fate has thrown us together again, and it will break my heart to lose this new sweet hope. Darling, will you forgive the past, and let the future make amends?"

Cissy had not thought last night that she would be won so quickly as this. She had resolved in her heart to be quite cold at first, and make her lover's second wooing very difficult.

But as Cameron said, the events of the day had made reserve impossible. They had come face to face with the past in all its love and pain.

So she could not steel her responsive heart to her lover's impetuous wooing. With a great burst of tears that revealed all her heart, she threw herself into his eager arms that clasped and held her with boundless delight.

And the woman whom Cissy had saved from exposure by her generous prayer for mercy, crept away to her room, muttering, in a fearful way:

"How strangely fate pursues me in this house! I thought I was done with my bitter past, but three of its ghosts have risen here to confront me with my sins! What a terrible blunder I made going into that room! But I did not dream of meeting my divorced husband there! Still, I might have guessed he would follow that girl, the one love of his life. She is indeed an angel, but alas! she would not intercede for me if she knew the thing I had done last night!"

CHAPTER LIII.

"I WILL NEVER FORGIVE HER!"

"Oh, loved one! where art thou?

Doubt whispers in my earMany and many a fear,And tells me thou art gay while I despair,Yet be the bright hours thine,If only thou art mine,I all the dark ones am content to bear."

The strange disappearance of her daughter had come to Mrs. Fitzgerald with the suddenness of a thunderbolt.

To lose her like this—the child she had loved so dearly and mourned so unceasingly—over whom she had rejoiced with such yearning love when found; oh! it was inexpressibly bitter!

In the six weeks that Geraldine had been with her the glad mother had lavished on her daughter everything that could make a young girl happy, withholding nothing except her approval of her love for Harry Hawthorne. Wealth had been poured out with an unstinting hand, to surround her and clothe her with beautiful things; she had been praised, petted, and loved by the whole household, and the two children, her half-brother and sister, had vied with each other in lovely attentions to their new-found sister.

Nothing had been lacking to make Geraldine happy—nothing except the love she had been forbidden to cherish.

Alas! this love had ranked above everything else in her tender heart.

"The world is naught when one is goneWho was the world? then the heart breaksThat this is lost which was once won."

The mother's heart was cruelly wounded by the desertion of her daughter.

"I will never forgive her!" she cried in the first agony of the shock. "She has proved herself the child of her wicked father by this heartless desertion of home and friends, and I can realize how little of my blood runs in the veins of the daughter I bore him."

In vain did Cissy intercede for her friend.

"Remember how young and loving she was, dear Mrs. Fitzgerald. Then, too, her lover was very charming—just the sort of a man to fascinate a young girl."

"He may have been as handsome as Apollo, and as fascinating, but he was not a good man, or he would never have persuaded a young girl to elope with him. Why did he not come frankly to me like a gentleman, and ask for my daughter's hand?"

"Dear Mrs. Fitzgerald, because he knew it would be hopeless. Of course our dear Geraldine must have acquainted him with your opposition to the marriage," said Cissy, gently, though in her heart she thought very strangely of Geraldine, asking herself over and over why the girl had chosen to deceive her so in asserting that she knew nothing of Hawthorne's whereabouts.

"She must have been in secret correspondence with him all the while, but I could not have believed it of Geraldine but for that note in her own writing," she said, sadly enough to the angry mother.

At first, Mrs. Fitzgerald had feared that Cissy was in the plot of Geraldine's elopement, but the young girl's surprise and grief were so genuine that she dismissed the doubt. "She has treated you shamefully, too, my dear," said the lady. "After inviting you here as a guest, and promising you such a charming time, it was abominable to go off that way and leave you in the lurch."

"Do not worry about me. My only concern is for you in your trouble. Geraldine acted willfully, I know, but there is one comfort. The man she has married is good and true, and cannot fail to make her happy."

"Ah, but, my dear girl, only think of what she has thrown away. Why, Geraldine was betrothed to a nobleman from her childhood, the owner of a vast estate in England."

"Perhaps that was why she ran away for fear of being forced into an unloving marriage, madame."

"Oh, no, that would never have happened, of course. I would not have wished her to marry unwillingly, nor would noble Lord Putnam have accepted an unloving bride. Perhaps, after all, he will wait for my Claire. She will be grown up in a few years, and bids fair to be as lovely as Geraldine," returned the lady, comforting herself with hopes of the future.

At that moment a servant entered the boudoir to announce the arrival of Cameron Clemens.

Cissy looked up with heightened color, saying:

"It is a gentleman we knew in New York. If you will excuse me, I will go down, and I will be glad to have you accompany me."

Mrs. Fitzgerald protested that she was not able to see any one, and excused herself to Cissy, who hurried down to the caller.

We have read in a former chapter of the result of that interview, so we will follow Cissy, after his departure, back to the presence of Mrs. Fitzgerald.

"I fear I shall have to return to New York in a few days," she remarked, feeling that delicacy would suggest her leaving after Geraldine's strange desertion.

But Mrs. Fitzgerald raised an indignant protest.

"No, Cissy, you must not go. I have grown very fond of you, and why should you not remain with me?"

Cissy thanked her for her cordiality, but said, blushingly, that she must go back to work. She was to be married in the spring, and she must earn her wedding clothes.

"Married? Oh, dear! And to the gentleman who was calling just now, I suppose?"

"Yes, madame," owned Cissy, with the loveliest rose glowing on her soft cheeks.

"Tell me all about it!" cried the lady, kindly.

Cissy thought that this would involve too long a story, so she said, simply, that she and Mr. Clemens had been engaged years before, and had quarreled and parted. Now they had made it up again, and she had promised to marry him in the spring.

"I have a charming thought," cried the lady. "You shall not return to New York. Stay with me as my companion and friend, and be married here."

"My dear lady, you are too kind—but it would be impossible. There is my trousseau to be thought of, you know."

"Certainly, child. I was thinking of that. Leave it to me to provide the trousseau as my wedding gift to you. What? Too proud? Why, aren't you to be my companion? And, of course, I shall owe you as much as you could earn at O'Neill's—and more," softly. "My dear girl, don't refuse. Think how unhappy I am, and what a comfort you can be to me."

Cissy saw that the offer was affectionate and earnest, and came from the depths of a noble heart, so she accepted it most gladly.

The days came and went, until it was almost two weeks since Geraldine's elopement.

They had looked every day for a letter from her, telling them where she was, and perhaps pleading for pardon, and to be permitted to see her mother again.

But not a line was received from the truant.

"She is cruel, heartless! her father's child, not mine," cried poor Mrs. Fitzgerald, trying to steel her heart against the truant.

But one cold, snowy day toward the last of February—could they ever forget that day—a card was brought to the lady in her boudoir.

She glanced at it, and turned deadly pale.

The card bore a name she had reason to hate.

HARRY HAWTHORNE.

It fell from her trembling hands, and Cissy, glancing at it, exclaimed, joyously:

"We shall hear of Geraldine at last!"

"I cannot see him!" moaned Mrs. Fitzgerald, tremblingly.

"Oh, yes, you will. Come! I will go down with you. Courage! You will fall in love with your son-in-law at sight, and forgive him for stealing your daughter!" cried Cissy, encouragingly, taking her hand to lead her down.

And in a few more moments they stood in the presence of a man so strikingly handsome and debonair that Mrs. Fitzgerald could not help from thawing toward him a little as Cissy presented him. He was well-dressed, princely in manners and appearance. As far as looks and culture went, her favorite, Lord Putnam, could not surpass the New York fireman.

He looked disappointed somehow, and after the first few words were passed, ventured straight to the point.

"Mrs. Fitzgerald, I think your daughter has told you of me. We are betrothed, you know, and I hope her heart has not turned against me with her accession to fortune. May I hope that you will also smile on my suit, and permit me to see Geraldine?"

They stared at him in amazement, the two startled women. Why, what could he mean, with those strange words and that confident air?

Cissy recovered from her trance of surprise first, and exclaimed:

"Mr. Hawthorne, what can you mean? Geraldine is not here. We supposed she was with you!"

"With me?—how strange! Why, Miss Carroll, I haven't seen her since Christmas Eve. Do not tell me that harm has come to my darling!"

CHAPTER LIV.

"WILL YOU BID ME GODSPEED."

"I reach into the dark, O Love!I reach into the dark.I cannot find thee; and my groping handsTouch only memories and phantom shapes.

"I call into the dark, O Love!I call into the dark.There comes from out the hush above, below,No answer but my own quick-fluttered breath."

Harry Hawthorne had sprung to his feet, pale with emotion, as he stood before Cissy, repeating the words:

"With me? How strange! Why, I have not seen her since Christmas. Do not tell me that harm has come to my darling!"

With the utterance of his words a terrible comprehension dawned on Mrs. Fitzgerald.

She understood that she had been horribly deceived, that Geraldine had not gone away to marry her lover, but had been entrapped into some terrible fate.

The fear of Clifford Standish's vengeance for the scorn she had heaped on him pierced her heart like a knife-thrust.

For two weeks Geraldine had been missing.

And no search had been made, because it was believed that she was safe and happy with her heart's choice, Harry Hawthorne.

But, instead, she had become the victim of a terrible doom.

The horror of her apprehensions overcame the mother's heart, and she fell forward in a heavy swoon.

When consciousness returned, she found herself lying flat on a couch, with Cissy bathing her forehead, and Hawthorne her hands, with *eau de cologne*.

She felt very weak and helpless, but as consciousness returned to her she groaned despairingly.

Hawthorne gave her a look of tender sympathy, and said:

"Mrs. Fitzgerald, can you listen to me a few moments?"

His gentle voice and manly looks inclined her heart toward him in spite of her prejudices against him, so she bowed her head affirmatively.

He went on:

"While we were trying to restore you to consciousness, Miss Carroll has told me the circumstances of Geraldine's disappearance. That note purporting to be from Geraldine was no doubt a forgery, and I fear she has fallen into the power of Clifford Standish."

Mrs. Fitzgerald groaned. Cissy sobbed aloud, and although Hawthorne would not permit himself to break down like a woman, his voice was very husky as he proceeded:

"A few more words and I must leave you, to institute a search for our missing darling. Will you bid me Godspeed?"

"Yes, oh, yes," and she held out her hand to him voluntarily.

When he took it he felt a warm, kindly pressure, and realized that in their common loss and sorrow humanity had triumphed over pride, and he could count on her as a true friend. Lord Putnam was momentarily forgotten.

Releasing her hand, he added:

"You may wonder at my delay in seeking Geraldine, so I will briefly explain: In the first place, when I found that the actor had abducted her on Christmas evening, I followed on the next train to Chicago. Four weary days I sought her, but all in vain. At length I met Standish one cold snowy evening on an obscure street, and demanded Geraldine at his hands. He assured me with such malice, that she was his willing companion, that I sprang at the dastard's throat in fury, and he stabbed me and ran off, leaving me for dead. Some kind Samaritans rescued and took care of me, but I kept the name of my would-be murderer a secret, for fear of drawing Geraldine's name into a scandal. Well, just as I became convalescent, I received news of the death of a very near relative that obliged my immediate return to New York. I sent for a detective, confided my secrets to him, and employed him to search for Geraldine in my absence. While I was away I received information that Geraldine had discovered her long-lost mother, and was safe with you. As this set my mind at rest about my betrothed, I paid and dismissed my detective, and determined that as soon as I had settled up some business matters I had on hand, I would return to Chicago and ascertain whether Geraldine's heart had remained true to me in her change of fortune, or if she would discard me for some richer lover. I arrived to-day, and came here full of hope and love to meet—this terrible tragedy of woe!"

He paused to steady his shaking voice, then added:

"But I believe I have a clew, and I shall follow it up. I go now to my detective. He is very clever, and I am very sorry I dismissed him. I feel sure he can help me to unravel this mystery."

The hope and courage in his voice inspired her to exclaim, eagerly:

"May Heaven help you—and bless you!"

"Thank you! Those words will inspire me to do my best."

He touched her hand with his lips, like a gallant knight, and bowing to Cissy, left the room.

But while Mrs. Fitzgerald lay unconscious, he had said to the young girl:

"Is there a governess in this house?"

"Yes, Miss Erroll."

"Has she ever carried on a flirtation with Standish?"

To his surprise, Cissy blushed, and stammered, replying:

"I should not like to answer that question unless you have very good cause for asking it."

She was generously eager to shield the woman's past if she could consistently do so.

But he answered, gravely:

"This must be considered a secret yet, but my detective wrote me that Mr. Standish was carrying on a flirtation with this Miss Erroll. Can she have been in collusion with him to kidnap Geraldine?"

"Good Heaven!" cried Cissy, paling at the awful suspicion that presented itself. She saw that she must tell all she knew.

But at that moment Mrs. Fitzgerald showed signs of reviving, and Cissy whispered, hurriedly:

"I can tell you all about Miss Erroll and Standish. They were lovers long ago, but I do not know if they have met recently."

Then the lady opened her eyes, and the subject dropped.

But when Hawthorne was gone, the horror of his suggestion staid in Cissy's mind, and she admitted to herself that it might be plausible.

For what if Standish, by threatening the woman with betrayal to her employer, had forced her to help him in his nefarious plot?

Cissy was so excited and indignant that she was on the point of rushing to Miss Erroll and taxing her with the crime.

But sober second thought restrained her.

She might frighten the woman, and cause her to run away out of reach.

She decided to leave it all to Hawthorne and the detective.

Meanwhile, she had enough on her hands to soothe the agonized mother, who was almost frantic with grief over the mystery of her daughter's fate.

She kept wringing her hands and sobbing:

"It is two long weeks since she disappeared. Oh, it is too late! too late! for any one to save my poor child now!"

Cissy shuddered at all that the words implied, but she cried, bravely:

"Do not let us despair. Although Geraldine's whereabouts are unknown to us, she is in the keeping of God, as she has always been, and surely He will protect her. Let us hope and pray."

Gradually she infused some hope into the mother's heart, and presently they knelt and prayed to God to restore Geraldine to their arms again.

Meanwhile, Hawthorne, as we will continue to call him for a little while, hurried to the office of Norris, the wonderful Western detective.

He found the little man in, and after a hurried greeting, said:

"I have called again about that case of mine."

"Ah, you wish to begin another search for the girl; is that it? I thought it strange you dropped it so suddenly when you got my report. But perhaps you had received news some way of the girl?"

"I had; but, Norris, that was a terrible mistake of mine letting you drop the case when you did. You were on the right track, though you did not know it. I am almost hoping you kept on watching, out of curiosity, after I paid and dismissed you. It will be worth much to you if you did," anxiously.

"But I did not, I'm sorry to say; for directly after I got your check I went off on a chase down South after some gold-brick swindlers. Fact is, I just got back from Richmond yesterday, after a stay of three weeks. But I ran the rascals down, though, after a very exciting chase. Tell you all about it," bustled the little detective, importantly.

"No, I don't care about it now," Hawthorne cried, impatiently. "You must hear my story first, for you must never pause now till that missing girl is found—the girl who was right under your nose all the time while you were watching the governess—Miss Fitzgerald, formerly Geraldine Harding."

"You don't say! Tell me all about it, sir."

Hawthorne went rapidly over all he had to tell, and then Norris said:

"The governess helped him, as sure as you're born, Mr. Daly."

CHAPTER LV.

DETECTED.

"If you could go back to the forks of the road,Back the long miles you have carried the load;Back to the place where you had to decideBy this way or that all your life to abide;Back of the sorrow and back of the care,Back to the place where the future was fair—If you were there now, a decision to make,Oh! pilgrim of sorrow, which road would you take?"

It would scarcely be believed that a young girl could be drugged and carried from her own room at midnight by a scoundrel, even in the great, wicked city of Chicago.

But such had been the fate of our pretty Geraldine, although only by the connivance of the governess had Standish been able to accomplish the daring abduction.

Having quieted her uneasy scruples by swearing that he meant to marry the girl—which, indeed, he was most anxious to do—Standish unfolded his nefarious plot, and by his threatenings forced her to consent to aid him.

He told her that the girl had flirted most outrageously with him once, then thrown him over for another, and he was determined to get even with the little jilt by making her his wife. He swore that nothing should turn him from his purpose of revenge, and unless Miss Erroll aided him in this he would send Mrs. Fitzgerald a letter on the following day, acquainting her with the past history of her handsome governess.

It was absolutely fiendish, his threat, but she doubted not that he would keep his word; so, promising all he asked, she hurried away from him, eager to escape the nipping winter blasts and the flecks of snow that kissed her cheeks with icy lips, the forerunner of a snow-storm that wrapped the earth in a snowy mantle long before the dawn.

When the young ladies returned from the theatre, Miss Erroll was bending over her desk, where she had been busy for hours, counterfeiting Geraldine's handwriting from a bit of manuscript she had stolen from her room.

She was an adept at this work, and succeeded in her task so well that the note she pinned on Geraldine's pillow somewhat later, was so cleverly done it might have deceived an expert.

When Geraldine went into her own room that night she found Miss Erroll waiting for her, instead of the neat mulatto girl her mother had employed for her exclusive service.

"Martha was called home by the illness of her mother, and begged me to help you if she did not return in time," she explained, smilingly.

The truth was that Miss Erroll had given the girl some drugged wine that sent her into such a heavy sleep that she was enabled to steal into her place.

Geraldine protested that she could do without assistance, but Miss Erroll insisted on remaining; so at last she was hurried into bed, and then the woman said, solicitously:

"Now a sip of this spiced wine the maid told me to keep warm for you, to prevent a cold after being out such an inclement evening."

Geraldine did not care for the wine, and she was not at all chilly, but she drank a little from the cup, just to escape the woman's importunities.

Then she laid her fair head down to rest, and in a very few moments was soundly asleep; and no wonder, for the wine she had drank had contained enough opium to keep her in a stupor for many hours.

Not till she was sound asleep did the woman go out, and then she stole like a shadow of evil omen through the darkened house, where she undid all the door fastenings, that Clifford Standish might have no difficulty in entering.

Returning to Geraldine's room, she cautiously dressed the sleeping girl in warm, thick shoes and stockings, and a thick blanket-wrapper, placing close at hand a heavy cloak and hood, evidently making her ready for a mysterious journey.

In the dressing-room beyond, she had already packed a hand-bag with clothing, which she now brought in and placed near the door.

While she was dressing her, Geraldine had stirred and moaned several times, but the influence of the drug held her senses bound too fast for her to awake; so Miss Erroll had everything ready, and was crouched in a chair waiting, when there came a low, soft scratching at the door, the signal agreed on between them.

She started, growing pale as ashes, her heart sinking in her breast. She had been hoping and praying that he would not come.

Stealing to the door, she admitted Standish, who was not a very pleasant object to see in his black crape mask.

Not a word passed between them, but she silently wrapped Geraldine in the cloak and hood ready for her journey.

The daring actor lifted the girl as though she had been a little child, and taking the hand-bag also, stole from the house undetected, and made his way to a sleigh that was in waiting around the nearest corner.

Then Miss Erroll, shivering like one in an ague fit, proceeded to finish her work.

She locked the door, and re-made the dainty bed, so that it had the appearance of not having been slept in that night.

Upon the pillow she pinned the note that she had written in Geraldine's hand, and to which she had signed Geraldine's name.

And, lastly, and just before leaving the room, she sank on her knees, and prayed with dramatic fervor:

"Oh, God, if Thou wilt hear the prayer of a wretch like me, I implore that Thou wilt watch over and protect from harm the poor girl whom I have betrayed into that wretch's hands!"

When the hue and cry arose the next morning over Geraldine's disappearance, she was as much excited as any, and her grief was as noisy as that of the others.

She was indeed grieved and remorseful over her evil deed, and she had only one comfort to offer herself:

"Self-preservation is the first law of nature."

She had saved herself, and, as the days dragged by, her first terror of discovery gave place to a conviction of safety. Not the least suspicion had pointed her out as the wretch she was. The children still remained devoted to her, Mrs. Fitzgerald was kind, Miss Carroll courteous, the servants respectful. She began to breathe freely again, saying, to herself:

"Why should I fret? Of course Standish has married the girl, and she ought to be glad to get such a handsome husband!"

She could not banish a little bitter jealousy of Geraldine, for once she had hoped to marry Standish herself, and the old passion still ached in her heart, though she had fled from him in horror when she learned that he had a living wife.

Now that two weeks had passed, she supposed they were married and happy, and some day there might be a reconciliation between the mother and daughter and the son-in-law who had so cleverly stolen his bride. Standish had promised that no matter what happened, his confederate's agency in the affair should never be known.

But she would not have begun to feel so confident of her position if she could have heard what the detective, Norris, was saying that day to Hawthorne.

"That governess helped him, as sure as you're born, Mr. Daly."

Hawthorne said, hurriedly:

"You may call me by another name henceforward—that of Hawthorne. I confess that Daly was an assumed one. And now, about this governess?"

"Yes, there's no time to lose, Mr. Hawthorne, in beating about the bush. That poor girl has been missing for two weeks, and God only knows what has come to her ere now. We must see this Erroll woman at once, and surprise her into confession by taxing her with the crime."

"A clever idea. Let us confront her at once," cried Hawthorne, with burning impatience.

"I'm with you to the death!" laughed the jovial little detective, springing to his feet, and within the hour they arrived at the mansion, and sent their cards to Miss Errol.

They had chosen Cissy Carroll to bear them, and the governess looked at her, pale with affright.

"I do not know these men, Hawthorne and Norris. I cannot see them," she declared at first.

But Cissy was firm.

"You must go down. They said their business was important, and they would not leave without seeing you," she said.

"I dare not see them! I am afraid!" faltered the guilty woman.

"Why should you be afraid? Have you done anything wrong?" demanded Cissy, sternly, for a terrible suspicion was troubling her mind.

The woman shot her a keen glance, and asked:

"Have you betrayed me?"

"No."

"Then I will see them, but they must have made a mistake. I am not the person they want."

Putting on an expression of bravado, she followed Cissy to the presence of the two men, who both rose and bowed profoundly, though they read the signs of guilt in her ghastly face. Then the detective said:

"Miss Erroll, will you kindly favor us with the address of your lover, Mr. Clifford Standish?"

CHAPTER LVI.

A REPENTANT SINNER.

"How can the patient stars look downOn all their light discovers—The traitor's smile, the murderer's frown,The lips of lying lovers?"

When that startling question fell on Miss Erroll's ears she gave a convulsive gasp, and sank limply into the nearest chair.

The skilled detective saw quickly that the woman was a coward at heart, and would not be able to sustain the air of bravado with which she had entered.

Advancing quickly to her side, he threw back the lapel of his overcoat, revealing to her frightened eyes his detective badge, and continuing:

"I am in search of Clifford Standish, and you must tell me where to find him."

She trembled like a leaf in a storm, and muttered, with weak defiance:

"How should I know?"

Norris answered, boldly:

"Because you have been in secret correspondence with the man for weeks. Because you were his confederate in the kidnaping of Miss Geraldine Harding."

The cry of a beaten animal burst from the cowering woman's lips, and her form shook with fear.

"You cannot deny it," added Norris, following up his advantage, while Cissy and Hawthorne looked on in breathless interest.

She lifted her pallid face and groaned:

"Who is my accuser?"

"I am, and this gentleman here, Miss Harding's betrothed, the Harry Hawthorne whom it was pretended in that forged note the young lady had eloped with. I have been watching you and Standish for several weeks, Miss Erroll, and had I not been called away by other business, you had never succeeded in that nefarious abduction. But I have facts enough to warrant me in threatening you with arrest unless you make a full confession!"

"Arrest me?"

Almost hissing the words, she sprang to her feet, glaring fiercely at him, but the flash of bravado did not intimidate the fearless little detective.

"Yes, you," he answered, coolly. "But, after all, I do not like to war upon a woman, even a bad one; so tell me the truth now if you want to escape a prison-cell."

Quaking with fear, she dropped back into her chair, covering her writhing features with her trembling white hands.

After waiting a moment vainly for her to answer, he asked:

"Where is Clifford Standish now?"

"I do not know."

"How long since you saw him?"

"Two weeks ago to-night."

"At the time of the kidnaping of Miss Harding?"

"Yes."

Her answers were given as if dragged from her under stress of fear, but it was plain that she meant to make the confession he demanded.

He flashed Cissy and Hawthorne a triumphant look, then said, briskly:

"Tell us all about that night and your share in it, as quickly as you can, for our time is very precious."

So, with her head drooped in bitter shame, and eyes downcast, lest she should meet their glances of scorn and execration, the beautiful woman whose sins had followed her so relentlessly, poured out the story of that night's wrong-doing, her heart sinking in despair the while, for before her she saw the dark future opening like Hades, so awful in its gloom.

And in all the bitterness of that moment the cruelest thought of all was that Cissy was listening to her confession of sin, and would hate and despise her now for her ingratitude after all the kindness she had showered on her worthless head.

Somehow, she had coveted Cissy's respect and good-will, and to lose them was most bitter to her pride.

The cup of her humiliation was full, but she had to drink it to the bitter dregs.

When she drew breath in silence at last, after telling of the note she had pinned on the pillow, Harry Hawthorne cried, indignantly:

"Why did you lend yourself to this terrible deed?"

Miss Erroll looked at Cissy and faltered:

"You can tell him why."

Cissy answered:

"I think he knew some dark secret in her past that she was anxious to hide, now that she is leading a better life, and he threatened her with betrayal unless she helped him to carry out his plot. Is it not so?"

"It is the truth. I tried to keep from doing it, but I could not get out of his power. Oh, how hard it is for a woman who has once done wrong to lead a good life again! The avenging fates pursue her to death or madness!" groaned the detected governess.

"But, now," cried Norris, impatiently, "now tell us where that fiend was to take Miss Harding after he placed her in the sleigh that you say he had waiting at the corner."

"He told me he had engaged an old woman to take charge of her till she consented to marry him. He said she was a terrible old woman, who lived alone on a farm about five miles from the city, and kept a savage bull-dog on the place."

"By Heaven! I know the place, and the woman!" almost shouted the detective. Then, calming himself, he added:

"She is Jane Crabtree, an old woman as big as a giant, who has been in the criminal courts twice, once for beating almost to death a child she had taken from the poor-house and secondly for the murder of her husband. He died of arsenical poison, and the woman was accused of administering it, but they could not prove it and she got off by swearing he committed suicide. But I always felt sure that she did the deed, for it was proved they led a cat-and-dog life. Since this happened, three months ago, it is said that she never permits any person on the premises, and keeps a large bull-dog unchained all the time; so, if Miss Harding is in the clutches of that old wretch, it is time we were moving toward her delivery. Come," and he motioned Hawthorne away.

In their haste to be gone they paid no more attention to the governess, and with a hasty adieu to Cissy, left the room.

The two women were left alone, and Miss Erroll crouched wretchedly in her chair, not daring to look up and meet Cissy's glance of scorn.

She started when the girl's voice fell on her ear—clear, cold, disdainful.

"What shall you do now?"

The woman lifted her face, deadly pale, but grown suddenly calm with a great despair.

"I must go away—at once!" she answered.

Then she fell at Cissy's feet.

"You, who have been so good already—grant my last prayer," she faltered.

Cissy looked down in silent inquiry at the haggard face.

"Do not tell Mrs. Fitzgerald of this story until I am gone out of her house forever. I love her and the darling children; they have been good to me, and I could not bear their reproaches. I will go now and pack my trunk, and send for it later. Let me steal out of the house, like the wretched outcast I am, before you tell them my miserable story."

"Your wish is granted," answered Cissy, huskily.

She went away then to her own room and sat a while in earnest thought.

Then she went to Miss Erroll's door and tapped softly.

It was opened by the governess, who had made such speed that her hat and cloak were already on and her trunk strapped.

"You are going now?" asked Cissy.

"Yes."

"Where?"

"To seek some humble lodging-house, and begin again the horrible struggle of a lonely woman for an honest living," the poor wretch answered, bitterly.

"Have you any money?"

"Fifty dollars that I have saved in the few months that I have been here— enough to starve on perhaps until I find another situation."

"Take this to help you," Cissy said, pressing a hundred-dollar bill into her hand.

"Oh, Miss Carroll, I cannot. You, too, are poor. It may be your little all."

"No, I have more. In fact, I received two hundred dollars yesterday from a lawyer in New York, who has been managing some lawsuits for me against a villain who brought a false claim against my grandfather's estate, and thus threw me penniless on the world. My lawyer has won the suit, and I shall have several thousand dollars of my own very soon."

"I congratulate you, Miss Carroll. You deserve all the good fortune that can fall to a noble woman. Heaven forever bless you. I accept your gift gratefully, because—because it—may save me, poor tempted wretch, from a life of sin."

"That was why I gave it to you. I hoped it might keep you in the right path."

"It shall! It shall! Oh, Miss Carroll, I am a repentant sinner, and since I am spared this time, I will never be tempted to do wrong again! I swear—I swear to you, in return for your angelic goodness—that I will repent my sins, seek God's forgiveness, try to lead a good life, and meet you—angel that you are—in heaven!"

She snatched Cissy's hand, pressed her burning lips upon it, and rushed from the house out into the blinding snow storm that darkened the air.

Then Cissy went to Mrs. Fitzgerald to tell her of all that had transpired, and to help her to bear the terrible suspense over Geraldine's fate.

CHAPTER LVII.

A NIGHTMARE DREAM.

"Once all was sunshine and brightness,Life had no sorrow or care;Love filled my soul with its brightness,As flowers perfume the air.Where now is Pleasure, the beauty?Where now is Hope's cheering beam?Where are those friends once all duty?All vanished, all gone, like a dream!"

We must follow the fortunes of Geraldine after being placed in the sleigh by her cowardly abductor.

Tucking the sleeping girl warmly under the heavy robes, he took the reins from the man he had employed to hold them, and drove off at a spanking pace for his destination, the old country-house of which Miss Erroll had told the detective.

As the night was propitious to his purpose, and the road remarkably fine, he reached the place in a short while, and without any misadventure.

The old woman, Jane Crabtree, in expectation of his coming, had muzzled the savage bull-dog, and came down the lane to the gate to meet him, as they had agreed upon.

The woman was a giant in stature, as the detective had said, and looked strong enough to floor John L. Sullivan with one hand.

In the light of the bull's-eye lantern that Standish flared into her eyes, her coarse face, with its straggling black locks blown about by the swirling snow, looked capable of committing any evil deed.

He dropped some twenty-dollar gold pieces into her hand, gave her some instructions, and drove his team toward the city. A few hours later he boarded a train for Cincinnati at daylight, and remained away five days, in order to throw the searchers for Geraldine off guard.

But as we have seen, the forged note, representing that she had gone of her own free will to marry her betrothed, had effectually prevented any hue and cry over Geraldine's disappearance.

So the villainous abductor had it all his own way, and for two long weeks, until Hawthorne's return, he was free to come and go as he chose in the prosecution of his designs against the poor girl.

As for the poor victim, who can judge of her surprise and terror on awaking the next morning from her drugged sleep, in a strange room, and guarded by an old giant of a woman, with the most villainous face she had ever beheld.

The night before she had fallen asleep in her own lovely, luxurious room, and the last sight her eyes had rested on was the handsome, smiling face of Miss Erroll, the governess.

But her sleep had been haunted by terrible nightmare dreams, and when she waked at last in that shabby room in the presence of her horrible old jailer, she thought that she was dreaming still.

Recoiling from the woman, she threw out her arms, groaning helplessly:

"Oh, those dreadful nightmare dreams! How they haunt me! Will not some one wake me, please? Martha, where are you? Come to me at once. Oh, Cissy! oh, mamma!"

Old Jane Crabtree came and stood over her scowlingly, snapping out:

"You an't dreamin', gal; you is wide awake!"

But it took her some little time to assure her captive that this was not a continuation of her terrible nightmare dreams.

When she at last convinced her that this was an awful reality, and boldly told her that Clifford Standish had brought her here in a drugged sleep, the terrible truth rushed over her mind.

"That wine Miss Erroll gave me was drugged! She was in the plot!" she cried, wildly.

The hag nodded sullenly, and Geraldine continued, passionately:

"He will never get my consent to marry him, never!"

And then she fell to pleading with the old woman for her liberty, promising to make her rich if she would only restore her to her friends.

But Jane Crabtree laughed her to scorn, sneering at the idea of Geraldine being able to reward her for her liberty.

Standish had cleverly prepared her for all that the girl might threaten or promise, by telling her not to listen to anything, as the girl was only a poor salesgirl from Siegel & Cooper's, on a salary of three dollars a week.

So the old witch grunted scornfully at her pleadings, threats, and promises, and presently went out, locking the door after her until she returned with a coarse breakfast of badly served food, from which the girl turned with loathing.

While she was absent, Geraldine rose and looked from the window to see if there was any chance of escape.

What she saw made her turn shudderingly back to the bright coal-fire, the only cheerful object in the poor room.

The window was very small, and the grimy panes were guarded by heavy iron bars.

Beyond these bars Geraldine saw a level stretch of country covered with a mantle of snow. A wild snow-storm was raging, and the wind drove against the shutters with terrible violence, banging them to and fro until the old house shook in the terrible gale.

She realized that she was in a farm-house, far removed from any other habitation, and that if she could have walked out of the house at that moment she must have perished in the deep drifts of snow while struggling to escape.

That terrible first day passed in alternate weeping and praying. Standish did not make his appearance, and Jane Crabtree remained down stairs, attending to her household tasks, except when she came up to replenish the fire and minister to the wants of her captive.

That first day Geraldine ate nothing. At night she sobbed herself to sleep.

The next day hunger drove her to partake of a little of the coarse food.

For three days the monotonous blizzard raged, and the snow grew deeper and deeper. Geraldine felt as if she should go mad.

She wondered despairingly if she should ever get free from the power of her cruel jailer, or if she should die here, as old Jane had boldly threatened.

The woman had become very impatient over Geraldine's continued weeping, and one day she said, roughly:

"You might as well hush that snivelin' an' make your mind up ter marry that man, for if you don't he'll kill you!"

"Kill me! He dare not!"

"He'll dare anything, and if he don't, I will. Sho! I don't mind killin' anybody. I beat a poor-house chile to death last year, and only three months ago I p'isened my husband with arsenic. An' that isn't all I done, neither, for——" She paused in the recital of her crimes, for the listener had dropped limply in a swoon, overcome by the horror of the story.

Oh, the weary days, and the terror-haunted nights! How did the poor captive drag through them? The wonder to her ever afterward was that she did not go mad.

At last Clifford Standish came.

It was a full week since he had brought her there and the storm had somewhat abated in violence, but the snow still lay deep upon the ground, and the wailing of the winter wind was like the knell of hope in her ears.

The door opened, and her cowardly abductor stood within the room, gazing at his cruel work.

Pretty Geraldine had wept till her brown eyes were dim and heavy, with purple shadows beneath them, and her cheeks all wan and sunken. She had not taken the trouble to exchange her blanket wrapper for the cloth gown Miss Erroll had put in the hand-bag. She had not given a thought to her appearance.

But even her disheveled locks and haggard looks could not quench the fire of passion in the villain's heart. He looked at her gloatingly, exclaiming:

"Good-morning, pretty Geraldine. I suppose that after your week with Jane Crabtree, you are glad to see even me!"

CHAPTER LVIII.

SENTENCE OF DEATH.

"Alas, a wicked man am I;With temper fierce, too prone to strife,And quick to wrath, my hands I plyTo evil deeds."

BENJAMIN HATHAWAY.

Geraldine gave the smooth villain a glance of measureless contempt as she answered, bitterly:

"The sight of his satanic majesty would be more welcome than you, Clifford Standish!"

"Still defiant!" he laughed, mockingly. "Why, I thought that a week of Mrs. Crabtree's society would bring you to your senses!"

"Say rather would cause me to lose my senses!" she retorted, bitterly, and there was a moment's silence, which he broke by saying, impatiently:

"I will come to the purpose of my visit, Geraldine, I wish to marry you."

"So you have told me before," disdainfully.

"Well, I tell you so again, and I am fully determined that you shall become my wife!"

"You have a wife already, you villain!"

"She died in New York recently, and I am free to offer you my hand in honorable marriage. Will you accept it, Geraldine?"

"Never! I would die before I would marry you!"

"It is the alternative you must accept unless you become my bride!"

The steel-blue glitter of his eyes was diabolical as he fixed them upon her, and continued:

"Of course you understand that I have run a great risk in bringing you here, and made myself liable to the law for kidnaping—that is, unless you marry me, and give the affair the color of an elopement."

He paused, but she did not speak, so he went on:

"No search is being made for you by your friends, for a note was left in your room, stating that you had fled to marry your lover, Harry Hawthorne.

Your mother believes that statement, and so there is not the least suspicion that I carried you off."

"You fiend!" she cried; then added: "But Harry Hawthorne will search for me!"

"Harry Hawthorne gave up the search for you weeks ago, and sailed for Europe."

"It is false!"

"It is perfectly true. Why he went, I know not, but I have read in a New York paper of his going. Believe me or not, as you will, my charmer, but you are entirely in my power, without hope of rescue, and I am desperate with love for you. I will not permit rivalry from any living man. Either my bride you shall be, or the bride of Death!"

She sat listening and shuddering before the terrible decision of his words, and the blue fire of his determined eyes. She felt that neither prayers nor tears would move him. He was mad with love, stubborn with a sense of power.

Changing his mood, he began to pour out in burning words all the mighty strength of his passion, pleading, raving, imploring her kindness in return.

He might as well have prayed to a statue, so changeless was the scorn of her silent lips.

He asked her, almost frantically:

"Do you understand that unless you marry me there is no appeal from the sentence of death?"

"Yes, I understand; but I consider death preferable to a union with you."

Angered by the scorn of her words, he retorted:

"It will be a cruel death, I warn you, at the hands of old Jane Crabtree and your body will not even have Christian burial. It will be flung into an old disused well on the premises, and the secret of your fate will never be known."

"Be it so. At least, you cannot murder my soul. It will return to the God who gave it," she replied, dauntlessly bravely, determined that he should not have the satisfaction of seeing her wince before his threats.

He rose, with a baffled air, exclaiming:

"I shall not consider this answer final. I shall give you one more week in which to decide your fate."

Geraldine's heart leaped with joy. Another week's respite! And who could tell what might happen in that time? She had been praying, praying, praying all the while. Perhaps God would save her from her enemy's wiles.

Smiling grimly, Clifford Standish continued:

"I shall leave old Jane to plead my cause with you, and I believe that she will prove a powerful advocate. So sure am I of her ultimate success, that in a week I shall return, bringing with me a justice of the peace, empowered with authority to join us in matrimonial bonds. If you refuse, I shall go away, leaving you in the hands of old Jane, to be tortured to death and buried in the old well!"

Not a word came from the white lips of the girl, but the scorn of her eyes was fiery enough to make him hurry from her presence with a stifled oath.

She saw him leave with a great strangling sob of relief, and murmured:

"Thank Heaven, he will not come again for a week. Something will surely happen in all that time."

But she did not know yet all the horrors that week held in store for her, or why Clifford Standish had smiled so grimly, when he spoke of old Jane's advocacy of his suit.

They had planned a desperate expedient.

Each day the cruel woman presented herself with the harsh question:

"Will you marry Clifford Standish?"

Geraldine always answered "Never!" and each time the old woman flew at her in a fury, and administered a severe beating.

"He told me to do it," she would exclaim, angrily.

The prints of her cruel hands would be left on Geraldine's tender face in crimson streaks; her arms and shoulders bore purple bruises on their whiteness, but though each day brought a more severe chastisement than the last, Geraldine's answer was still the same:

"Never! Never!"

Her daily portions of food grew less in quantity, and more inferior in quality, so that only the severest pangs of hunger forced her to swallow the coarse mess. But for the hope of rescue, she would have left it untouched, and starved herself.

The old fiend began also to neglect the fire, so that the freezing winter winds, as they swept across the snow-covered prairie land, penetrated the cracks of the old frame house and chilled poor Geraldine until her fair face looked blue and pinched from the cold.

"I shall beat, and starve, and freeze you into consent!" snarled wicked old Jane, in a rage at the girl's stubbornness.

"You may kill my body, but you cannot bend my will!" answered the resolute victim.

But from weakness of the body her hopefulness began to fail. She cried out that God had forgotten her; she ceased to pray for rescue; she asked only that death would come quickly.

But the slow days and nights dragged on till the week was at an end, and still the strength of youth kept life in her sore and aching frame.

Late that afternoon old Jane came up stairs.

"He is coming. I see the sleigh off in the distance now. He will bring the justice to marry you to him!" she snarled.

Geraldine did not answer; she had already been beaten and kicked that day so that she was barely able to rise from the chair where she was crouching.

The woman continued, threateningly:

"If you do not marry him, he will leave you here for me to kill. Do you know how I shall do it?"

"No."

"I shall turn the dog on you. He has been kept without food two days, to make him savage. He would tear a stranger to pieces. He has never seen you, so when I 'sic' him on you, he will spring at your throat and make mincemeat of you. While you are still warm and bleeding, I shall throw your body into the old well!"

It was horrible to listen to her, but Geraldine only trembled and hid her face. Two weeks of misery had inured her to such brutality.

"I must go now and chain up Towser, so they can get in," added the old wretch, going down, after locking the door as usual, to receive her guests.

They came in, Standish and the justice of the peace he had bribed to accompany him—a villain, if ever a man's face spoke truly, who would stop at nothing if tempted by gold.

The actor whispered to Jane Crabtree, nervously:

"Has she consented?"

"No—although I've half-killed her tryin' to break her will."

Curses, low and deep, breathed over his lips; then he said:

"Well, we won't go up stairs to see her yet. We're half-frozen with this beastly cold, anyway, so we'll thaw out over the fire and a bottle of wine."

CHAPTER LIX.

WEDDED TO HER CHOICE.

"'Oh, darling', she said, and the whispered wordsIn a dreamy cadence fall,'Can I help but choose thee who art the bestAnd the noblest among them all * * *And since in thine eyes I shyly readThat thy thoughts hold a place for me—I bring thee a love, and a heart, and a life,And consecrate all to thee!'"

They drew up their chairs to the glowing kitchen fire, smoked, drank, and even played a game of cards, for now that the final moment had arrived, the villain's nerve began to fail him, and he began to realize his crime in all its enormity.

And while he lingered there, dreading the consummation of the crowning act of his villainy, along the road he had traveled another sleigh was speeding toward the farm—a double sleigh—and in it were seated Harry Hawthorne, Detective Norris, and two stalwart policemen detailed on special duty for this occasion.

Fast flew the gallant horses under the gently urging hand of the driver, until they were in sight, then Norris exclaimed:

"There's the old house now. And, see!—a sleigh at the gate! Perhaps Standish is there now, the villain! We will be extremely lucky if we catch him on the spot!"

At the same moment, Standish tossed off a bumper of wine, exclaiming:

"Here's to the bride, the beautiful heiress! Come, let's get the ceremony over!"

The three conspirators filed up stairs and into the room where Geraldine, more dead than alive, crouched in her chair in terror of their coming.

Standish, whose spirits were much elated by generous potations of wine, crossed over to her, crying, gayly:

"Give us a kiss, pretty one! I've come to marry you at last! Here's the preacher—justice, I mean. He can tie the knot just as well. Hello, Jane! if you're the bridesmaid, get her up on her feet by my side, will you?"

The justice planted himself in readiness to perform the ceremony, but Geraldine would not permit any one to drag her up from her seat.

She fought off their hands with a wonderful strength, born of desperation, and shriek after shriek, loud, agonized, ear-piercing, burst from her pale lips.

Perhaps it was the sound of those defiant shrieks that drowned the sound of bells as the second sleigh dashed up to the gate, and the men tumbled out pell-mell into the lane.

But the winter wind bore to their ears the sound of Geraldine's awful cries, and their feet seemed winged, as, headed by Hawthorne, they rushed up the lane and threw themselves altogether against the locked door.

It yielded and fell in with their united weight, tumbling all together upon the kitchen floor.

But each sprang to his feet and followed the sound of those frantic shrieks up a rickety stair-way to another locked door.

"Now all together again, lads—push!" shouted Hawthorne, and under the strong onslaught the second door yielded, the lock fell off, and they were on the scene of action.

And, oh, what a scene!

Clifford Standish and the old woman had dragged Geraldine from her chair, despite her desperate shrieks and struggles, and were holding her up between them, while the half-drunken justice mumbled over the words of the marriage service.

The conspirators, thus taken by surprise, dropped their victim and turned to fly, but the clubs of the agile policemen quickly strewed the floor with three groaning wretches.

As for Hawthorne, he thought only of Geraldine. She flew to him, and he clasped her in his arms, crying:

"Oh, my love, my love! I have come to save you!"

It was a tender meeting, but its pathos was quite lost on Norris and the policemen, who were busy putting handcuffs on the three prisoners, whose dose of clubs had reduced them to a dazed condition that made them easy to conquer.

The surprise had been a complete one, and extremely successful—so much so that all three of the conspirators were taken away as prisoners by the jubilant Norris and the two policemen.

And, to dispose of the subject at once, we may add that all three were committed to jail, had a speedy trial, and were convicted of kidnaping and conspiracy. An indignant judge and jury awarded them the severest sentence under the law, and they were sent to prison for a long term of years during which their energies were expended in labor for the State of Illinois.

———————————

It would be too great a task to describe the joy of the Fitzgerald household that evening when Harry Hawthorne restored Geraldine to her home, or their grief and indignation when they learned the terrible persecutions she had suffered.

Mrs. Fitzgerald's gratitude to Harry Hawthorne was boundless.

She scarcely remembered the existence of the English nobleman, whose title she had so ardently desired for Geraldine.

She realized how true was Hawthorne's affection when she saw him weep the bitterest tears over the cruel bruises that for several days empurpled the poor girl's face and hands—marks of the brutal blows she had been given by Jane Crabtree while trying to force her consent to marry Clifford Standish.

"He loves her with the devotion of a noble heart, and I will not stand between them, even though he is only a poor fireman. Besides, he really saved her life from those murderous wretches, and it belongs to him," she thought, generously.

So, when he came to her a few days later, asking her for the second time for her approval of his suit for Geraldine's hand, she accepted him with pleasure for her son-in-law.

And then she said, with a smile:

"But I hope you will not carry my dear girl away from me when you are married. This house is large enough for us all."

Thinking that he was poor, she wished to make the future as easy for him as possible.

But Hawthorne answered:

"I thank you for your generosity, but I have a home in England, and a widowed mother awaiting me."

"I do not understand," she said, wonderingly.

Just then Geraldine and Cissy came in, with the two children, who were enjoying the freedom of having no governess at present.

Mrs. Fitzgerald called Geraldine to her side, kissed her beautiful brow, and said:

"I have just given you away, my darling, to your worthy lover."

Geraldine blushed deeply, as Hawthorne drew her to his side and said:

"Dearest, I have just been telling your dear mother that our home must be in England when we are married. Indeed, I have a letter of introduction from my own mother to yours, which I must now deliver."

He bowed gracefully to Mrs. Fitzgerald, who opened the letter with a mystified air.

Directly she looked up, exclaiming:

"But this is very puzzling. The letter is from my English cousin, Lady Putnam, to introduce her son, Lord Leland Harry Putnam."

"I am he, Mrs. Fitzgerald," the young man said, with another low bow, but it took many minutes of explanation to convince her of the truth, and then she said, beamingly:

"But why did you deceive us?"

"Can you not guess? I wished to test Geraldine's love, and to win your regard as simple Harry Hawthorne, the poor fireman. I have succeeded, and now I am perfectly happy."

So were they all, if their radiant faces were an index of their feelings, and Lord Putnam made Geraldine blush very brightly when he added:

"My mother and sister told me to tell you that they will come to America to our wedding, and they hope it will be soon, as Amy especially is anxious to see this country."

When he brought Ralph Washburn and Leroy Hill to call the next day, they sounded the praises of beautiful Lady Amy so persistently that Geraldine was in love with her new sister before she ever saw her, and she wondered which one of the handsome young lovers would win the charming beauty.

She persuaded Cissy to be married on the same day as herself and Cameron Clemens, although very impatient for the marriage, consented to the postponement to please the two fair brides.

"Won't it be just too lovely to be married on the same day, Cissy, and cross the ocean together on our bridal tour and spend our honeymoons at Castle Raneleigh? We must write and tell the Stansburys and Odells, and send them invitations," cried pretty Geraldine, who was so happy in her love that she wanted all her old friends to rejoice with her when she was wedded to her heart's dear choice.

The happy day is set for June, dear reader, and I am invited to the double wedding.

(THE END.)

9 789362 093905